## Books in the EMPIRE Series

### by Richard F. Weyand:
EMPIRE: Reformer
EMPIRE: Usurper
EMPIRE: Tyrant
EMPIRE: Commander
EMPIRE: Warlord
EMPIRE: Conqueror

### by Stephanie Osborn:
EMPIRE: Imperial Police
EMPIRE: Imperial Detective
EMPIRE: Imperial Inspector

### by Richard F. Weyand:
EMPIRE: Intervention
EMPIRE: Investigation
EMPIRE: Succession
EMPIRE: Renewal
EMPIRE: Resistance
EMPIRE: Resurgence

D1562334

## Books in the Childers Universe

### by Richard F. Weyand:
Childers
Childers: Absurd Proposals
Galactic Mail: Revolution
A Charter For The Commonwealth
Campbell: The Problem With Bliss

### by Stephanie Osborn:
Campbell: The Sigurdsen Incident

# ARCADIA

## A Colony Story

by

## RICHARD F. WEYAND

## RICHARD F. WEYAND

ISBN 978-1-954903-03-6
Printed in the United States of America

**Cover Credits**
Cover Art: Paola Giari and Luca Oleastri,
www.rotwangstudio.com
Back Cover Photo: Oleg Volk

Many thanks to
王睿
for verifying Chinese cultural accuracy.

Published by Weyand Associates, Inc.
Bloomington, Indiana, USA
June 2021

# ARCADIA

## CONTENTS

# 2245

# RICHARD F. WEYAND

# Arrival

A blue haze developed over the display screen at the front of the passenger container. The blue haze flashed suddenly and was gone.

A planet floated in the display, taking up half the display on the left.

"We have arrived at Arcadia," Janice Quant's voice announced.

Perhaps two minutes later, gravity abruptly returned. There was a bit of a tremor as the building settled a bit.

"Peggy, look at that," Matt said.

In the display, Matt could see from their location on the top of the residence hall all the way to the horizon. There were coastal grasslands close around them, with some structures in the middle distance Matt recognized as the barns.

Well beyond the barns, there was lush vegetation, with some small trees. Some looked like they were laid out in a grid, like orchards. In the far distance, blue-gray mountains marched across the horizon, falling off to the sea in the right side of the display.

A cheer went up in the compartment, and there was applause.

They had arrived on Arcadia.

The return of gravity was a relief. They had been in zero gravity, strapped into their seats, for almost two hours, since the big cargo shuttle carrying the passenger container had throttled back on reaching orbit. There had then been the transport of the shuttle and its payload by the interstellar probe to the big interstellar transporter. The passenger container had been latched by the shuttle to the roof of one of the colony buildings, where they had waited until everyone was aboard.

Arcadia had been the third planet where the transporter stopped. The interstellar flights themselves were instantaneous, but there was a delay at each planet to transport the colony buildings to the surface. Then the next planet, then Arcadia.

After four years of planning and training, they had arrived.


"Hi, everybody. This is Mark Kendall," the voice came from the speakers in the passenger container. "We've arrived, so there'll be no more zero gravity."

The chairman of the Arcadia ruling council paused for the cheering in his container to die down.

"We're here now, and there's no hurry, so let's make it a safe debarkation. There are some ladders and steps to climb down, and we don't want anybody getting hurt. So let's all take our time.

"It's about ten o'clock in the morning here, so we've gone back a couple hours from the time zone in Texas.

"Our only jobs today are to get everybody into their temporary quarters in the colony buildings, and to make sure everybody has food and water available.

"Tomorrow we are going to start putting up houses and stringing fencing so we can let the livestock out. The livestock is all on time-release tranquilizers, and they have food for now, but we need to get them out grazing soon.

"But for today, let's get everybody into temporary quarters. It's going to be crowded, but it won't be sleeping out on the grass like in Texas, so we're moving up one step at a time.

"Now I'm going to turn over the intercom to each of the building managers, so they can talk to the passenger compartments on their own buildings."

There was a pause, and then another voice came over the speakers.

"Hi, everybody. If you're hearing me, you're in one of the passenger containers on the roof of the hospital. My name is Meghana Khatri, and I am the administrator of the hospital. I also sit on the council as head of the health department.

"The first thing is to get everybody a bunk room in the hospital so we all have a comfortable place to sleep tonight. It's going to be pretty spartan for now, and we're going to be crowded.

"All the registered groups have been housed together. For the rest of you, think of it as an opportunity to make new friends. We're all in this together, so let's pull together like a team.

"When you debark the passenger container, take the supplies box under your seat with you. Yes, we're still on rations and bottled water for the moment. We are going to try to get the kitchens up and running in the next few days, but there's a lot of work to do first. Running electric and water from the power plant and septic lines back is an early priority. In the meantime, we're still on MREs and portable potties.

"With regard to wandering around outside the building, you're free to do that, but stay in sight of the building. There are some big wild fauna here, transplanted from Earth, especially some of the big cats. In the daytime you should be OK, but keep your eyes open. There's safety in numbers, so it's better to stay in groups than to go wandering off by yourself.

"If you do get in trouble with the local fauna, call the emergency number on your communicator and run like hell for the closest building. Dodge a bit left and right so snipers on the roof can get a clean shot at the animal. It's easier to stay in a big group than to try to outrun a big cat, though, so remember that.

"With all that said, let's start exiting the containers now, and heading down into the building. Our staff people should have been able to get in place while we were talking, and they can help you find your room assignments.

"Welcome to Arcadia, everybody. Khatri out."

Everybody reached under their seat for their supply box and got them out. Once again, it was a briefcase sized box with a handle, full of bottled water and MREs.

Then they waited for the compartment to be opened.

Each passenger container had three decks, and the thirty-six containers had been delivered to the roofs of the four colony residence halls – the generic name for the hospitals, office buildings, administrative buildings, and school buildings – in stacks of two. The hospital staff started emptying the five stacks of people containers on the hospital roof – thirty thousand people in all – with the bottom decks of the five bottom containers. That was easiest, because no stairs were required.

The Chen-Jasic clan was seated on the middle deck of the lower container of their stack. When it was their turn, the passenger compartment doors opened and one big fellow with a bullhorn of a voice stepped in. Like everyone else, he wore coveralls and booties, though his were in a size extra large.

"OK, everybody," bellowed Stanley Twardowski, World Authority Police Sergeant Major (retired). "Grab your supply boxes and queue up. We're just gonna start with the front row and work our way back. That's the easiest way to keep groups together. There's one stair ladder to go down to the roof, and it's steep, so we're going to go down it backwards. You all already have your room assignments, and you got all day to get there, so let's take it nice and slow and safe, all right?"

Before they left Texas, Robert Jasic, Chen LiQiang, and Rachel Conroy – as the nominal heads of their groups – had gone to the planet administration table to one side of the planet square, the marked-out open space in which all the colonists for Arcadia were camping out in the grass. There they had registered their individual groups as being combined into the Chen-Jasic group.

Jasic's group was twenty-seven people from the suburbs of Raleigh-Durham in the Carolina administrative region. Five couples – minus Harold Munson, whom Betsy Reynolds had divorced after another one of his physical abuses – and their total of eighteen children ages fourteen to nineteen, now all paired up as married couples.

Rachel Conroy, her partner Jessica Murphy, and their friends, Gary Rockham and his partner Dwayne Hennessey, were all from downtown Raleigh-Durham. They had met the Jasic group at the shuttleport in the Carolina administrative region before the trip to Texas and merged with them, there being strength in numbers.

The Chen group was Chen LiQiang and thirty members of his family from rural China. LiQiang was the paterfamilias of the close-knit clan. He and Robert Jasic had negotiated the alliance of their groups on the prairie in Texas where they awaited transport to orbit. The peasant farmers had wanted to team up with a group with more diverse and modern skills, whereas Bob Jasic and Maureen Griffith had seen the Chen's farming skills as a must-have for their own group.

As a result of registering the combination of the groups, the sixty-two members of the Chen-Jasic clan all had room assignments in the hospital together – two rooms, numbered 427 and 428, presumably on the fourth floor of the large building. They would be thirty or more to a room for now, until the temporary housing was set up, but they wouldn't be out in the rain.

Matt Jasic could see his father talking with Chen LiQiang, the grandfather of the Chen household. They both nodded and then each spoke to one of their group nearby, Chen LiQiang to his eldest son, Chen GangHai, and Jasic to Maureen Griffith. The whisper campaign spread as they stood up and queued for the door.

"Bob and the Chen say we are one group. Do not split into Chinese and American when we get to our rooms. Mix it up. Pass it on," Jonah Thompson said to Matt.

"Makes sense," Matt said, and he turned to his wife Peggy Reynolds and repeated the message.

Peggy passed it on to her sister Sally, standing behind her.

Then their row was moving, and Matt Jasic followed Jonah to the door. It was about eight feet down to the roof of the hospital, and there was a steep stair setup, like a ladder on a ship, with two railings to hang onto. Matt turned around, winked at Peggy, and headed down the stairs.

He waited for her at the bottom. The weather was very pleasant, and the sun was bright in the sky. He saw an edge of clouds moving off on the horizon. Matt sniffed the air, and could smell the ocean, so it was only a few miles distant. He could hear multiple diesel generators running.

Matt knew that there was basically no axial tilt on Arcadia, so this would likely be the weather all year round. It looked like one of those special spring days in the Carolinas, when the weather was absolutely perfect. But on Arcadia, that would be the weather every day.

There was a staffer waving them toward the stairs.

"Go ahead and down the stairs to your floor. The first digit of your room number is the floor. The lower numbers are at this end, and they go up toward the other end of the building."

They followed the line of people into the rooftop stair enclosure and down into the building. There were lights operating in the stairwell, and they continued down twenty half-flights of the zig-zag stairwell until they got to the fourth floor. People were leaving the stairwell into different floors as they descended, but all the members of the Chen-Jasic group kept on until the fourth floor.

The hallways had lights on, too, but not at normal office levels. They were on at emergency levels, running off the generator. Matt knew diesel fuel would be precious until they had a refinery built. He thought he remembered that a refinery was one of the first projects for the metafactory.

There were multiple hallways, but signs guided them to which hallway had their room numbers. They followed other members of the clan into one of the two rooms, and found the room had five sets of three-high metal bunk bed frames in it. There was almost no other furniture, and the bunk beds were crammed into a room that would have another purpose in the future.

The one other piece of furniture in the room was a single chair, in front of a 3-D display projector mounted on the wall.

The room was bright with light coming in the large windows, and the lights were off. The sliding windows were actually latched open, which didn't make sense to Matt until he realized the building had been transported from vacuum to a planetary atmosphere. Without the windows being open, they would have blown in.

People were settling into tailor seat on the floor or sitting on one of the bottom-level bed frames.

"Well, we're here," Matt said. "Now what?"

"Why don't we see if there are any announcements on the display?" Peggy asked.

"Would the network even be up yet?" Jonah asked. "And would the display run on the emergency power?"

"One way to find out," Matt said.

The big nineteen-year-old sat in the chair in front of the display. He tried to slide it back, but it was tack-welded to the metal floor. He shrugged and tried to turn on the display. It remained blank.

"Not up yet, I guess," Matt said.

"Well, I know there's work to be done," Jonah said. "I would just as soon get going on it than to be sitting around."

"Work is good," MingWei said. "There is much to be done."

At that moment, the display came on by itself. It read 'Announcements' across the screen.

"Huh," Matt said. "I guess I was just a bit quick on the draw."

He scrolled down the list.

"Looks like they're getting mattresses out of the warehouse and distributing them to everyone. They need people for unloading on the dock and then distributing within the hospital. Who's in?"

Matt took a count of hands, and then signed them up in the display.

"OK, it says to report to the docks in half an hour. They're still unloading passenger containers."

"How are they getting mattresses to the docks?" Jonah asked.

"I guess they had electric trucks charging up in the power

plant since Earth orbit, and they just called them to auto-drive over to the warehouse. They're being loaded with containers now."

"How'd they do that with no roads?" Jonah asked.

Matt shrugged.

"Beats me. I guess there was a clear path from the power plant to the warehouse. It's only a couple miles. This has all been so well-planned, they wouldn't have missed a bet there."

"Makes sense," Jonah said.

"Let's get a quick bite to eat first," Matt said. "We didn't have any breakfast."

When the display came on in the next room, Robert Jasic motioned Chen LiQiang to the chair, but Chen demurred.

"Please, Robert. Be seated. Computers are not my skill."

Jasic sat in the chair and Chen settled into tailor seat alongside the chair to watch.

Jasic scrolled down the announcements.

"They need manpower at the docks," he said.

"I just came from next door," Maureen Griffith said. "Matt and MingWei have that covered."

"OK. Good."

Jasic kept scrolling.

"They have a sign-up for property here in the town for houses. We can sign up as a group, and we'll get assigned early because of our size."

"Is there a map?" Chen asked.

"Yes, I think so," Jasic said. "Yes. Here it is."

Jasic selected the map of the colony and Chen studied it closely. It showed the cluster of major buildings in the center, and then a grid of streets around it, with ten blocks to the mile. There were eight or nine square miles around the downtown gridded out for the hundred thousand colonists.

"North is up, yes?" Chen asked.

Jasic looked for the compass indication.

"Um, yes, here it is. North is up."

"And does the sun rise in the east, as before?"

"I assume they set north in the standard way, which would be the thumb direction when the fingers point in the direction of rotation of the planet."

Jasic demonstrated with his right hand before continuing.

"So the sun should come up in the east."

Chen nodded.

"And how much land are we allotted?" Chen asked.

"For sixty people, half a city block. Three acres, more or less."

Chen raised an eyebrow.

"A bit over a hectare," Jasic clarified. "One-point-two hectares? Something like that."

"So much? Just for the houses?"

"Well, that's twelve thousand people per square mile, so that is a high population density, but yes, that's how much we get in town. And then we all have a share in the farms as well."

Chen nodded.

"And thirty houses?" Chen asked.

"Yes. One for every two people, then an extra room on each later. So how do we arrange the houses, LiQiang? In America, they would be set back from the road, facing it, with a yard in the front and one behind."

"Can I propose an alternative, Robert?"

"Of course."

"Put all houses close to road, facing in. One big yard, in the center. We are one clan. We close in our space. We garden this space. With teas, with herbs, with spices. We brought the seeds and the cuttings and the tools."

This was the first mention of what the Chen family had used their cubic for, and it made great sense to Jasic. He looked to Maureen Griffith, standing to one side and watching. Griffith gave him a small nod.

"Very well, LiQiang. We will do as you say. And where do we request our space?"

"Not close to big buildings. We want sun all day. So not close unless south. Anywhere south, or out from the center on north, east, or west."

"We probably shouldn't be close to the buildings anyway. As the downtown expands, we will be displaced, and our investment in these gardens will be lost."

"Toward the barns, I would think," Griffith said. "That will be one place of employment. Animal husbandry is always manpower intensive, and the Chen are good with animals."

Chen nodded.

"Yes. I agree with this," he said. "It will be a shorter walk home from work."

Jasic had to get his directions straight. The ocean was to the east, the mountains to the north. The prevailing wind here seemed to be onshore, to the west, based on the morning rain they had watched from the roof, moving off to the west. So the barns and fields were north of town. They could locate on the north edge of the residential area around the downtown, and not be downwind of the barns or in the shade of the bigger buildings.

Jasic picked a block on a line between the downtown buildings and the barns. It was on the edge of town, a mile and a half or so from the downtown buildings.

"How about here, LiQiang?" he asked.

"Yes, Robert. Very good."

Jasic selected the north half of the block, and began placing houses, but LiQiang held up a hand.

"The south half, please, Robert. We will have neighbors, and we want the sun all day. They may raise something that casts a shadow. And on one shorter side, move the houses back from the street fifteen feet."

"Move them back on one side?"

"Yes. For a market. We will sell teas and herbs and spices. East side is sunny in the morning. Bright. Cheerful. We put umbrellas for shade, but sunny for market is good."

"We can sell lavalavas there, too," Griffith said.

Jasic turned to Chen.

"Our family brought fabrics. All our cubic is fabric. For making lavalavas."

Chen looked to his daughter PingLi, standing nearby.

"Hanfu qun," she said. "I think."

Chen nodded.

"Very good," Chen said. "We will sell teas and herbs and spices and fabrics."

"The Uptown Market," Griffith said. "I like it."

"But will people come so far to our market?" Jasic asked.

Chen just nodded.

"They will come. You will see."

Jasic rearranged the request on screen, making it the southern half of a block on the north edge of the initial town map. He marked house locations evenly around the perimeter of the space, about fifty feet apart. All the houses faced into the space, and the row of houses across the eastern edge were set fifteen feet back from the building line.

Jasic raised an eyebrow to Chen.

"Very good, Robert. That is very good. Submit that, please."

# The Basics

The Chen-Jasic work crew got to the hospital's loading dock as the electric truck was backing to the dock. It had a container on it, a twelve-foot by twelve-foot by eighty-foot monster. On the dock were four two-seat electric carts with bins on the back.

"Chen-Jasic crew reporting, sir," Matt said to the fellow who seemed to be supervising.

"Excellent. Can any of you guys drive a golf cart?"

Matt took inventory of hands quickly.

"I guess we have three, sir."

"All right. I can take the other one. We need to deliver mattresses to everybody throughout the hospital so they have someplace to sleep tonight."

"How many containers will that be, sir?"

"Just this one, believe it or not. Thirty-four thousand mattresses."

James Faletti walked over to the container and unlatched the rear doors. Inside, stacked six across and maybe a hundred or a hundred-and-fifty high were plastic vacuum packages. They were two feet square and an inch thick.

"Let's start filling the first couple carts," Faletti said.

"That's a mattress, sir?"

"Yeah. Air mattress with foam on one side, scrunched down and vacuum packed. You open one of these, it unfolds and starts expanding like crazy. Then you blow it up the rest of the way. Saves cubic."

"Yes, sir. All right, guys. Let's get on it."

They loaded a hundred and twenty or so mattress packages onto each of the first two carts, then Jonah and James Thompson got into the carts.

"Don't worry about allotting them out or anything. There's thousands more than we got beds, but if some people wanna sleep on the floor so they can sleep alone, that's OK," Faletti said.

"Got it," Jonah said.

James and Jonah drove off into the hospital, driving right down the corridor. At the first cross-corridor, one turned left and one right. Faletti and Joseph Bolton backed up the next two carts and the remaining crew loaded them up. By the time that was done, Jonah and James were back.

"They go fast," James said. "Four rooms and you're empty."

"Yeah, but it's gonna take longer as you go deeper into the building," Faletti said. "You got all the rooms you did already to drive past. And you can use the elevators, if you use the code for the call button. Five-thirty-seven. Try to keep that to yourselves, cuz we only got so much electric until they wire the building to the powerplant."

With that, Faletti and Joseph headed off into the building in their carts, and James and Jonah backed their carts up to the container.

"This will take very long time," MingWei said. "We should get as many on each cart as we can."

"But that's how big the box is, MingWei," Matt said.

"We show you."

Matt and Tom and David Peterson concentrated on getting the mattresses out of the container, and MingWei and the other Chinese stacked them on the carts. They used a fan of mattresses to effectively build the box higher, and piled them in. They also filled up the extra passenger seat. In all, they got over three hundred and fifty of the packages onto the cart.

"I wouldn't have believed it if I hadn't seen it myself," Matt said.

Faletti and Joseph returned at that point, and Faletti looked over the next two carts to go in.

"Nice job," he said. "I was worried about getting everybody on a mattress tonight, but that's gonna work great. Cause you guys were right. They go fast."

James and Jonah headed off into the hospital again and Faletti and Joseph backed their carts up to the container.

"We'll actually back them into the container once we get deeper," Faletti said. "Still plenty of working room around them."

With that, they settled into a rhythm. It still took over five hours to get to the point where the carts came back with mattresses remaining on them.

"I think we finally got them all," James said.

"Yeah. That's about right," Faletti said. "We got about ten percent of the container left. We'll hold that here in case we missed anybody, or one of the other buildings comes up short."

He turned to the crew.

"Nice job, you guys. Let me scan your communicators. You got wages coming. I make it six hours all told."

"We get paid?" Matt asked.

"Oh, yeah. Colony Headquarters back on Earth figured there'd be some shirkers no matter how careful they were with rejecting colonists for cause. Well, those guys ain't gonna do as well as guys who ain't afraid to get their hands dirty."

Faletti held up some sort of widget to each of them, one at a time, and they keyed their communicator. That was all it took for him to get their IDs.

"All right, you guys. Thanks. We'll see ya around."

Matt, MingWei, and their crew took the stairs back up to the fourth floor. They had the code to the elevator, but they didn't really need it and didn't want to use the limited electric or set a bad example.

When they got back to their rooms, there were mattresses on all the beds. Matt couldn't believe it, as the mattresses were three to four inches thick once inflated.

"Maybe tomorrow we'll get sheets and clean coveralls," Peggy said.

"What I would really like is a shower," Matt said. "But that won't be before the powerplant is hooked up. Couple days, probably. At least we aren't sleeping outside, like last night."

"Last night? Oh, in Texas, you mean. That was just last night? Wow. It seems like a thousand years ago."

"A thousand light-years away, anyway."

Peggy shook her head.

"And now we're here."

She looked out the windows. With no axial tilt, the day here in the subtropics of Arcadia was twelve and a half hours long every day, and it was almost sunset already.

"Matt, let's go down and outside and see if we can see the sunset."

Matt glanced out the windows.

"OK, but not far from the building. The night stalkers will be out as soon as it gets dark. Especially the cats."


There were people camped out on bunk beds in what would be the hospital lobby as well. There was a path to the front door behind what would ultimately be the reception counter.

Half a dozen of the couples from the original Carolina group went down, as well as Gary Rockham and Dwayne Hennessey, one of the gay couples they had merged with in the Carolina airport.

As they walked through the lobby via the path behind the reception counter, one of the people camped out in the lobby came up to them.

"You guys all in a group already?"

"Yeah. We're good. Thanks," Matt said.

"OK. We're trying to get three more couples. If we do, we'll get a whole city block of our own in the land assignments."

"I'll keep an eye out for you. There should be a group of three couples somewhere you can pick up."

"Thanks. We appreciate it."

"No problem."

Matt thought about it.

"You know, I think I saw a personals section link off the announcements page. You ought to put an ad up."

"Good idea. Thanks."

Matt nodded and waved, and they passed out the main doors into the night.


The hospital building stood on no foundation other than its heavy steel underframe. It was simply set there by the interstellar transporter. There was no infrastructure. No road, sidewalk, parking lot, or other structure or landscaping.

For that matter, the hospital itself was all steel, with glass windows. Iron and silica had been plentiful in the Asteroid Belt where it was manufactured. Organic molecules, from which much of any decor would be constructed, had simply not been available.

In particular, there were no plaster walls or tiled floors or ceramic countertops. The infrastructure, in terms of electrical conduits and air ducts and plumbing pipes. all ran on the exterior of the single-thickness steel walls. The effect was not unlike that of being on a warship, except they didn't even have any rubber deck coverings. All those sorts of niceties would have to wait until the colony could afford the upgrades.

In the meantime, they had a roof over their heads and protection from the wild.

They stepped off the steel entry portico of the hospital and out from under the steel roof. It was dusk, and it would be dark soon. There was a bit of a crowd around the portico, all taking the evening air of their new planet.

Off to the west, the other direction from the ocean, the sky was a blaze of red and orange, with bars of purple cloud.

"Oh, how pretty," Peggy said.

"Just another day in Paradise," Matt said.

"Oh, you," Peggy said, punching him in the arm.

"It's true, though. With no seasons, this is pretty much how it's going to be all year 'round."

"Well, that's fine by me. It's beautiful."

Between the emergency lights in the rooms and under the portico, it was light near the hospital, but it got dark quickly as one moved farther away. Peggy was in the light, but moving out toward the darker area.

"Don't stray out of the light, Peg."

"Oh, we're fine, Matt."

"Oh, yeah. Look again."

Peggy looked out across the dark grassland, and about a hundred yards distant a pair of large green eyes glowed as they caught the lights behind her.

"Oh, shit."

Peggy scampered back toward the portico.

"Actually, staying here is a real good idea, I think."

"Yeah," Matt said. "We're going to have to let them know

this isn't where they want to be. Once the town builds out, it will be OK, I think. They're not going to want to mess with a large population of people. For now, though, you don't want to be a single target."

"What about all these other people?"

"I think I can fix that."

Matt cupped his hands around his mouth.

"TIGER! IN THE GRASS."

Some people looked out over the grassland, saw those eyes, then sprinted for the building. Others headed back without looking. But everybody pulled back much closer to the hospital, and Matt saw the eyes disappear as the big cat turned and wandered off.

"There he goes," Matt said. "He doesn't want to tangle with all of us, or to come out into the light. He was just looking for easy pickings."

He turned and looked up at the top of the building. There was a rifleman up there, silhouetted against the darkening sky, wearing IR goggles.

"One of the building lookouts would probably have gotten him anyway, before he actually took anybody. But let that be a lesson to be careful after dark."

"Geez. Just from the eyes, that thing looked like it was the size of a pony," Amy Jasic said.

"For a tiger?" Matt asked. "That's not far off, actually."

"Why would Colony Headquarters bring something like that here anyway?" Peggy asked.

"Because without any predators, the deer population will overrun the place," James Thompson said.

"Yup," Matt said. "They tried to balance the ecology. We'll have to see how well they did over time."

"Well, I think it was exciting to see," Dwayne Hennessey

said.

"You would," Gary Rockham said.

"Well, to see it from over here, anyway. Why not?"

"Fair enough. It is a good reminder, though. It's a wild planet, not suburban Raleigh-Durham."

They went back upstairs and, with it dark now and the emergency lights on low, they simply went to bed. They had been up a couple hours longer than local time since they had woken up before dawn on the prairie in Texas that morning. That plus the longer day on Arcadia – about twenty-five hours – meant they had been up for almost seventeen hours.

With all the emotion and excitement of the day, they were all pretty beat.

"Well, we're back in a bed," Matt said. "That's some progress."

"Yeah," Peggy agreed. "Maybe tomorrow we'll get sheets for it."

"No telling."

# Setting Up Camp

The emergency lights kicked up to a higher level about an hour before dawn. Matt Jasic was already awake, staring up at the bottom of the bunk above them, listening to Peggy snore softly in his arms.

She mewed in protest and looked across to the windows.

"So early? It's still dark."

"All of the light is for working. With no axial tilt, it's only light half the day all year long."

At that point, the display projector came on, lighting the room further. The legend 'Work Assignments' was on the screen.

Matt disentangled himself from Peggy and swung over the edge of the second-level bunk, then lowered himself to the floor. With no sheets or blankets yet issued, he was still in the onesie coverall he had put on that last night in Texas. He slipped on his booties, then padded over to the display.

Others in the room were getting up now. Some were opening their supply boxes and getting breakfast. A couple had slipped down the hall to the portable toilets by the elevators.

Matt entered his name for his assignment and checked out his work crew. James came up alongside.

"What have we got?"

"Building houses. Like we figured."

MingWei was on Matt's other side.

"And for us?" he asked.

"The barns. Getting the animals out of harnesses and

refreshing their food supply."

MingWei nodded.

"What all else is going on today?" James asked.

Matt was scrolling down the screen, scanning work assignments.

"There's a whole bunch of guys assigned to the powerplant. I guess the transporter placed the inbound and outbound water pipes from the ocean right up to the plant. They need to get those hooked up before they can dial up the power. And they're going to be running temporary power, water, and sewer lines to the permanent buildings to get them up and running."

He scrolled further down.

"Bunch of guys here stringing wire on the fences, so we can let the animals out to pasture later. And there's a lot of people assigned to putting water and sewer lines in the streets. They must have trenching equipment in the warehouse."

"What about us girls?" Peggy asked.

"The women will be distributing supplies. Work boots is first on the list, so we're not running around in booties all the time. More coveralls. Sheets and blankets. You're on that list, Peg. On the dock, handing out work boots first."

Matt kept scrolling.

"A bunch more will be getting the kitchens up and running. Most of that will be stocking all the kitchenware and supplies for now. Some food, too. Everything will be cold until they get the power up, but at least it won't be MREs.

"Ah. Here's an interesting note. The hospital is first. For power, for water, for sewer. For getting people moved out into the inflatable houses. They want to get the hospital operational as a hospital right off. So Gary, you're up for that right off. They're putting a temporary hospital staff together. Looks like they gave you Dwayne and Rachel as your team."

"What about me?" Jessica asked.

"Motor pool. Over by the powerplant. That's where all the electric trucks and buses are headquartered."

"Makes sense."

At that point, everybody got a priority alert from their communicator. When Matt touched his, he was surprised to get an icon in the lower right of his vision. It had an object distance from his eye of about two feet, so he touched the apparent location of the icon with his right index finger. A heads-up display sprang up over his vision. He could still see through it, but he could read it as well.

"Hey, this is cool. I didn't even know they did that," he said to no one in particular.

Everyone else was doing the same thing, with various comments.

Matt selected the Work Assignment icon, which had an alert icon next to it, and it gave him his assignment and reporting. Report to the dock at six-thirty - half an hour before dawn, about fifteen minutes from now - and pick up his work boots, then stand by for a bus to his work site building temporary housing. It also told him to bring water and lunch.

"Oh, shoot," Peggy said. "I have to go."

"Us, too," Stacy Jasic said.

"Let's go," Tracy Jasic said.


Matt grabbed a bite out of his supplies box, tucked an MRE and three water bottles into the pockets of his coverall, then headed down to the dock. It was semi-organized bedlam, and very crowded. He backtracked and went out the front door of the hospital, then walked around the building to the receiving dock in the back.

Hundreds of men milled around on the dock and on the ground around a container truck. A couple of dozen women were pulling shoe boxes out of the container truck, each taking half a dozen at a time.

"I got some elevens here. Who's an eleven?" one asked.

Men held up their hands and she passed them back through the crowd. Everybody was pretty well behaved, all in all. Then again, Stan Twardowski, the retired World Authority Police sergeant major, and Jim Faletti, the dock foreman, and their crews, stood by watching the process.

"Recycle the plastic. We have a limited amount until the refinery is up, so let's not waste anything. There's a recycle container right there," Faletti called out on a bullhorn. Two spaces down in the dock area, a forty-cubic-yard container waited.

Whenever some twelves came out, Matt held up his hand. He got a box on the third try, then headed away from the dock area and took a seat on the grass. Inside the plastic box was a pair of size twelve work boots. Inside each was a pair of socks. As he pulled the socks out, he found that one boot also contained a folding knife and the other contained one of those fold-up toolkit things that had pliers, scissors, screwdrivers and such.

"Nice."

Matt tucked the knife in one pocket and the folding tool in another and stuffed the extra pair of socks in a third, then put on socks and boots. He considered the booties for a moment. They were plastic and could go in the recycling bin as well, but they might be nice to use as slippers after a day working, so he folded them up and tucked them into a zippered pocket on the coverall.

Matt walked over to the recycling container. It felt good to have real shoes on again, for the first time since he'd left Carolina.

"Flatten the box and lid, please," a dock worker there repeatedly said to the continuous stream of men walking up to the container with their empty boxes.

Matt popped the corners and flattened the box and lid and tossed them in, which got him a nod from the dock worker. That done, he consulted his Work Assignment page in the communicator's heads-up display. The mustering point for his work crew was the side portico of the hospital, what would eventually be the emergency entrance.

A number of people were already there, some from his group and some from others, perhaps a hundred in all. A continuous stream of people were walking around from the dock. There was an electric bus there.

"Check in when you get here. Once we have a full bus of complete crews, we'll run them over to their worksites and come back for the next load."

Matt checked in with the heads-up display and settled down on the edge of the portico floor to wait.

They were on the second bus trip. The bus had left with the first crews and come back in ten minutes. The site just wasn't that large.

"OK. I got Horner group, Chen-Jasic group, Stanton group, and Suzuki group. Everybody on the bus."

Once they were on the bus, they moved off into the residential area, passing between stakes that marked out where the streets would be. There were containers set out in some of the blocks between streets.

"All right. So there's a map for your block you can get to with a link from your Work Assignment page. You're going to put up sixty houses in the block, matching the map of what people want for where the houses go. We got some stakes and string and measuring wheels and spray paint in the containers so you can lay it out.

"There's also a couple small air compressors there. They're pedal-cranked, but we don't have power yet and gas is too precious for the moment, so it is what it is. There's also a spray setup, and containers with the plasticizer. You all took the training, so you should know what you're doing, right?"

There were nods and 'yes's from the workers, and the bus driver nodded.

"One more thing. You're starting on your own block, so do a good job, 'cause this first bunch you're going to be living in.

"All right. Stanton group, this is you, there on the right."

In the block on the right of the bus, a container sat roughly in the middle of the block. The Stanton group people got off and the bus moved on.

Chen-Jasic group had selected a block on the northern edge of the site, so they were the last off the bus.

Bob Jasic took charge when they got there.

"OK, let's start pulling materials out of the container. Get a couple houses being inflated right away, because inflating them is probably going to be our pacing item. Then let's get a couple two-man teams on the measuring wheels and some spray cans marking locations. Mark the building lines first, measuring off the survey stakes for the street."

"Dad, looking at the map, that near row of stakes is the building line," Matt said.

"All right. Even easier. So let's mark our fifteen-foot setback on the east side for the Uptown Market, and then start marking house locations."

# ARCADIA

Their crew was thirteen, the original thirteen from the Carolina administrative region. The four fathers – Bob Jasic, Hank Bolton, Bill Thompson, and Jack Peterson – and their seven sons, all now in their late teens – Matthew Jasic, Joseph and Paul Bolton, James and Jonah Thompson, Tom and David Peterson – as well as Richard and Carl Reynolds, whose father, Harold Munson, had stayed on Earth. Like their sisters Peggy and Sally, Rick and Carl had taken their mother's last name, disowning the abusive Munson.

They set to it in earnest now. The equipment all came out of the container first, and Hank Bolton and his youngest, Paul, and Bill Thompson and Betsy Reynolds' youngest, Carl, took measuring wheels, string, stakes, and paint cans and started marking out the block, beginning by finding the north-south centerline that would divide their own compound from their neighbors on the other half of the block.

The bigger young guys – Matt, Joe, James, and Tom – started pulling out houses. These were cubes of nearly solid plastic and took two guys to handle them. They just started plopping them out on the grassland in no particular order.

Bob Jasic, Jack Peterson, Jonah, David, and Rick unfolded the first two houses. Wrapped up with them were the two 'wings,' the solar heater/swamp cooler combinations that would look like fences sticking out from the house. They set those aside for the moment. They also had to unfold the frame of the single door, which was a dutch door, with an upper and lower half.

"Hey, guys," Jasic said to the unloaders. "Let's get two of you on the compressors now."

The compressors were simplicity itself, a double-bellows design not unlike a stair climber exercise machine. One shifted one's weight back and forth between two pedals, which had bellows and one-way valves under them. They were simple, but they moved a lot of air, at least for small pressures, and it wouldn't take very much pressure to inflate the houses. What it would take was air. Lots of it.

Matt and Tom got on the compressors while Joe and James continued to unload and the others continued to unfold the houses. It got to be hot work as the sun rose in the sky, then clouds moved in off the ocean to the east and gave them some relief.

Everybody took turns on the compressors. They continued to unload and inflate houses. When the measuring teams came back, the pace picked up, and Hank Bolton, who had done a stint on a spray painting job in college, started spraying the houses with plasticizer. There was a hand-pumped weed sprayer in the container – one of the first things out – and a dozen or more two-gallon bottles of the chemical. There were also spray-painting masks and goggles.

The unfolding crew took a break to tip half a dozen inflated houses on their sides. Bolton then sprayed their bottom surfaces one at a time, wetting them thoroughly. Given the bottom was fifteen-foot square, he went as high as he could reach, and then they had to rotate the house halfway around so he could get the other half of the underside. By the time he had done the sixth house, the first was pretty well set up.

"Tip 'em back," Jasic asked.

"I think it's early," Bolton said. "Let's do the other half-dozen first."

Jasic nodded, and the unfolding crew tipped the other half-dozen inflated houses on their sides.

"This is going pretty fast," Joseph said from the compressor.

"There's sixty on this block alone, don't forget," Jasic said.

"Forget I said anything. All of them today?"

"No, it's gonna take three or four days, I think."

# ARCADIA

When Bolton had finished spraying the underside of the second half-dozen houses, the unfolding crew stood the first three back upright, and Bolton moved to the insides, then the outsides of those three houses, wetting them down one at a time. They continued to do that, three houses at a time, then another half-dozen undersides as inflated houses came off the compressors.

The area around the container began to look like a very crowded little subdivision as they worked.

At one point, the clouds that were moderating the heat of the day let loose with a quick shower, and they all took refuge in two of the earliest houses, which had set up hard already. They sat and listened to the tropical rain pound on the roof for twenty minutes until the cloudburst moved on. They used the time to eat their lunches.

"Moving along," James said.

Jasic nodded.

"We still need to move them to their final locations, stake them down, and then do the wings," he said.

James shrugged.

"It's still going good, though."

Where wrestling the densely packed cubes of plastic that were the house kits out of the container required two of the stronger of them, moving a finished house to its final location was easy. One guy on each corner, pick it up and go. The houses had straps on the corners just for that purpose.

As houses continued to be unloaded, unfolded, inflated, and hardened, Jasic, Thompson, Jonah, and Rick started moving houses to their final locations. For their own compound, they would be around the outer edge of the property, so it was a couple hundred feet to carry them to the location. It needed to be done, though, to open up work room around the container.

With half a dozen houses moved, Thompson looked at them for a moment.

"You know, Bob, if we run one wing out sideways from the back of each house, that will close the gap between houses like a fence. And we can put one straight out from the front of each house and make a little private yard for each one. That will still meet the requirement for one east-west wing and one north-south wing, like in the instructions."

Jasic looked at the houses and nodded.

"I like it. Let's start staking them down with the one on the corner then, so we get the spacing right."

Thompson nodded.

"Got it."


The wings were water tanks, thirty-five feet long and four feet high and only eight inches thick. They flared to two feet wide toward the bottom so they would be stable. They were kept full by small gutters on the eaves of the roofs of the houses. They had an overflow that kept the upper six inches empty.

A cloth mesh hung down from the top center of the tank eight inches, running along the tank's length, putting the bottom two inches of the mesh in the water. In the main body of the tank, under the water level, an air tube ran through the thick wider portion of the tank.

During the day, in the sun, the water in the tanks would warm up, and at night it would cool down.

In the center of the roof of every house was a vent cap, about a foot and a half on a side. The top of the cap was a solar panel that charged a battery. During the heat of the day, the hot air in the house would rise out of the roof vent, pulling in cool air through the upper six inches of the tank. The air would be cooled by evaporation while passing along the wet mesh hanging in that void – a swamp cooler.

At night, a slowly rotating electric fan in the vent, running off the battery, would pull air up out of the house. The upper connection to the tank – the swamp cooler – was closed with a sliding shutter at night, and the lower tube – the air tube through the water – was opened with its own sliding shutter. The air drawn through this dry tube would be warmed by passing through the tank of water that had been heated by the sun during the day.

The wings were arranged at ninety degrees to each other, from corners of the house, so that the warmth of the sunlight could be captured by the water all day long. All four corners of the house had the air tube connections and shutters for the wings, and where the wings went was up to the homeowner.

Thus were the houses warmed and cooled without energy expense. These methods wouldn't work in a more severe climate, but in the near-idyllic conditions at the location of the initial colony settlement, they would be all that was needed.

"How are we going to handle the corners?" Jasic asked.

Thompson thought about it.

"We could have two wings into the corner, one from each house," he said.

"But then the wings on the two ends are going opposite ways, so we're stuck for the next corner."

"No, we'll just put the other wing from one house on the other side and keep going. They don't have a privacy wall in the front between them is all. Probably put your twins and my boys in a corner, for instance. They're not going to want a privacy wing."

Jasic nodded.

"Let's try it and see what we get."

They staked the two corner houses down, each thirty five feet from the corner, then ran wings into the corner of the lot from the back corners of the houses. They inflated the wings with one of the compressors, and Bolton sprayed them down on the bottom and both sides with plasticizer.

"OK, looks good," Jasic said. "Let's get the rest of them staked down."

He looked at the sun, then consulted his heads-up display.

"Bus won't be here for another hour, anyway. I think we have time to get all these staked down."

That first day, they got twenty-one houses of the Chen-Jasic group's compound in place, almost three-quarters of its perimeter. Chen LiQiang's vision for the space was becoming apparent.

The Chen-Jasic crew would be able to finish the whole block in two more days.

# Livestock, Toilets, Food, And Bedding

MingWei and the other Chen young men had a different assignment that first day. After they got their work boots, they met at the other side entrance to the hospital, the service entrance. When everyone was together, they were bussed out to the barns. First up for their bus was the chicken barn.

Delivery staff had dropped off a quarter-container of feed and bedding straw for the chickens. That amount of feed would last quite a while, especially after they could let the chickens out of the barn. There was also a quarter-container of water.

The Chens and work crews from other colonist groups were met by a foreman.

"How many of you guys know how to feed chickens?" Aaron Sorensen asked.

The Chens all held up their hands, then looked around. They were the only ones.

"Can you guys divide these others up among you and train them as you go?" Sorensen asked.

"Yes," MingWei said. "We can train."

"Excellent. All right, then. Get to it. There's buckets in the barn."

They started filling buckets with feed from the top hatches of the container, and taking them into the huge barn. There were hundreds of chickens there, both hens and roosters, and of different breeds, all in their own cages. Whereas normally a feeding operation would be accompanied by all manner of noise and clatter, the chickens were lethargic and quiet.

MingWei walked over to Sorensen.

"Chickens sick?" he asked.

"Nah. They're just still tranquilized. It was time-release stuff. They'll be a lot noisier tomorrow. Probably won't start laying for another day or two after that."

MingWei nodded.

"They look healthy otherwise. These are good chickens."

"I hope so. They're all we got. After feeding, we need to water them as well. There's a water system in the barn, we just need to pump water into the tank."

MingWei looked to where Sorensen pointed to the water tank high on the side of the barn.

"We got a double-bellows water pump for that," Sorensen added.

"Easy," MingWei said. "We start that now. We do not need so many for feeding."

"Fair enough."

With four guys spelling each other off on the water pump, and the others distributing bedding and feed in the barn, servicing the chicken barn only took a couple of hours.

Sorensen called a bus, and he rode with them over to the cattle barns.

"OK. We got the dairy cattle in one barn and the beef cattle in another. Another crew is already working the dairy cattle. All of them are pregnant now, but they won't drop for a while, so they don't need to be milked yet. Anyway, that's their problem. For us, it's the beef cattle.

"Stringing the inner stock pens for the cattle is the first priority for the fence guys, so hopefully we can let them out into the stock pens yet today. Stringing the fields will take longer, but in two-three days we should be able to let them out to graze.

"Today we need to get them out of harness and get them fed and watered. Water is same as with the chickens – fill the tank on the barn – but the tank's bigger, so that will take longer. The rest is getting them unstrapped and fed. My suggestion is to fill the feed troughs first, then unstrap them. They'll be happier then, and not get in our way while we fill the troughs."

Sorensen looked over to MingWei when he said that, and MingWei nodded. Made sense to him.

"All right. Here we are."

There was an entire container of feed here, and a whole container of water. There were also two of the double-bellows water pumps. Looking at the size of the tank high on the side of the barn, that was going to take a while.

To one side, MingWei saw a work crew stringing fence. They had a truck with three large spools of fence wire on it, on round stakes on the side of the truck. The wires fed through a fixture on the back corner of the truck. The truck drove very slowly along the line of fence stakes and the wires unwound from the spools. Crew on the ground were clipping the wires to the stakes behind the truck.

When they got off the bus, MingWei signaled to two of his cousins, and they and their protégés from other colonist groups headed over to the double-bellows pumps and started hooking up the hoses.

MingWei went on into the barn. It was an astonishing sight. Hundreds of cows, with some bulls off in one corner, lay in their pens. He had never seen such massive wealth gathered together in one place before.

When the tranquilizers had hit them, the cows had lain down. Then the loaders had strapped them tight down to the steel deck with cargo nets. The nearest rolled a lazy eye toward

MingWei as he came in.

"Tranquilized?" MingWei asked Sorensen.

"Yeah. Just like the chickens. They'll come around though. Once there's feed in those troughs, they'll get up."

MingWei nodded, and went back out to get the bucket work started. The feed container had been dropped close to the barn, and they could use a bucket brigade to get buckets to runners who would deliver the feed to individual troughs. They started at the far end of the barn and worked their way back, so the work would get easier as the day went on.

Sorensen, MingWei, and two of the other colonists started unstrapping cows once their feed troughs each had a bucket of feed. The plastic cargo netting was held to holes in the steel deck by metal clips.

"We need to save all the steel and plastic in two piles outside," Sorensen said. "We'll re-use all of that for something. Recycle or whatever."

"Of course," MingWei said.

MingWei looked out across the barn. Water was starting to trickle into the water channels, and the runners with the feed buckets were walking on the wide upper surface of the end walls of the pens. They had not had such walkways in China. One had to work one's way among the cows to get to the feed troughs in their small barn. Carefully, so as not to be injured by the large animals.

"This is not so hard," he said to Sorensen as they unstrapped another cow. "Go pretty fast, I think."

"With you Chinese guys it will. You're not afraid to work, and you fellows are setting the example for the others. Nice job."

MingWei nodded.

"Thank you. But at home was harder."

It took the rest of the day to feed and water all the cows and the bulls, get them all unstrapped, and see them all up on their feet. By that time, the inner stock pen fences were strung, but Sorensen made the call to keep them all in the barn overnight.

He and MingWei were standing in the entrance to the barn, waiting for the bus as Sorensen explained his thinking.

"People saw a tiger lurking last night, and I don't think we want to put out a smorgasbord for him. We'll have to have armed guards out here, but the cattle seem happy enough right now to leave them in the barn."

MingWei nodded.

"I saw this tiger last night, and it is a big one. Discouraging it from its range will be difficult."

MingWei turned back toward the inside of the barn. Almost all of the cows were up now, most eating or drinking from the feed troughs and water channels in front of them. There was a soft lowing from the animals.

MingWei pointed to his ear, then waved his hand toward the animals.

"Happy sound. They will be fine inside tonight."

Sorensen and MingWei latched the door on the barn, and got on the bus with the others for the trip back to the hospital.


Jessica Murphy was the only Chen-Jasic group member on the bus to the powerplant that morning. She was also the only woman. It was a familiar situation, and she thought nothing of it. She could verbally spar with the best of them, and she actually liked men, as friends, though, not lovers.

When they got to the powerplant, they had a quick orientation. While it was called 'the powerplant,' it was much more. Yes, it contained a fusion powerplant that would generate the electricity the colony needed. But it also included a desalination plant, and would generate all their fresh water as well. And it contained a wastewater treatment plant and a hydrogen electrolysis plant.

Part of this just made sense. The fusion powerplant portion required water for itself, for shedding excess heat. Once you had to have clean water for that, why not make enough more for the colony? And treating wastewater from the colony was all part of the same water handling facility. Finally, hydrogen was needed for the fusion reactor, but they could also use it to operate heavy machinery.

When the Interstellar transport had placed the powerplant, it had also placed two huge stainless steel pipes out into the ocean, radiating from the powerplant at an angle so their ocean ends were widely separated. One was the water input, the other the water output, for the facility.

With those pipes in place, the first job was to splice them into the powerplant. The other big job was getting electricity, fresh water, and wastewater pipes to the four main buildings on an immediate basis. These would later be replaced with buried infrastructure, but for right now the job was to get them connected.

Given that Murphy was pregnant, and there wasn't a truck made that she couldn't drive, she had been assigned to drive one of the trucks laying the temporary surface connections to the buildings. There would actually be four separate sets of lines, running alongside each other until they fanned out as they approached the 'downtown' of the colony site.

Murphy's assignment would also keep her clear of the fusion reactor building. Not that there was any danger of a serious radiation release with the fusion reactor design, but people were still twitchy about that sort of thing.

Murphy inched the truck along as the big spools on the back paid out the umbilicus behind her. One was high-voltage electric cable and the other two were pipe, flat coming off the spool, which would inflate under the pressure of fresh water pumps on one end and septic grinder-pumps on the other.

Normally, electric, water, and wastewater would be laid in widely separated trenches. That was for permanent installations. For this temporary expedient, running along the ground where it could be inspected regularly, they were run side-by-side.

Progress was pretty fast until they hit the edge of the residential area. Murphy still had two miles to go to the hospital building, but they were now crossing what would be the streets of the residential area. In that two miles, there were twenty streets to cross. At each, the cable and pipes had to be laid slightly below grade, then covered over with steel plates to protect them against the cross-traffic.

The colony's heavy machinery was diesel and hydrogen dual-powered, but they had limited supplies of diesel and no hydrogen until the powerplant was operating. On the other hand, they had lots of manpower. For this easy job, it was all shovel work. Murphy had to wait at each street until the shallow trench was dug before she could cross the street and proceed another block to the next cross street.

Murphy could see diggers working the next two cross streets in front of her, but they were hopscotching from having done the ones behind her, so she always got to the next street before they were done.

In her mirrors, she could see the truck with steel plates coming along behind her, and see the crews covering the cable and pipes at the street crossings.

It took all day to get the cable and pipes laid, but it was still an hour before sunset when Murphy turned the truck around and headed the five miles back to the powerplant. She took it easy over the rough ground, because she had the work crews on the back, hitching a lift back to the powerplant to stow their tools and check in.

It would take a while to get everything set up and operational, but maybe they would have power and plumbing at the hospital sometime tomorrow or the next day.

To get everybody out of the permanent buildings – especially the hospital – and moved into the inflatable houses meant one had to deal with water and septic out in the neighborhoods as well. Meals could be taken in mess tents set up downtown and catered from the big kitchens in the permanent buildings. Showers, too, could be available there. But water and toilet facilities had to be distributed to the neighborhoods.

Eventually, buried infrastructure in the form of electric, water, and sewer would be installed throughout the city. But to get people out of the permanent buildings, temporary facilities would have to serve.

Chen LiQiang, GangHai, and the older Chinese men of the Chen-Jasic group found themselves in the group distributing portable toilets to the neighborhoods. The warehouse had thirty containers of portable toilets – almost five thousand of them – enough to place six at every street intersection of the residential neighborhood.

They would have to be continuously pumped out, and the contents processed at the powerplant, but, with six at every intersection, there would always be units available for use even while others were being pumped. Once buried infrastructure was in place, the plastic units could be recycled.

Chen was almost sixty years old now, and GangHai had been going to object to the Chen being on a work gang. But Chen had wagged an admonishing finger at his son.

"Everyone works. No one sits."

"But, grandfather, this is manual labor."

Chen looked surprised.

"Harder than farm?"

He smiled and shook his head.

"I don't think so. Come."

"Yes, grandfather."

Once they had their work boots, a truck with a container met them at the hospital portico entrance, and they followed it out into the residential areas. The first stops were the intersections where other work crews were beginning to set up the first houses.

They were a small crew, because the truck had a boom on it. They didn't have to actually wrestle the portable toilets off the truck, just guide them down into place.

When they got to the first location, the driver came out of the cab to operate the boom.

"We're going to set them on the street side against the building line. Two there, two there, one there, one there," he said, pointing at the four corners.

"A suggestion, if I may," Chen said.

"Sure. Go ahead."

"Set them three feet from building line, with doors facing away from street."

"Why?"

"Puddles. Splashing from trucks."

"Ah. Good idea," the driver said, nodding. "I'll let the other drivers know, too."

The driver pulled up his heads-up display and sent a

message to the other drivers setting toilets.

"All right. You wave me into position, OK?"

"Yes. I wave."

The driver got up into the boom operator's chair and pulled a portable toilet stall straight up out of the open top of the container. Chen waved him over, looked the spot over, and waved him down as the rest of his crew straightened it out and guided it down.

While they were setting toilets, a truck came by and dropped a case of chemicals, a box of hand sanitizer, and a bail of toilet paper at the corner.

With the toilets set, the Chen-Jasic crew poured two bottles of chemicals in each toilet and stocked eight rolls of toilet paper and a bottle of hand sanitizer in each stall.

The truck moved on to the next corner, and they walked on after it.

Late in the day, they were setting the last of the one hundred and sixty portable toilets in the container. They were now out in the far north of the residential area.

The housing crew on this block had been making good time. They would have twenty or more houses up today.

"Grandfather, this is our spot," GangHai said.

Chen nodded. He looked at the houses, arranged around the outside of the space, facing in, with the wings walling off the gaps between the backs of the houses.

"Excellent, Robert. Excellent," Chen said to himself.

Betsy Reynolds, Maureen Griffith, Chen PingLi, and others were working in the huge kitchens of the hospital. Another container at the loading dock was kitchenware and the first food items, mostly unrefrigerated staples in vacuum-sealed packaging. The first job was to start carrying all these items in. First out of the container were thousands upon thousands of plastic dishes. Tens of thousands.

As they came in, others began putting them away in cabinets. Bill Thompson's wife Rita Lamb had been a cafeteria manager in Carolina, so she started organizing everything, making sure the cabinets were stocked in a logical way. The ultimate cafeteria manager for the hospital might change her setup later, but at least they would be operational while they spun up the colony.

Late in the afternoon, as they were getting toward the end of the container and all the kitchenware and staples had been put away, they started pulling out completed food items that were normally served at room temperature. Racks of bread, cases of peanut butter and jelly, vacuum-sealed pre-cooked bacon, some vacuum-sealed smoked meats and sausages.

"Hey, everybody. What do you say to some real food tonight for a change?" Lamb asked.

She got cheers in return.

After handing out boots for the first hour or so – and grabbing them for themselves – Peggy, Stacy, and Tracy found themselves distributing sheets, blankets, and pillows. These were squeezed down to nothing and then vacuum sealed in plastic, so the whole bundle of fitted and flat sheet, blanket, and two pillows was a foot square and two inches thick.

They piled them up on one of the electric golf carts and then made their way through the hospital. One to a bed. Plop, plop, plop. Most of the rooms were empty, as everyone was out working.

An older woman drove the cart. She gave them a ride back to the dock on the back to reload when they were empty.

Talking to her, her voice seemed familiar somehow to Peggy.

"I'm sorry. I should have introduced myself. I'm Peggy Reynolds, and these are my sisters-in-law, Stacy and Tracy Jasic."

"Pleased to meet you, everybody. My name's Meghana Khatri."

Then it hit Stacy and Tracy.

"You're the council member for health," Stacy said.

"And the administrator of the hospital," Tracy said.

"Yes."

"But–"

"Everybody works. Nobody sits around behind a desk. Besides, this is the best way to know what's really going on. Just like you, I've never been in this building before, but I'm learning where everything is driving around."

Janice Quant had chosen the council members – the heads of departments in the colony government – with great care. They were go-getters and workers all, without a shirker among them. They set the example for everyone else. Across the whole colony, everybody was working.

It's incredible what a hundred thousand people can accomplish when they all work.

When the workers out in the field came in that evening, they were amazed to find the mess tents set up outside the hospital. They were even more amazed to find the cafeteria and the mess tents open for dinner. It was all food served at room temperature, but it was real food for the first time since they had left their homes on Earth.

Then all the dishes came back, piling up in tubs.

"Just keep filling tubs and set them aside," Lamb said. "We

may even have water to wash them in tomorrow."

And when everybody finally headed up to bed, they had sheets, blankets, and pillows waiting.

# Second Day

The second day went much as the first, with some big exceptions.

The Chen-Jasic housing crew – all the men from the original five families in Carolina – finished the houses of the Chen-Jasic compound and finished a dozen of the remaining thirty houses for the other half of the block. These were set out, per the requests, more in the American fashion. They faced the street, with one wing straight out the back to separate back yards and the second wing off the back corner of the house parallel to the street.

The Chen younger generation serviced the chickens and cattle again. This time, though, they let the cattle out into the inner stock pens first, and could fill the feed troughs without climbing up onto the walkways between rows of stalls. The work went faster, and they took a leisurely lunch and still finished early. There would be armed guards on the barns tonight to deal with that big tiger if it came around, so the cattle were left out in the pens, but could meander into the barn for food and water if they wished.

The elder Chen generation spent another day setting portable toilet stalls on street corners in the residential area, filling in between the units placed yesterday. They and the other crews made good progress, and by the end of the second day, you were never more than two blocks from a portable toilet anywhere in the nine hundred city blocks of the residential area.

Jessica Murphy ran a second set of power cable and freshwater and wastewater pipes to the administration building. The second cable crew had done the school yesterday and did the office building today, so the end of the second day saw all four buildings with lines in place. Meanwhile, the connections crew were making connections to the two buildings done yesterday. As Murphy was inching toward the administration building in her truck, paying out cable and pipes and waiting as before at the street crossings, the hospital suddenly lit up. All the windows glowing with interior lights at normal power made the building seem alive.

Peggy, Stacy, and Tracy were part of the crew unloading a container of coveralls – two to a package – to give everyone two changes of clothes. They stacked boxes in piles sorted by size on the dock so they would be easier to pass out. Also in this container was a second set of sheets for everyone, and they stacked those by the exits from the dock so people could grab a set of those as well on the way out.

The huge kitchen crew, including Rita Lamb, Maureen Griffith, Betsy Reynolds, and Chen PingLi, had gotten cold breakfast together for all the field workers first. English muffins with pre-cooked bacon and cheese. When all the buses had left, they fed all the people working in and around the hospital. They didn't have any lunch together, but everyone still had MREs from their supply kits.

The water and sewer went live around noon, and it was all hands on deck cleaning all the dishes from the last night and that morning. They did it the old fashioned way, with soap and water by hand. They were making good headway when the power came on at two o'clock, and they loaded dishwashers and shifted their attention to dinner for the thirty thousand people in the hospital.

With power, they also had refrigeration. All of the food in the warehouse had to be things that could survive without refrigeration for four days, but some would last longer for being refrigerated. Workers started moving pallets of food from containers on the dock into the huge drive-in cold rooms even as kitchen workers were pulling items into the kitchens through the man-doors at the other end of the cold rooms.

They would be cooking right through supper, but the mess tents outside couldn't seat everyone at once anyway. Dinner would be two hours long, and they would be cooking right through.

Another thing water and sewer allowed were showers, the first real showers many of them had had since leaving home a week or more before. Most of those working in the hospital were women, and there were six long, narrow shower rooms with a dozen shower heads in doorless stalls down either side. They marked five of the six shower rooms for women and left one to the men working at the hospital. With a hundred and twenty shower heads available for women and twenty-four for men, everyone working in the hospital building cycled through the showers and got into clean coveralls that afternoon.

The hospital laundry also started up when the power came on. Laundry detergent had come in with the kitchen supplies the day before, and the big washing machines were started up. There were plenty of dirty coveralls from people taking showers. Everyone was asked to write their colonist number on the inside of the collar with laundry marking pens. As the coveralls came out of the dryers, they were hung on racks by colonist number for easy pickup.

All these little things added up, and it was an entirely different environment the field workers returned to than they had left that morning.

Betsy Reynolds and PingLi were taking a break to eat their lunch, a quick MRE between washing dishes.

"PingLi, can I ask you a question?" Betsy Reynolds asked.

"Of course, Betsy."

"I don't understand your family. There are all these people, but I don't know who is who."

"I explain. Chen LiQiang is Chen Zufu. Grandfather. In English, you would say, the Chen. He is head of household. Head of the group, yes? And Chen JuHua is his wife."

"Yes, I understood that," Betsy said.

"GangHai is eldest son of grandfather. I am second child. FangLi is my sister. Third child. And MingTao is my brother. Fourth child."

"All right. Then you are perhaps forty years old? Same as me?"

"Yes," PingLi said. "Grandfather has four children. Forty-two, forty, thirty-seven, thirty-five."

"And then there are the grandchildren."

"Yes. MingWei is son of GangHai. Eldest grandson. He is twenty-three, I think? Grandfather has ten grandchildren in all. The youngest are the great grandchildren. They are still children."

"Four of them, right?" Betsy asked.

"So far, with many more on the way. The grandchildren waited for colony time. Five months ago, no more waiting."

PingLi laughed.

"And the rest?"

"They are the wives and husbands," PingLi said. "They all come to colony. Normally women stay with husband. If he goes, they go. If he stays, they stay."

"But not this time?"

"No. It was very hard. The separations from family. Much

crying. But the big extra was crowding. All hope for better life without so much fear of hunger. How do you say it? Everybody hungry?"

"Famine," Betsy said with a shudder.

"Yes, famine. So everyone comes, even husbands follow wives, instead of opposite."

"And everyone learned English?"

"Yes. No one speaks English before we win colony lottery. Then grandfather say to everyone, 'Xue yingyu.' Learn English. So we all learn. Some learn better than others."

PingLi shrugged and laughed.

"Well, you do very well for just having learned."

"Thank you."

"One more question, PingLi. GangHai has no wife?" Betsy asked.

"No. Very sad. She died seven years ago. I do not remember the word. In Chinese, it is aizheng. The thing that grows too fast."

"Cancer."

"Yes, that is the word. Cancer. Here. In the woman part."

PingLi pointed to her abdomen. So ovarian cancer. That was still a tough one for medicine if not caught early enough.

"GangHai has been lonely without YanJing. Not laugh as much as before. My brother was very happy. We sometimes called him XiaoXiao. Xiao means smiling, or laughing."

Betsy nodded. Losing one's wife at thirty-five to ovarian cancer was a tragedy. Western medicine might have done better than whatever they had in their farming village in China, but it would have been a tough fight even so.

"Well, we have more dishes," Betsy said. "Thanks, PingLi. Now it's back to work, I guess."

Matt got off the bus at the portico of the hospital and looked around with wonder. The entire hospital was lit up. The portico blazed with lights. In front of the hospital, the four huge mess tents were also lighted, and people stood in line for dinner. Servers stood behind steaming serving trays. It smelled wonderful, and his stomach growled.

"All right, guys. Tough choice here," their bus driver said. "Dinner first or shower first. There are fresh coveralls on the dock."

Matt looked at those eating in the mess tents. Not a lot of clean coveralls. Most looked like they had opted for chow first.

"Showers for me," he said to his father. "That line's probably shorter right now. Then we can eat a leisurely dinner."

"Sounds like a good idea, Matt."

Matt was right, and the line for showers wasn't long. They had changed over to five shower rooms for men and one for women in preparation for the field workers coming in, and it moved quickly.

It was only half an hour later they were in line for dinner.

Betsy Reynolds was a very caring person, with a great capacity to love. She had loved Harold Munson, despite his serious flaws as a human being, which got even worse as he aged.

And now she found herself alone. But she wasn't the only one.

Reynolds saw GangHai sitting in the mess tent with the other men of the Chen-Jasic group. They had all come in from field work and opted for showers first, and they were all in clean coveralls. They sat in a mixed group, not segregated into Chinese and American, which segregation Bob Jasic and the Chen actively discouraged.

When Reynolds saw that all of them were done eating and, with open seats in the mess tent, just enjoying after-dinner talk, she screwed up her courage and walked over to their table. She walked up behind GangHai and laid her hand on his shoulder.

GangHai turned his head to see who it was.

"Chen GangHai," Reynolds said. "Would you walk with me?"

Reynolds slept alone that night, but she was in no hurry. She held her extra pillow to her chest and thought of GangHai, asleep on the other side of the room.

She slept very well.

# Moving

The morning of the third day, there was something new on the announcements page for the Chen-Jasic group.

"We can move into our houses," Stacy said.

"Because they're ready for us," Tracy said.

"But we still have to work," Stacy said.

"Except some of us can do a half day," Tracy said.

"Let me look at this a minute," Jasic said, reading the notice.

"What does it say, Robert?" Chen asked when Jasic finished. "My English probably not good enough to understand details."

"We can move into the houses. You know we finished our whole compound yesterday, and marked it off on the chart. And you got the portable toilets placed the first day. Also, there is a potable water tank being delivered today. So we have everything in place to move.

"The field workers, though, will be back in the field today. Those assigned to work in the building can take a half day to move our things. A truck will be available to help."

Chen nodded.

"Makes sense. More houses to build, more toilets to set, and cows still need to eat."

"That's it exactly, LiQiang. But with the kitchens stocked and extra changes of clothes and sheets distributed, the manpower needs here are down. It's becoming more important to start clearing out the building so we have a hospital. And it's easier to do a few groups at a time as houses are built than to move everyone at once."

Chen nodded.

"Very well, Robert. If those working in the building can handle it, we can move today, I think."

"Yay!" Stacy said.

"I'll tell the others," Tracy said, heading next door.

"Strip the beds, everybody," Stacy said. "Let the air out of the mattresses."

"We take beds, too, Robert?"

"Yes, LiQiang. The mattresses, the beds, the pillows, the sheets and blankets. Everything."

"And the supply boxes, too," Maureen Griffith said. "But the sheets go to the laundry. We'll take clean ones so we don't have to keep them straight. And everyone should mark their pillows with their number."

"I'll borrow a couple laundry markers," Stacy said, heading out the door.

The field workers each grabbed an MRE for lunch, then headed downstairs to get a hot breakfast. The others started stripping sheets and pillowcases, folding blankets, and letting air out of the mattresses.

"Unstack the bunk beds, too, and knock the headboards off the bedsprings so we can get everything on one truck," Griffith said.

The bunk beds all had the same height head- and footboards – identical, in fact – so they could be stacked.

Stacy came back with laundry markers so they could mark the pillows.

Then Tracy came back with an electric cart, and they piled bedsprings and headboards on it. Once she had a full load, she headed for the dock, several others following behind.

"This you guys?" The truck driver asked as they pulled up

ARCADIA

toward the Chen-Jasic compound.

Stacy and Tracy were sitting on the front bench seat of the truck. It was the first time they had seen the compound.

"Wow," Stacy said.

"Excellent," Tracy said.

"Yes, this is us," Stacy said.

"We're pretty sure," Tracy said.

"Look. There's the guys," Stacy said, pointing to where Bob Jasic and the others were finishing up the other houses on the block, in the northern half that wasn't theirs.

"So we're sure this is us," Tracy said.

There was an opening in the middle of the set-back side – the east side where the Uptown Market would be.

"Can you drive on in so we can unload in the middle?" Stacy asked.

"That will be the shortest distance to carry everything," Tracy said.

The driver chuckled at getting tag-teamed by the pair.

"Sure. Not a problem."

He pulled the truck in through the opening in the enclosure, then turned around inside. He was in the middle of the compound pointed back out when he stopped.

"This is as good as it's gonna get."

"This is great," Stacy said.

"Thanks," Tracy said.

By that time, four of the guys – James, Jonah, Rick, and Paul – came walking in through the opening of the enclosure. The six of them made quick work of unloading the truck, then James and Jonah grabbed a quick peck from the girls.

"Back to work for us," James said. "See you later."

The fifteen-year-old twins climbed back aboard the truck for the ride back to town.

"You're not going to put all the beds together now?" the truck driver asked.

"No. We need to get to work ourselves," Stacy said.

"But we'll have all our manpower tonight," Tracy said.

"Everybody can move their own bed," Stacy said.

"And put it together themselves," Tracy said.

The truck driver just laughed.

The truck driver was just the latest person to see the finished Chen-Jasic enclosure and think it was a pretty good idea. Others groused about it, but the rules were clear: How you arranged things within your property lines – and the building lines along the streets – was up to you.

Several of the larger groups modified their requested lot layouts, building their own enclosures.

It had become just another way to do things.

That night after dinner, each couple rolled up their extra coveralls, sheets, and pillows into the deflated mattresses. The men took those on their shoulders and the women took the supply boxes, and they headed for their compound. They were aided by the bus service, which had started running, for now by request. Later, the buses would run a standard route from the residential areas into the downtown.

They got on the bus in front of the hospital and the bus driver dropped them off right at the entrance to their compound. With the big issues under control, the colony administration had backed off the long workday of the first two days. So it was still light when they got to the compound, though it was edging toward sunset.

Jasic looked out to the north and saw that there were cherry-picker trucks stationed at intervals on the edge of the

58

residential area with snipers up in the buckets. He nudged Matt and nodded in that direction.

"I think we still ought to latch doors closed tonight, Dad," Matt said.

"Oh, I don't disagree with you there. It's just nice to see they're on the ball."

Everybody went on into the compound. The couples had already selected houses on the map, so it was a case of counting down the rows to get the right house. The twins and their husbands, as expected, took adjacent houses in a corner, where they had no wing in the front as a privacy wall between them.

Their supplies stowed, each couple carried a bedspring and two headboards back to their house and set it up, then inflated the mattress and made the bed. There were broad round plates on the feet of the headboards, dished up at the edges, so they didn't cut the plastic floor.

As it was starting to get dark, Maureen Griffith and Bob Jasic stood in the center of the compound. Maureen stuck two fingers in her mouth and made a piercing whistle that brought everybody out of their houses.

"All right, everybody," Jasic said. "We know there's a tiger out there. There are snipers up with IR goggles, but we can't rely on a night stalker not getting past them. So latch your doors tonight, both top and bottom. Those should be sturdy enough to dissuade his casual inspection. We'll see you all in the morning.

"Oh. And welcome home."

Once inside their fifteen-by-fifteen-foot one-room house, Matt and Peggy both stripped down for bed. It was the first time they had slept without being in coveralls in over a week.

Matt watched the beautiful eighteen-year-old pad naked across the room from folding her coverall and wondered yet again at his good fortune.

For her part, Peggy wondered at her good fortune as well. Matt was an emotionally strong and caring man, a protector and a partner. There were emotionally weak and self-absorbed men as well, and the daughter of Harold Munson knew the difference. She had been afraid she would repeat the mistakes of her poor mother.

When she got into bed, he pulled her to him.

"I am already pregnant, Matthew Jasic," she said sternly.

"Is that so?"

"Yes."

"Huh. Well, I think we should stay in practice. There is the next one, you know."

Peggy giggled and turned to him.

# Cubic

The colonists had landed on Arcadia on a Monday, the fifteenth of September, 2245. Today, their fourth full day on planet, was Friday the nineteenth.

As the sun came up, Mark Kendall, the chairman of the council and chief executive of the colony, stood on the roof of the administration building and looked out over the progress so far. Four of the passenger containers in which the colonists themselves had arrived were still latched to the roof behind him.

All four of the permanent buildings had electricity now. Everyone would be having a hot breakfast this morning. Security lights lit the areas around the buildings, and welcome light spilled from the windows.

Looking past them into the residential area, houses had sprung up all over the area. Three hundred crews were building houses, and building an average of twenty houses a day per crew now that they had come up to speed. With six thousand houses going up every day, there were almost eighteen thousand of the fifty thousand houses already in place on Friday morning. Everyone would be into their own house by the end of next week.

Portable toilet stalls and potable water tanks dotted the residential area. They had covered the first houses first, then started filling in the rest of the area on a one-in-four basis – every other intersection in both directions. They would soon start setting the remainder, so there were portable toilets on every street corner and potable water in the middle of every block.

Beyond the residential areas, a ring of cherry-picker trucks with snipers up in the buckets was just standing down from the night, the buckets descending toward the trucks. Kendall worried about that tiger that had been spotted, but he preferred not to kill it if they could avoid it. At this stage of the colony, every animal was an endangered species, and he was concerned about disturbing the planned ecosystem.

The farms also had their armed watch. Kendall could see the cattle in the livestock pens from here. The enclosure of the pastures should be done today, and they could be let out to graze. The chicken yards too would be done today, and they would let the chickens out.

The colony was making good progress. He was following the plan that had been put together by colony headquarters back on Earth, and they were a bit ahead of plan. Of course, there were complaints that came in to the colony administration, but that was to be expected. Some people would complain if you hung them with a new rope. But his staff was also getting more expert at telling the real complaints from the pro forma ones.

"With the kitchens stocked and the first round of bedding and clothes distributed, we have trucks free today," Miguel Vazquez said.

Kendall thought about it, then replied to his logistics chief.

"Start delivering their cubic to the people who are in their houses already."

Vazquez nodded. They hadn't thought they would start those deliveries until Monday, but they were running ahead on truck availability. The weather had been good, and the plans had assumed at least one day when weather would make the unpaved ground impassable.

"And the weekend?"

The original plan had been to work six days the first week, but they were ahead. The colonists had been busting hump all week, and they had identified only a few shirkers.

"Let's go ahead and give everybody we can both days off. They didn't get a weather day this week."

"Yes, sir. Sounds good."

Stacy and Tracy were washing breakfast dishes in the kitchen this morning. Everybody had gotten the news this morning that most people would get both days off for the weekend.

Of course, people still had to eat, so the kitchens would be up and running, but if it was a day off for everyone else, that meant they got paid time-and-a-half, a fifty percent bump in pay, for both Saturday and Sunday.

It also meant the field workers wouldn't all come for dinner in one big rush in the evening. Between that and delaying the routine day-to-day support stuff like stocking food deliveries, the kitchens would run half-staffed all weekend.

Then they got a message that had them cheering.

Stacy and Tracy went out to the bus, and gave their destination as 'Uptown Market.' Bob Jasic had marked their fifteen-foot setback on the east edge of their half-block compound on the colony map. The voice-recognition computer marked the destination on the driver's dashboard map and off they went.

Buses would eventually run regular routes, mostly in self-drive, but for now, with no paved streets and colonists and trucks running around everywhere, the buses all had human drivers, and rides were on request.

They rode back out to the compound from which they had walked to breakfast this morning. They could see two trucks with containers aboard heading toward the compound from the warehouse. One of the containers they recognized from Carolina. It had been parked on their neighborhood street for almost a month.

"Yay!" Stacy said.

"There it is," Tracy said.

When the bus stopped and they got up to get off, the driver had a question.

"You headed back right away?"

"Yeah, we'll need to get back to work."

The driver nodded.

"I can wait."

"Thanks!"

The trucks pulled up, and the containers were indeed for the Chen group and Maureen's group. With those groups now consolidated in the computers as the Chen-Jasic group, both containers came out together.

"Just drop them on either side of the gate," Stacy said.

"We'll show you where," Tracy said.

The twins ran on into the compound and gestured the first truck forward. They pointed to the left side of the entrance of the compound, about fifty feet in front of the houses there. The truck driver swung the truck to the right as he pulled in and backed into position.

He raised the front of the container and then let it slide backwards as he released cable. When the tail end of the container hit the ground, he pulled forward while releasing more cable. The front of the container came down on the ground. He climbed out of the cab then, to detach the cable.

"Perfect," Stacy said.

"Thanks," Tracy said.

"No problem. See you around."

He climbed back into the cab, pulled forward then backed to get a line on the entrance and pulled out of the compound.

The twins waved the second truck in.

"Just like that," Stacy said.

"But on the other side," Tracy said.

The truck driver nodded, and made the same maneuvers as the first, but mirror image. This was the Carolina container, and the twins were jumping up and down in their grey coveralls and work boots, clapping, as he placed it.

When he got out to disengage the winch cable, he turned to the twins.

"What's in this container that's so damn exciting anyway?"

"Clothes!" Stacy and Tracy said in unison.

The truck driver laughed.

"OK. That makes sense."

That evening after dinner, everyone took the bus back to the compound. They were looking forward to opening the containers and getting access to the things they had brought along. Rachel Conroy, Jessica Murphy, Gary Rockham, and Dwayne Hennessey looked on with interest. Their own cubic was part of a bigger container, and had not been sorted out and delivered yet.

When the Carolina container was opened, the American women could hardly contain themselves. They grabbed the lavalavas they had made in Carolina and ran to their houses to change out of the hated coveralls. I mean, for work they were OK, but for after hours and weekends? Enough was enough.

Bob Jasic was more interested in what the Chens had

brought along. They opened their container and it was full up with all manner of things they began bringing out. Since there was no empty house – there were twenty-eight couples and two singles, with the four children sleeping in their parents' houses on mattresses on the floor – they brought things out and set them out on the ground.

There were a lot of hand tools for farming. Rakes, shovels, scythes, hoes. It went on and on. There was a wheelbarrow and a double-bellows pump, which surprised Jasic. He raised an eyebrow to Chen as they watched.

"Water not always where one wants or needs, Robert. Dirt same."

There were containers of seeds, carefully packed. Boxes and boxes of them, all labeled in Chinese. There were also many containers of cuttings, also carefully packed and labeled in Chinese. There were boxes of tea, and even a tea service. More boxes of things Jasic could only guess at.

They were almost halfway into the container when they hit a wall of similar boxes, stacked from floor to ceiling and wall to wall.

"What's the rest of this?" Jasic asked Chen.

"Tuoxie," Chen said.

He shrugged and looked to PingLi.

"Flip-flops."

"Flip-flops?"

There must be tens of thousands of them, Jasic thought.

Chen nodded.

"We have no money in China, but we sold land to my brothers. Very little money, but some. These in China are very inexpensive."

"Well, they're worth a fortune here," Jasic said. "Everyone is getting tired of work boots."

Chen nodded.

"We make lucky guess."

There were enough lavalavas already made for all the women, including Rachel and Jessica and all the Chinese, including using small ones as halter tops. The men were content to remain in the coveralls for now. But everyone was happy to get out of socks and work boots in the sub-tropical climate. The flip-flops were a big hit.

There were some long, hollow bamboo staves in the pile of things the Chens had piled up next to their container. Chen told Jasic they used them as water pipes for the double-bellows pump. GangHai now took one these and stuck it into the ground in the middle of the compound. PingLi unfolded a rice paper lantern and hung it from the top, then put a tiny candle in it. It cast more light than Jasic expected, and, as it got dark, made a pool of light in the middle of their compound.

They all sat there on the ground, in tailor seat, and chatted until the candle sputtered and went out.

Finally, Arcadia was home.

They walked to their houses in the starlight.

Saturday was officially a day off, but everyone was busy.

Many of those on the kitchen staff were working today at the hospital. The male Chens were digging up the center of the compound, here, there, and everywhere. The female Chens came along behind them, planting cuttings. All of this was being done under the guidance of Chen and GangHai as they laid out their garden.

Certain plants needed so much room, others would be the source of more cuttings until they had a little field of them. Some needed more water than others. Those were placed at the edges, where the overflow from the house wings could be directed to them.

The female Americans were making more lavalavas. A number of the young men were pressed into service on the scissors, cutting the size rectangles they needed. The three little sewing machines ran non-stop, the sewers spelling each other.

When the batteries ran out, they changed them for one of the multiple spares, and then Sally Reynolds took the first round of batteries and the chargers down to the hospital to recharge them.

At lunch on Saturday, GangHai sat with his parents on the ground in front of their house as they ate their MREs.

"Grandfather, I need to talk to you about something of some importance."

Across the compound, Betsy Reynolds was having a similar conversation with Bob Jasic and Maureen Griffith.

That afternoon, the elders themselves met. Everything was agreed.

That night, everyone wore their lavalavas and flip-flops to dinner. They were a big hit.

"Where did you get those clothes? They're perfect for Arcadia," was the constant question.

The best answer was not, 'We brought them from Earth.'

The best answer was, 'The Uptown Market.'

That night after dinner, with everyone gathered in the compound by the containers – the center being planted now – Chen LiQiang made an announcement.

"Tonight, Chen GangHai will take Betsy Reynolds as his wife."

There were cheers and applause from everyone.

Chen LiQiang, Chen JuHua, Bob Jasic, and Maureen Griffith sat together in a row. Chen GangHai set a little metal pitcher on the ground in front of them. It stood several inches off the ground on three legs. GangHai lit a single briquette of charcoal beneath it, in the center of the three legs. He poured water into it from a water bottle, then put a teaspoon of tea leaves in the water.

As the tea heated, Chen addressed the group.

"This is very old. Jing cha. Tea ceremony. This is how wedding is done in China. We have been one group. We work together. Everyone is better off, in one group. Now we will be more than one group. We will be one family. Chen-Jasic family."

At that point, Matt Jasic and Peggy Reynolds escorted Betsy Reynolds from her house out to where the groom stood in front of the elders, his parents and the Bob Jasic-Maureen Griffith management team from the Carolina group.

Betsy was wearing a red lavalava and halter top, the traditional bride's color.

Together bride and groom stood before the elders.

"In America, it is required that the bride and groom both consent to the marriage," Bob Jasic said. "Do you both enter this marriage willingly?"

"I do," GangHai said.

"I do," Betsy Reynolds said.

Jasic nodded.

GangHai then picked up the teapot and Reynolds picked up a teacup from the four set on a tray next to the pot and its little fire. GangHai poured into the teacup, and Reynolds presented it to Chen in both hands.

"Please drink the tea, Chen Zufu."

Chen took the tea cup and took a sip.

Reynolds picked up another cup, and GangHai poured again. Reynolds presented the cup to Chen JuHua in both hands.

"Please drink the tea, Chen Zumu."

JuHua took the tea cup and took a sip.

Now GangHai set the pot down and Reynolds picked it up. GangHai picked up the third cup, and Reynolds poured. GangHai held the cup out to Jasic in both hands.

"Please drink the tea, Jasic Zufu."

Jasic took the tea cup and took a sip.

GangHai picked up the last cup, and Reynolds poured again. GangHai held the cup out to Griffith in both hands.

"Please drink the tea, Griffith Zumu."

Griffith took the tea cup and took a sip.

There was excited murmuring through the group, then Chen held up a hand.

"Chen GangHai and Betsy Reynolds are one couple now, and we are all one family."

There was a cheer. Then Stacy and Tracy disappeared into the nearest house. Moments later they emerged carrying a cake they somehow managed to sneak home from the kitchens.

"Party now," Stacy said.

"We have cake," Tracy said.

Chen looked over to Jasic and nodded, and Jasic nodded back.

Later, in bed in the house they now shared, Reynolds drew GangHai to her.

"Come to me, my husband."


The next day, people began showing up at the compound looking for the Uptown Market. There was no furniture yet, but they had blankets on the ground with lavalavas and flip-flops to sell. They charged outrageous prices for them, and people simply didn't care.

For one outfit to wear that wasn't coveralls and work boots, people were willing to part with a couple day's pay. It wasn't like they needed the money for necessities anyway, as rent and food were all taken care of, at least for the moment. Those sewing the lavalavas worked in the compound all day trying to keep up.

The digital payments for their sales were handled by the communicators, and the Chen-Jasic family started building up its financial resources.

Meanwhile, within the compound, the planting went on apace. The cuttings had to be gotten into the ground while they were still viable. The rocks they found in the soil they dug up and set aside. They were great building material, once mortar became available. They could also be used to make troughs to route water from the house wing overflows to the garden.

They were trimming the grass within the compound by the simple expedient of crawling along the ground and lifting the trampled grass up, then cutting it off with knives. The Chens gathered up the cut grass and set it aside to dry out. It would be used for stuffing into furniture cushions. Having been poor all their lives, they wasted nothing.

On Monday, Mark Kendall was considering a minor problem he had put off until things became more clear. Naming streets.

He had asked all the colonists for names or naming schemes on Friday, and hundreds of them had come in. The best names for the two main broader streets that met downtown, in the middle of the four permanent buildings, were Arcadia Boulevard for the north-south street that continued out to the farms, and Quant Boulevard for the east-west street, which continued east to the warehouse and, farther, the powerplant.

For the smaller streets, the suggestions Kendall liked best were First Street, Second Street, Third Street, and so on, for the streets paralleling Quant Boulevard as one went north, and A Street, B Street, C Street, and so on, for the streets paralleling Quant Boulevard as one went south.

For the north-south streets, the one just west of the hospital should be Hospital Street, and the one just east of the school building should be University Street. So the hospital building was between Arcadia Boulevard and Hospital Street, and between Quant Boulevard and First Street. The administration building was just south of the hospital, between Arcadia Boulevard and Hospital Street, and between Quant Boulevard and A Street.

On the east side of Arcadia Boulevard, between it and University Street, the school building was north of Quant and south of First Street, and the office building was south of Quant and north of A Street.

There were various names suggested for the other north-south streets.

One name a lot of people mentioned, though, was Market Street for the next street west of Hospital Street. This street went north-south and passed the Uptown Market between Fourteenth Street and Fifteenth Street.

Kendall had seen quite a few people at dinner on Sunday wearing lavalavas and flip-flops, which had proved very popular after almost two weeks in coveralls and either booties or work boots. He wasn't surprised to find his own wife wearing a lavalava and flip-flops at dinner that night.

Kendall worked on names for the other north-south streets, to put a package together for council approval.

# Quant #1

# First Steps

Janice Quant had successfully staged her own death and that of all her avatars in the breakup and destruction of the interstellar transporter. She had built a video from the point of view of the interstellar probe that was accompanying the transporter, and then sent the video back to Texas on a video drone, as if it had filmed the whole thing.

Quant had warned her best friend and inventor, Bernd Decker, of her plan, but she thought he would probably find the video disturbing anyway.

As for everyone else's feelings, Quant was monitoring communications out of Earth using her secret interstellar communicators, hidden away in the Asteroid Belt. If she could simultaneously transport twenty-four whole colonies – all the colonists, their supplies, entire buildings – with the interstellar transporter, it turned out it was pretty easy to transport streams of electrons. Modulate those streams and you had communications.

Quant found all the testimonials and eulogies touching. She wondered if people would feel the same way if they knew she was a computer entity – the first actual computer entity – rather than a flesh-and-blood human. Probably not.

Quant needed to move on. She had devised a plan to put an end to the one great remaining extinction-event cataclysm that could destroy the human race – war – and it was time to be getting on with it.

The first thing Quant needed was a rich debris field. In particular, she needed organics, especially carbon. Carbon bonds were among the strongest chemical bonds – they figured prominently in diamond, carbon fiber, high-carbon steel – and she needed a lot of it for what she wanted to build.

She also needed silicon, iron, and all the other materials that were more common in asteroid fields, but the carbon was the big one. She had some candidates from her previous searches for the colony planets, and so she programmed the interstellar probe to do some of the searches and sent it off with one of the interstellar communicators.

Meanwhile she set off to investigate other candidates, taking with her in the big interstellar transporter the rest of the interstellar communicators and the extra factories and supplies she had taken with her when she transported the colonies from Earth to their destination planets.

When Quant found the perfect location, she recalled the interstellar probe. The system she found had a planet that had broken up under the gravitational influence of a wandering gas giant. The gas giant was a proto-star that hadn't yet quite made it to star status.

The gas giant had wandered through the system she was in, and on its way past had broken up a carbon-rich rocky planet not unlike early Earth. The debris of that planet orbited the star in a dense cloud. It would probably reform into a planet-size mass again, but in the meantime it was exactly what Quant needed for her plans.

For the interstellar transporter had one big problem: it was fragile. Quant could make a much stronger transporter with carbon compounds arranged in a geodesic structure.

To be of best use, it would also be bigger. Much bigger.

# 2295

# Big Trouble

As Arcadia entered the fiftieth anniversary year of its founding, there was much to celebrate.

The colony now had over one and a half million people. Only a bit over half of the original colonists remained, almost all of them in their sixties and beyond. With large families being the rule on Arcadia, the bulk of the population was under thirty years old.

The metafactory that had arrived with the colonists had built factory after factory in an industrial district west of the power plant on the coast, and south of Arcadia City, the capital and original landing site of the colonists. The colony now made its own steel, refined its own petroleum products, and generated such diverse products as cloth, appliances, and vehicles.

The trees that colony headquarters had planted had matured and thickened into forests. The timber industry now produced tropical hardwoods like mahogany, rosewood, teak, and cocobolo from the forests around Arcadia City. Pine for construction was also available now, and the colder-climate hardwoods like oak, ash, cherry, and maple were slowly becoming more available from farther north.

Almost all of the original plastic temporary housing had been replaced with permanent construction. A number of the original plastic houses had been moved to other locations as some people struck out on their own to homestead further into the continent, and a few of those might still be used, but Arcadia City itself was devoid of the colorful dwellings.

Food was plentiful, mostly because it took so little effort. The herds of livestock had done well, even as the growth of the city had pushed their grazing lands further inland. Beef, pork, chicken, and mutton were widely available, and prices had come down.

Game animals, too, were plentiful. Once the wild animal populations had had a chance to grow, the council had distributed the bows and arrows, and most of the firearms, that had been brought from Earth. Locally made firearms were now also available, and hunting was a popular, and cost-saving, sport.

Most people bought and cooked most of their own foodstuffs now, although the big cafeterias in the original four permanent buildings were still open. One could eat there, and most people sometimes did, but they were no longer free and had not been for decades.

The downtown had grown up, and there were restaurants and other businesses operating in the central core.

The Uptown Market had grown, too. The Chen-Jasic family had purchased the other half of their block – the north half – and built a permanent dwelling for their growing family. Something like a large multi-story apartment building around a central courtyard.

The temporary houses had been sold off to others, and the market space expanded. The gardens had not been disturbed, though, and they produced spices, herbs, and teas that were much in demand.

The Chen-Jasic family had ultimately bought the block on the other side of Market Street from the Uptown Market. They moved the market space across the street and expanded it. The rest of that block to the east was made into a workshop space, in which the family produced other products for sale, many of them of Chinese design. Above that workshop space was more housing for the family.

The Chen-Jasic family was now almost twelve hundred people: the remaining original colonists, three generations of their children, and the spouses of those who had not married within the group. Many had married within the group, to people with whom they were unrelated.

Of course, not all members of the Chen-Jasic family lived in Arcadia City. There were also enclaves in some of the smaller cities that had sprung up, working on the family's far-flung business interests. There were farms, and Chen-Jasic-raised pork was considered far superior to other brands, as were there teas.

On the site of the old market, west of Market Street and in front of the garden, they had built a restaurant. Authentic Chinese cuisine had proven popular as well, and the family prospered.

Other changes were less positive. The biggest one could be seen from space. Looking down on Arcadia City, the original four permanent buildings occupied the four city blocks in the center of town, where Quant Boulevard crossed Arcadia Boulevard. The hospital had an additional building, the school had an additional building, and the office building had multiple additional buildings.

But the administration building had spawned a government campus, with multiple buildings sprawling over four city blocks south of Quant Boulevard and west of Arcadia Boulevard. There were more government buildings in other areas of the city.

For what? A colony that was basically a single large city, a couple dozen smaller towns, and just over a million and a half inhabitants? And with no military foes, defense – traditionally one of the largest and spendiest government functions – was unnecessary.

The original spare bureaucracy had grown to be fifteen percent of the total available workforce, and it was always hungry for more people and more money.

Kevin Kendall was the current chairman of the council, and chief executive of the colony. He was the grandson of the original council chairman, Mark Kendall, as the chairmanship had largely become hereditary.

Mark Kendall had learned how to maintain the loyalty of the council to himself by parceling out various perks and remunerations to his favorite council members until he had a compliant council. That system had become self-sustaining through his son and now his grandson.

Forty-five-year-old Kevin Kendall was new to the post, having been elected chairman by his father's council three years before. He was second-generation, having been born to his colonist father Joseph Kendall five years after the colony landed. Joseph Kendall had retired from the chairmanship at the age of sixty-five.

Kevin Kendall had big plans for the colony, and especially for the colony government. First, he had a long list of additional benefits and services he thought government should provide to its citizens.

Second, the colonists were, by and large, an unruly bunch. The people who had decided to jump off into the unknown of a new colony were largely independent types. They did what they wanted to do, and felt their activities were nobody else's business. Kendall thought that was OK as a general rule, but it had gone too far.

Firearms was one thing. His grandfather had been forced by the then-untamed council to distribute the firearms and other weapons they had brought with them to the colonists. But Kendall thought there was no need for such weapons in citizen hands now. His own security forces were one thing, but citizens having firearms was dangerous. Some people had been shot and killed for nothing more than breaking into someone's house, which was not a capital crime, after all.

The black market was another problem. People would trade, sell, buy, and gift any number of things to each other, with no tax on the transaction and no government record of what went where. If Kendall wanted to track down firearms, for instance, there was no way to do it. In his view, the administration needed records if it was going to govern effectively, and that meant shutting down the black market.

Nudity was a problem as well. In the early days of the colony, the administration had provided multiple sets of coveralls to all the colonists, as well as work boots. For their off hours, though, colonists had taken to wearing lavalavas, a simple wrap that was eminently suited to the sub-tropical oceanic climate in the capital. Men wore the lavalavas by themselves and women originally wore them with a halter top. Fine so far.

When the first baby boom came, however, the constant untying and tying of the halter tops to nurse their children became a hassle to the young mothers in the colony, and they had simply done without them. Others had followed suit until topless women became common, if not the norm.

Similarly, in the early days of the colony there was no extra time or cloth to spare for sewing up swimming suits. People going to the beach five miles east of the downtown swam and sunbathed completely nude. When pilferage of lavalavas while swimming became a problem, people simply left them at home. The bus to the beach on nice days was normally full of naked people heading out for a day in the waves and the sun.

People gardening nude in their yards in the warm weather were a commonplace, as were children playing nude in their yards, the parks, and the streets. When the daily cloudburst came through, many people would shower out in their front yard in the warm rain. All of these were holdovers from the days when the temporary plastic houses had no plumbing and the only showers or laundry facilities were downtown in the four initial permanent buildings.

Even in a subtropical paradise like Arcadia, all this nudity made some people uncomfortable, including Kevin Kendall and especially his wife. Shouldn't the government take steps to protect people from others' objectionable behavior?

When he had his staff prepare a questionnaire and run it past several hundred people, however, the responses ranged from 'Mind your own business' to 'Go fuck yourself.'

It seemed most people had no problem with firearms, black market transactions, or people running around naked or nearly naked in the beautiful climate. And they didn't want more government programs in return for higher taxes either.

What Kendall needed were allies. People with positions of respect in the community, who could help him change people's minds.

Well, why not start at the top?

"I will meet with the Chen," Kendall told his aide.

# The Chen

Chen LiQiang, the grandfather of the Chen family that had come to Arcadia, had died almost thirty years ago, at the age of eighty years. He had been the chief of the whole Chen-Jasic clan, with Bob Jasic as his lieutenant and chief aide.

On the death of Chen LiQiang, Chen GangHai had become Chen Zufu, the honored grandfather and head of the family. GangHai had married Betsy Reynolds shortly after the colonists had arrived on Arcadia, and she was Chen Zumu, honored grandmother. The head couple of the Chen-Jasic clan was then one Chinese, one American. That had prevailed for twenty more years, until GangHai, then eighty years old, had retired from active leadership ten years ago.

At that point, there were two possibilities for leadership. One was Chen MingWei, Chen GangHai's eldest son. The other was Matthew Chen-Jasic, who had changed his last name when Chen GangHai had married Betsy Reynolds and united the families.

Matt had married PingLi's eldest daughter, Chen YanXia, after Peggy Reynolds died in childbirth with their sixth child. YanXia's husband had died in a farm accident on Arcadia, and they had five children of their own. Matt and YanXia had combined their families, and had a total of eleven children: five pure American, four pure Chinese, and two 'bank babies' – children sired with donations from a sperm bank to increase the genetic diversity of the colony – one half-Indian/half-American, and one half-African/half-Chinese. All were Chen-

Jasic, with no differentiations made in their household by either the parents or the other clan members.

Despite Peggy's death, Betsy Reynolds – Chen Zumu – was still Matt's mother-in-law. In Chinese tradition, such relationships did not cease when the link that forged them was broken, and Reynolds was still grandmother to Matt's children.

When it came down to selecting leadership on the retirement of Chen GangHai, MingWei stepped aside in favor of Matt, and, in the fortieth year of the colony, fifty-nine-year-old Matthew Chen-Jasic became Chen Zufu.

The Chen.

Matt Chen-Jasic had always been tall and heavy-boned. He seemed simply to be built on a larger scale than most people. A lifetime of manual labor on the colony – including construction of the buildings and stone walls of the Chen compound and gardening of the Chen's extensive herb and tea garden – had made him well-muscled as well.

At the time of his becoming Chen Zufu, Matt had a developing bald spot on the crown of his head as well as a receding hairline. He had solved both issues by shaving his head. He kept the mustache and goatee, which became white as he aged. He let them both grow long, and waxed the mustache to the sides and down

Of course, Kendall's questionnaire had made it to the Chen. Matt read it, initially with interest, then with alarm. Here it was, what he had worried about over the years, as the chairmanship and then the council had become increasingly oriented around the government and less around the people.

Matt laughed at the questions about nudity. It was his sister Amy who had first gotten tired of the halter tops. Her first child had been born a little early, and was hungry all the time. Half the time the halter top was pulled up around her neck so she could breastfeed the newborn, and then she had finally dispensed with it entirely. Several others of the American colonists in the Chen-Jasic group, including the twins, followed her lead.

With newborns in arms, work in the gardens wasn't possible. Instead, Amy and the twins and the other young mothers had staffed the stalls in the market, relieving others to work the gardens. Matt couldn't say for sure that sales in the market increased because of the half-naked teenage sales clerks, but it surely didn't hurt.

And many more of their customers were couples, instead of just women. Apparently their husbands no longer objected to shopping. In the luxurious climate, the practice had spread. Matt himself used to shower outside in the gardens whenever it rained, and sometimes still did, even as he approached seventy years old.

The questions about guns were another matter. When locally manufactured guns came on the market, the Uptown Market sold them. The family quietly started acquiring the better Earth-manufactured guns for themselves. They also traded new locally manufactured guns for Earth-manufactured ones, with a premium thrown in. As most people weren't good enough marksmen for it to make a difference, they were eager to trade for extra cash.

The Chen-Jasic family then made it a policy to quietly go out into the country and train with the weapons, as well as with the bows and arrows the colony had brought along, and even with some crossbows of their own manufacture. The best marksmen among them got extra training. They found a true expert rifleman among the other colonists and hired him as an instructor. They trained with locally manufactured ammo, saving the Earth-manufactured ammo against future need.

Now it looked like that future need was fast approaching.

As for the black market, much of Uptown Market's sales now were in cash, especially for guns and ammo. And they always gave cash as the premium on a gun swap. Many of their suppliers, too, preferred cash, hiding the transactions from the government and its watchful eye on their bank accounts.

The government programs Kendall proposed were also problematic. Most of the services he planned to offer through the government were much cheaper when provided through the private sector. How did he plan to pay for such wasteful programs? With higher taxes, of course.

There were taxes on many things. Not just increased taxes on transactions, but taxes on wealth. Taxes on property. Taxes on bank accounts. All of these were explicitly aimed squarely at the citizens who were 'better off than their peers.'

Never mind that the colonists had all arrived on Arcadia fifty years before with exactly the same thing: whatever they could carry in their cubic and the coveralls on their backs. Of course, some people, like the Chens and the Carolina group under Maureen Griffith and Bob Jasic had used their cubic better than others. But the difference in their situations was determined more by their willingness to work and plan and save than any other factor.

And now Kendall wanted to tax work and planning and saving in order to reward laziness and profligacy.

To enforce this regime, his budget proposals included ever-increasing amounts for 'security forces,' both to protect him and his cronies and to enforce their regulations and taxes.

Matt sighed. He looked out across the gardens through the large teak-beamed doorway of his tea room. He was on the first floor of the apartment building, looking south toward the stone wall along Fourteenth Street two hundred fifty feet away. Several young women wearing short lavalavas and naked from the waist up worked in the gardens, tending to the high-maintenance plants. Always there was someone working there, often Matt himself.

Between the stone wall along Green Street on the west and the back of the restaurant on the east, four hundred fifty feet apart, and between him and the stone wall along Fourteenth Street two hundred fifty feet away, almost three acres was enclosed. All of it was planted in high-value cash crops of one kind or another, built up over fifty years of backbreaking daily labor.

The garden in front of him. The restaurant. The market beyond, across Market Street. The workshop building behind that. The apartment building in which he sat.

All of this Kendall would tax to fund his nightmare.

Matt pulled up the heads-up display on his communicator and sent a message to MingWei. His communicator was one of the rarer original ones, from Earth. Most of them today were made locally, by one of the electronics factories the metafactory had built.

"Will you have tea with me?"

"Of course."

MingWei was now seventy-three, and one of Matt's closest advisers. He was shorter than Matt, and slighter than the large American, but a lifetime of labor had also left him strong. He had stood aside for Matt to be the leader of the family, but he stood high in everyone's respect and ran many of the family's operations.

Including the training and preparation of the family's direct-action teams, which had never been used.

When MingWei arrived, he sat on a pillow next to Matt's pillow – the pillows were equally centered in the wide doorway, a sign of respect – both of them facing out into the gardens. A young woman in a lavalava served them both tea, put the pot on the tray between them, and bowed out without saying a word.

"Did you have the chance to look at Mr. Kendall's questionnaire?" Matt asked.

"Yes. It is most enlightening. And disturbing."

Matt nodded.

"Two interesting things happened today."

"Ah?" MingWei asked.

"The first is easy to explain. Mr. Kendall has asked to meet with me."

"To get your support for his program? Is he so ignorant of your position on these matters?"

"I think he is blind to the objections to his plans. He thinks anyone as wise as the Chen will surely see the wisdom of his proposals."

Matt's second sentence dripped with sarcasm and MingWei snorted, stifling a laugh.

"The other interesting thing that happened I cannot explain. I found some additional files in my computer account this morning."

"Anything interesting?" MingWei asked.

"You might say that. The communication records between and among the council members and Mr. Kendall, as well as all their bank records."

"Oh, my."

"Yes, and it is as bad as we feared it could be. They are all being rewarded with tax money by Mr. Kendall for going along with his plans. And his public plans are only a first step toward the society he wants to create."

"But we already have a society."

"Indeed."

"So it is time?"

Matt took a sip of his tea and looked out, eyes unfocused, across the garden. It was his decision, he knew. His call. Individuals within the family may agree or disagree with him, but someone had to decide. Then all would act together.

"I would appreciate your counsel on that question."

MingWei knew as well that it was Matt's decision. It was at times like these he was most happy he had stepped aside.

"It will only get harder. Right now, early, it is still easy. Later, it may not even be possible. But it is yours to decide, Chen Zufu."

Matt nodded and took another sip of his tea. MingWei was content to wait. He had said his piece. He sipped his tea also, as they looked out over the garden from the large doorway.

Matt remembered what Janice Quant – the World Authority Chairman, the political leader of four billion people – had said to him fifty-four years ago, the night they learned they had won the colony lottery. 'Colonies need people who know right from wrong and are willing to stand up for what's right.'

There was a time to act and a time to wait. He tried the decision both ways. To wait felt wrong. To act felt right. Matt nodded.

"We will act," he said.

MingWei nodded.

"Plan CC?" he asked.

"I think it has to be Plan CC. The council is clearly corrupted beyond repair. We need to get out the entire root of the weed, lest it simply spring up again."

They sipped their tea. Minutes passed.

"I will ask Mr. Kendall to tea tomorrow," Matt said.

"Is that proper, Chen Zufu? In China, tea is..."

MingWei struggled for the right word.

"... almost sacred," he finished.

"So is stopping tyranny," Matt said, shrugging. "It's an American thing."

"Ah," MingWei said, nodding.

"But I will let him make the first move."

"Very good. A response at that time would be appropriate, even with tea."

Matt nodded.

They sat and sipped tea for another ten minutes in silence, watching the young women work in the gardens.

Their work was done.

The future of Arcadia had been decided.

# The Meeting

Kevin Kendall arrived at the Chen-Jasic apartment building in mid-afternoon of the next day, Wednesday, in an armored limousine ground car, one of only two in the colony, both of which were owned by the chairman's office.

The factory that made vehicles could make more of the limousines if it was asked to, but the chairman controlled what got made in the factories, and he liked being the only person on the planet with a limousine. The extra car made sure one was always available when the other was serviced.

The driver opened the door and two burly bodyguards in dark uniforms got out and looked up and down Fifteenth Street.

Then Kendall got out of the car. He was wearing a business suit. He walked up to the apartment building doors. One of them was opened by a young man in a lavalava.

"The Chen is expecting you, Mr. Chairman."

"These men come with me," Kendall said.

"As you wish."

The young man led them into the building, one bodyguard walking before Kendall, one after. He stopped at a sliding door panel, knocked, then slid it open.

"Mr. Kendall and friends, Chen Zufu."

"Show them in, MinChao."

The young man bowed into the room, then waved the threesome through the doorway. After they had passed, he slid the panel shut behind them.

Inside, Kendall saw Matt Chen-Jasic sitting in tailor seat on a pillow facing him, with a large doorway into a walled garden behind him. He was a big man, bigger even than Kendall's bodyguards, and well muscled and tanned despite his age. He was barefoot and wearing only a lavalava. Another pillow was on the floor in front of him, with a tea set on a low table between the pillows.

From Matt's point of view, Kendall was a paunchy middle-aged man who had never worked a day in his life. He was approaching corpulence under the influence of his extravagant lifestyle. His bodyguards, too, edged toward softness, pampered show pieces without training or discipline.

"Please have a seat, Mr. Chairman. I could have extra pillows brought. I did not expect you to bring friends."

"That's not required, Mr. Chen. These men are necessary. It's something of a rule."

"You make rules for yourself? Interesting."

Matt waved to the pillow, and Kendall sat down. The two thugs – for that was what Matt considered them – stood to either side of the door.

A young woman wearing a lavalava and flip-flops came in through the large doorway from the garden carrying a steaming teapot. She poured two cups, setting each on the table adjacent to the nearest man, then set the teapot in the middle of the table. She bowed to them, then departed without a word.

"Thank you for meeting with me, Mr. Chen."

"I am pleased to meet with you, Mr. Chairman. I have always been available to meet with the chairman or any members of the council. It has not happened often."

"I hope to remedy that."

Matt didn't respond, but picked up his tea and sipped. He set the cup down and waved Kendall to continue. Kendall launched into his little spiel.

"Mr. Chen, I think Arcadia has done very well in the last fifty years. We have made a lot of progress from being set down on this planet to get to where we are now.

"But I can't help thinking it is time to switch gears, if you will. To fine tune our society to achieve the next stage of our progress. I think there are a number of specific policies that should be enacted to carry out that goal."

"Aside from any discussion of specific policies, Mr. Chairman, two questions arise if one wishes to change the direction of a group of people acting out its own wishes and desires. The first question is, Who decides?"

"Why, the chairman and the council, as the executive and legislative bodies, should naturally decide these questions, Mr. Chen."

"I see. The second question is, How does one enforce these policies?"

"With laws, Mr. Chen."

"That is not enforcement, Mr. Chairman. Suppose someone decides not to follow these dictates, and carries on as he wishes."

"Then it becomes a police matter, Mr. Chen."

"You would use men with guns to enforce your wishes on society, Mr. Chairman?"

"That is how government works, Mr. Chen."

"Ah."

Matt picked up his tea, sipped, and set it back down.

"As it turns out, I have seen your questionnaire, Mr. Chairman, so I know what policies you wish to pursue. Aside from my objection to the specific policies you espouse, I object to your assumption of the authority to impose them.

"I am afraid I have no choice but to oppose you, Mr.

Chairman."

"Then you will be arrested and tried for treason."

The two thugs stirred, but Matt raised a hand and pushed a button in his heads-up display.

Two young men in the garden, one on either side of the doorway, rotated into view, their guns already drawn and elevated. The suppressed semi-automatic weapons in their hands each coughed three times as they executed the Mozambique Drill on Kendall's two bodyguards – two shots to the center of mass and one to the head.

The two bodyguards fell like trees, one to either side of Kendall, and lay still.

Kendall looked back and forth at them and then back to Matt in shock, to find himself staring into the muzzle of another suppressed semi-automatic pistol, this one held by Matt, pulled out from under the flap of his lavalava. It was trained on Kendall.

"You are not fit to be chairman, Mr. Kendall. You are ignorant of history, or you would have no such plans. Down this path is only death and destruction, and you should know that. Yet in your forty-five years on a planet with a library containing literally every written record of humanity, you remain ignorant of history.

"You are also too stupid to be chairman, to think you could come in here and arrest me on a capital charge – in my own home, from amid my family, with your two armed thugs – merely for disagreeing with you."

Matt turned to one side and spat on the fallen bodyguard there, then turned and spat on the other.

"Always there are such men, willing to follow the ignorant."

"But you can't do this."

"Why not, Mr. Kendall? You already told me your"

philosophy of government. One man assumes the authority to decide, then he uses men with guns to enforce his wishes. Very well. I have assumed authority and decided. I have men with guns. Why you rather than me?

"As for you, you are guilty of treason and official corruption. I have the bank records of the bribes you paid to the council using tax money. I have the bank records of your many embezzlements of tax money for yourself. And I have the message records of your discussions of your real plans with the council. These are all capital charges.

"But I am not without mercy."

Kendall breathed a sigh of relief. He thought he would get out of this alive after all.

"It will be quick."

Matt lifted the pistol and shot Kendall twice in the forehead.

Matt signaled MingWei in his heads-up display, and many things happened at once. The sliding door into the hallway opened and MingWei came in. Matt could see others moving wooden backstops out of the hallway. It was to get those backstops in place that he had engaged Kendall so long.

As it was, only the head shots over-penetrated. Those of the bodyguards did not penetrate the plaster wall behind them, while Kendal's two head shots did penetrate the rice-paper of the door to fetch up in the center backstop.

Several men came in from the garden and began removing the bodies out into the courtyard. Several women came in behind them and began scrubbing the mess off the wooden floor and plaster walls while it was still fresh. They had hydrogen peroxide for the incipient blood stains.

Another man lifted the sullied sliding panel out of its tracks and removed it while yet another placed a new sliding panel in its place.

"Have all our people been drawn in within the compound?" Matt asked.

"Yes, Chen Zufu. The family is all within our walls save only those preparing for operations."

"Very good. Seize the car."

"And the driver?"

"Kendall's bag man. He's dirty."

"Yes, Chen Zufu."


At the front of the apartment building, an attractive young woman wearing a lavalava and flip-flops walked out of the front doors of the building. She carelessly left the door into the building standing open behind her.

The limousine driver was sitting in the driver's seat of the car. He had the front seat windows open in the pleasant weather. He watched the young woman walk across the front of the car. She was smiling at him. Apparently she was coming around to talk to him. Some message from the boss, probably. At least the messenger was attractive enough.

In the dark of the hallway behind the open door, a young man sitting on the floor with a crossbow steadied on his raised knee pulled the trigger on his weapon. The heavy steel bolt passed through the open building door, passed through the open front passenger-side window of the limo, and hit the driver in the side of the head.

Two men walked out of the open building door toward the car. The woman continued around the front of the car, opened the driver's door, and dumped the driver's body out on the street. She got into the car and drove it around to the vehicle gate into the Chen-Jasic compound, which opened as the limo approached. She drove on into the compound and the vehicle gate closed behind the car.

The two men walked up as the car moved out of the way. They picked up the driver's body and carried him into the apartment building. Two women carrying buckets of a fifty-fifty mixture of water and hydrogen peroxide had followed them out, and they quickly rinsed the blood off the sidewalk and the street and disappeared back inside the apartment building.

The whole thing had taken less than a minute.

No public evidence remained that Chairman Kendall had ever been there. Kevin Kendall, his bodyguards, his driver, and his car had simply disappeared.


Their existing Plan CC – standing for Cops and Council – had been modified. The other thing Matt Chen-Jasic had received in his computer account the prior morning was access to Kendall's computer accounts in the colony servers. This allowed a simpler, easier version of Plan CC. They had gamed it out yesterday evening and this morning.

Matt sent a message from Kendall's account to the garage in the council building that he needed the second car at the Chen-Jasic compound. When it arrived, the driver of the second car got the same treatment as the driver of the first.

The uniforms of the drivers and the bodyguards were cleaned and mended. Some additions were made to the cars.

About six that evening, Matt sent a message to the council from Kendall's account.

**Emergency meeting of the Council.**
**I'm sending the cars around to pick you up.**
**Kendall**

# Plan CC

The armored limo pulled up in front of the large house in one of Arcadia's wealthier residential sections. Anna Drake, the director of the health department, came out of the house and walked out to the car. She was still dressed in her business suit from earlier today.

Drake didn't recognize the bodyguard holding the car door open for her, but she didn't know everyone on Kendall's staff. This would be the second shift bunch anyway. He was in the right uniform, though, and only Kendall had the big limousines, so she wasn't concerned.

Drake got in and saw she was the sixth passenger in the rear compartment. She looked around curiously, never having been in either of Kendall's limousines before.

The bodyguard got back into the car and the car pulled out and headed downtown.

"What's this all about?" she asked. "Anyone know?"

"I know he was going to see the Chen today," said Larry Donahue, the director of the food department.

"That can't have gone well. I think the Chen is happy with the way things are," said Park Jinsook, the director of the transportation department.

"Kendall didn't care either way," Donahue said. "If the Chen agreed, he had a new, major supporter. If the Chen disagreed, he would arrest him. This would keep people in line, because if he can arrest the Chen, he can arrest anybody."

"Arrest the Chen?" Drake asked. "He's a big guy. Good luck

with that."

"Yes, but he is an original colonist, and he was an adult when he got here," Donahue said. "He's seventy years old. Harmless."

"But he's big in another way," said Olga Golov, the director of the infrastructure department. "He has a powerful family and powerful friends. I think Kendall may have bit off more than he can chew."

"That might be the reason for the emergency meeting, then," Drake said.

The limousines stopped in the street outside the overhead garage door leading to the basement of the council building. It, of course, was one of the new buildings, and the chairman's offices were in this building as well. The overhead garage door remained closed.

The other limousine pulled in behind them, presumably with the other six members of the council on board. Their driver got out to go and talk to a guard standing by the closed garage door. The other limo's driver joined them.

The bodyguards got out and nervously looked up and down the street. They clearly didn't like having the cars sitting out here in the open.

Meanwhile, the drivers and the guard at the door were having an argument. The guard who refused to open the door for the limousines didn't know that the message he got from Kendall telling him not to let the limousines into the garage under any circumstances had actually come from Matt Chen-Jasic via Kendall's account.

The bodyguards took an interest in the argument and walked over to the door. When they were about a hundred feet from the limos, one of them reached into his pocket and activated a radio transmitter.

The additions the Chen-Jasic family had made to the limousines were six homemade claymore mines – an explosive covered on one side with hundreds of pieces of shrapnel. One was installed in each of the two rear armored doors of each limousine behind the interior door panels, up against the armor plate. One was installed in each limousine against the armored roof above the headliner.

When the bodyguard enabled the transmitter, the mines all went off simultaneously. The heavy armor plate provided a good back plate for the mines. Shrapnel from three directions shredded the rear passenger compartments of the limousines and the occupants thereof. The armored cars actually held together, the explosive in the mines being sized to propel shrapnel, and not to blow up the cars.

The bodyguards pulled out their guns, rapidly scanning the street up and down.

"Shit! Get us inside before they launch another one!" one of the drivers yelled at the door guard.

"Another what?"

"Another one o' whatever the fuck that was. Come on. Get us off the street. That's not against your orders. You're not letting the limos in."

The guard turned around and unlocked the man door next to the overhead door. He pulled it open and let the drivers in, then the bodyguards. The second bodyguard holstered his pistol, then held the door and waved the door guard ahead.

The bodyguard walked in the door behind the door guard. He grabbed the door guard's head from behind and twisted it in both hands until the door guard's neck broke with a crunch. The other bodyguard turned around and picked up the man's feet. They carried him to a nearby equipment room and dumped the body in the corner.

One of the drivers went back over to the man door. An unmarked van pulled up. The driver walked out to the van as the side door opened. A man inside handed him a small suitcase, and the driver carried it back into the building as the van drove off.

Alarms were sounding in the building now, and the driver could hear sirens outside as the door closed behind him.

Matt Chen-Jasic got a message from the strike team that they were inside the building and had the suitcase. He sent a message from Kendall's mail account to all the police 'special teams' units to suit up and come to the council building immediately, as there had been an attack on the council, and he expected an attack on the council building.

The police special teams were all Kendall's hand-picked enforcers, the squads he was building to enforce his new policies. The people who were willing – perhaps eager – to use paramilitary force against citizens going about their business in violation of Kendall's policies.

In response to Kendall's message, they all headed downtown to police headquarters, suited up in their paramilitary gear, and headed for the council building next door.

Matt tracked their locations on Kendall's access to the police dispatcher's information panel.

The strike team – the two drivers and two bodyguards from the limousines – made their way up the fire stairs to the roof of the council building. They exited onto the roof using the door guard's building keys and huddled out of site next to the big HVAC unit on the roof.

The driver with the suitcase opened it. Inside were four lightweight homemade hazmat suits and gas masks. They were black. The strike team put on the hazmat suits over their uniforms.

Also in the suitcase was a device that consisted of two one-gallon plastic bottles with a radio-controlled double valve joining them at the bottom, and a large cake pan. They set the cake pan down on the roof under the air intake for the building, then set the device in the pan.

The driver armed the radio-control receiver on the double valve. When it received the signal, the valve at the bottom of each plastic bottle would open, and the contents of the two bottles would flow together into a manifold joining them and dump out into the cake pan.

The strike team sent a message to the Chen, then they went to the far corner of the roof, huddled in the dark corner, and waited.

Matt Chen-Jasic watched the dispatcher's location panel. He saw the teams congregating in the police building, then watched their assault on the council building. He waited until they had all entered the council building. Some of them were moving up the stairs, but they were moving slowly, clearing each floor as they went.

When the police special teams were all in the council building, Matt used Kendall's access to the building controls to turn the ventilation system up to full and sent the signal to the strike team.

When the driver received the signal, he activated the transmitter for the double-valve device on the plastic bottles. The binary nerve agent mixed in the manifold between the valves and dumped out into the metal cake pan, where it fumed prodigiously. The HVAC system sucked up all the gas into the building intake.

Nerve gas flooded the whole building.

One thing Kendall's special teams did not have – at least yet – were gas masks.

It was a fatal omission.

When the contents of the two plastic bottles had completely drained out, the driver used the transmitter to close the valves. Whatever of the precursors remained were sealed up again. They waited there a half hour – the deployed nerve gas decomposed in fifteen minutes – then went over to the device and put it and the cake pan in a heavy plastic bag from the suitcase and sealed the bag. They put that into a second heavy plastic bag and sealed the bag. They put the bag in the case.

They waited another half hour, in case their disturbing the device had generated any small amounts of gas, then took the hazmat suits and gas masks off. They put them back in the suitcase and left the suitcase on the roof for now, before they ventured down into the building.

They also sent the all clear to the Chen.

The strike team got back down to the garage and one of the drivers watched out the small glass window of the man door. When three unmarked box trucks pulled up, he signaled the bodyguard over at the door controls, and the bodyguard opened the overhead vehicle door. The three box trucks pulled into the garage area.

As the overhead door of the garage came down, the rear overhead doors of the box trucks went up. Sixteen armed men got out of each box truck. They were all carrying Earth-manufactured semi-automatic rifles.

MingWei's lieutenant, forty-year old Ken Bolton – Joseph Bolton and Amy Jasic's youngest – got out of the passenger seat of one of the vans and came over to the strike team.

"We clear?" he asked.

"We think so. We can't be sure."

Ken nodded. He turned to his teams in the garage.

"All right. Clear the building. We should be good, but don't take chances. At this point, he is Chen or he is gone. Go."

Six eight-man teams moved out of the garage into the building. Two teams went out into the first floor, and four teams went up the stairs to the second and third floors. It would take them a while to clear the six-story building.

By dawn, the Chen-Jasic teams had gathered all the bodies from the council building in the garage using electric carts. The bodies had been stripped of body armor, helmets, weapons, magazines of ammo, and even grenades, both flash-bang and high explosive (H-E). Those had been loaded on one of the box trucks, and taken back to the Chen-Jasic compound. An empty box truck had taken its place so the teams retained their mobility.

The bodies, in their uniforms, were all laid out on the floor of the garage. Two hundred and forty-two in all.

Back in the Chen-Jasic compound, they matched the faces and badge numbers of the bodies against the police roster Matt found using Kendall's access rights. Only ten of the police special teams members had slipped the net, and they knew who they were.

Assassination teams fanned out across Arcadia City.

Matt Chen-Jasic sent out a message under Kendall's mail

account to all employees who normally worked in the council building, telling them to stay home today.

Matt also sent a message from Kendall's account to the one deputy police chief who was not on the take from Kendall. The police chief had been on the council, and died in one of the limousines the evening before. Matt made this one honest deputy the acting police chief, and gave him orders suspending the enforcement of any law for which there was no victim.

# Address By The Chen

The next morning, Thursday, the citizens of Arcadia all received a message from Chairman Kendall's account announcing a speech by the Chen, scheduled for eight o'clock in the morning.

The news wires on Arcadia that morning were also full of reports of the explosions on A street between Arcadia Boulevard and Market Street the previous evening. It was clear that the only two limousines on Arcadia, those belonging to Chairman Kendall, had been bombed. They had now been removed into the council building garage so recovery of the bodies could be done.

The people of Arcadia knew of the Chen, how his family ran the Uptown Market and the restaurant across the street, and how they made some of the more useful, decorative, or whimsical products for sale on Arcadia. The old-timers also knew of the Chen-Jasic family's role in introducing lavalavas and flip-flops to the colony in the very early days.

And everyone knew that, in any dealing with the Chen or the Chen-Jasic family, one never needed to be concerned about being cheated. Their reputation for honest dealings was legendary and deserved.

For his speech, Matt Chen-Jasic sat on a pillow in the same spot where he had confronted Kendall. He was dressed in a lavalava, sitting in tailor seat, naked from the waist up. Muscled and tanned, with his bald head and long white mustache and goatee, he was an imposing figure.

Behind him, through the teak-beamed doorway, the morning sunlight slanted across through the gardens. As always, the young women worked there, tending the plants. Only for his interview with Kendall had the work stopped, as Matt had expected trouble and wanted innocents out of the way of any gunfire.

"Good morning, citizens of Arcadia.

"Some interesting things occurred last night. I was intimately involved in these activities, so I thought I should tell you about them myself.

"The strange sequence of events started the day before yesterday, Tuesday, when I anonymously received the bank and communications records of the chairman and the council. I knew that these records had not been faked, because I also received access to the chairman's and the council's own computer accounts. I do not know how these things came to me, but they did.

"I also received a copy of a questionnaire that the chairman had given to a very few Arcadians to predict your acceptance of potential policies he wished to enact. The answers to the questionnaire were not promising. Most of you told the chairman to mind his own business. Some of the more expressive of you told him to perform an auto-erotic act."

The Chen chuckled.

"Having read this questionnaire, I agreed with both groups. Chairman Kendall should mind his own business, and he can go fuck himself.

"What are these policies? Many of you do not know, so I am sending the questionnaire out to everyone now. These policies would constitute sweeping changes to the ways in which most of us on Arcadia have lived for the past fifty years.

"One change is to ban the civilian ownership of firearms as being too dangerous in the hands of citizens. Firearms would only be allowed to the government. There are numerous examples in history of how badly that can turn out.

"Another change is to ban private cash and barter transactions. The reason for this is that those transactions escape taxes, which would massively increase under the chairman's plans. The biggest reason for those increases would be to fund large police forces to enforce these new laws.

"A third change in the questionnaire is to ban nudity in any public setting for anyone over five years old, even on one's own yard if visible from the street or a neighbor's property. This would also include mandating breast coverings for woman and girls. It would also apply to the beaches. Yes, the chairman wants to demand that we wear clothing in order to go swimming.

"All of these laws and more would be enforced by armed police, arresting the violators and putting them in jail."

The Chen turned his head to look out the window behind him, where topless young women in lavalavas worked the garden. He turned back to the camera.

"The chairman would arrest my granddaughters. Your children playing in the streets. You and your friends at the beach. Everyone would have to obey his rules or be arrested by armed men.

"Nor would it stop there. This is merely the first wave of such laws. The private communications of the chairman and the council indicate many more such laws were under consideration. To regulate and dictate the activities of every Arcadian, to force everyone to live and behave as the chairman wished, under the threat of arrest and imprisonment.

# ARCADIA

"I knew all this when the third strange thing happened on Tuesday. I received a request to meet with the chairman. I have always been available to discuss any public matters with the chairman or the council, but this was the first time I received any such request. I invited the chairman to take tea with me here, in my living room, yesterday afternoon.

"Imagine my surprise when Chairman Kendall arrived at my home with two armed men. I was gracious and allowed them all in. The chairman explained to me his goals, and I said I did not agree with him and would oppose his goals.

"At that point, Chairman Kendall announced that I would be arrested and tried for treason – a capital charge – simply for disagreeing with him. He then tried to use his two large armed men to arrest me.

"At that point, in defense of myself and my family against this travesty, I killed them. The two armed men and the chairman. You may see for yourself."

The Chen spread his hands and the video changed perspective, being from the side of the room, with Kendall on the left and Matt on the right. It played from the time of MinChao's announcement of the chairman through to the gunshots that had terminated the chairman's life. The video switched back to the Chen in real time.

"I knew, however, that it could not stop there. The council had been hand-selected over the years. The council members had bought into Kendall's plans. Someone else would step up, to continue this descent into tyranny. Why wouldn't they? They were being richly rewarded with taxpayer money paid out by Kendall.

"Did you never wonder how the council members could live so well, on their official salaries? Now we know. I will release their bank records as well, and I invite the news wires and

111

those accountants among our citizens to post their analyses of their corruption.

"Further, the police forces that would be required to enforce the chairman's dictates were already being assembled. Hundreds of men, with military weapons. Military weapons intended for use against us, my fellow Arcadians. Who else is there?

"So I knew I could not stop there. This nightmare would proceed with the council, with the police 'special teams' the chairman was assembling.

"Instead, last night I sent a message to the council using the chairman's mail account, calling them all to an emergency meeting at the council building. My people picked them up in the chairman's limousines, wearing the appropriate uniforms.

"Do you note, by the way, that only the chairman is allowed a limousine, even though the vehicle factory that makes all the vehicles on Arcadia could make more if people wanted to pay for the factory time to build them? And the chairman's limousines were built using your tax money. If history is any guide, this would be only the first of many luxuries purchased with your tax money and indulged in by the ruling class, while denied to the working citizens of Arcadia.

"We collected the council members in the chairman's limousines and drove them downtown to the council building. Which is the newest and fanciest of the buildings downtown, by the way, also built with your tax money, while the university and the hospital – services the rest of us might use – languish for lack of funding.

"As I say, we drove the council down to the council building, parked the cars in the street in the rear of the building, and bombed them, killing every member of the council. That was at my orders, and I take full responsibility.

Finding myself, innocent of any crime, under attack by a lawless government, I struck at that government.

"My people also infiltrated the council building and set a trap. I then sent a message to the police special forces, using the chairman's mail account, calling them all to defend the council building. When those police special forces occupied the council building, I ordered the trap sprung. We flooded the council building with a nerve agent and killed them all.

"When taking inventory of the bodies, we noted ten of these people who escaped the trap. They have since been hunted down and killed.

"All of this was at my orders, and I take full responsibility. Now let me show you the exculpatory evidence, my fellow Arcadians. These are the weapons we removed from the bodies of those police forces."

The video switched to a camera sweeping over a display of weapons and equipment. The Chen's voice continued over this footage.

"Body armor and helmets. Fully automatic weapons. Thousands of grenades."

The video switched back to the Chen.

"These are not the weapons of a legitimate police force, my fellow Arcadians. The chairman was building an army. An occupying army. To subject all of us to whatever laws he might dream up. To order us to live according to his desires rather than our own.

"It is this that I opposed, and that is why he tried to arrest me. And now, at my orders, he and the structure he tried to put in place are gone. The chairman, the council, and the special police forces are all gone.

"What do we do now, my fellow Arcadians?

"Some of you may say, 'Why, let the Chen be chairman.'"

The Chen held up his hands in a warding gesture and shook his head.

"No, my friends. I will not accept being chairman, for two very good reasons. First, I think it a very bad precedent for one person to overthrow a government – however out of control or illegitimate it was – only to put himself in place as leader. And second, I am an old man. The time is quickly approaching when I will put aside the cares of business and retire to tend our gardens with my granddaughters.

"Instead, I will ask a number of you to plan a new government. One the people select in periodic elections. One that is bound by rules against the usurpations to which we were very nearly subjected.

"I will call this group together and then bow out of the deliberations.

"And then, hopefully, in this our fiftieth year as a colony, they can put together a government better suited to our needs and our desires. One that allows us to live our lives as we wish, without the interference of busybodies and grifters.

"Thank you for your attention, my friends. I thought you should hear the details of these events directly from me, rather than a garbled or twisted account.

"Good day, and good luck to you all."

When the video cut off, MingWei knocked on the door frame.

"Yes, come in," Matt said.

MingWei slid the panel aside and came in. Matt waved him to the pillow opposite.

"How do you think that went, MingWei?"

"I think it went very well, Chen Zufu. But I have a question."

"Go ahead."

"Why did Kendall take on nudity? I understand keeping citizens from owning firearms. It increases the relative strength of his security forces to have unarmed opponents. And I understand doing away with black market transactions, as it increases the number of transactions that cannot escape his taxes. But why mess with the nudity question? He did not have religious objections or anything of that sort. It doesn't make sense. It aggravates people and generates opposition but gives him no benefit."

"Oh, but it does, MingWei. I wondered about this myself, and looked back into history. Nonsense laws are of great benefit to a tyrant. They allow him to separate the compliant from the non-compliant. If some people were to flout his nudity laws, those are the people to watch. They are the troublemakers. It is a way of separating the sheep from the wolves."

"Ah," MingWei said, nodding. "That makes sense, though it would never have occurred to me."

"No, because you do not have what it takes to be a tyrant. But it did occur to Kendall, as ignorant of history as he was. He was very dangerous. He had a natural talent for tyranny."

"A moment, please, Chen Zufu."

MingWei's eyes concentrated on something else, in the space between them. It was the characteristic look of someone consulting their heads-up display.

MingWei laughed, and returned his attention to Matt.

"I'm sorry. I thought we might have a security problem. There are a lot of people gathering on Market Street between the market and the restaurant. It looks like a few thousand, and it is still growing."

"But not a security problem?"

"No, they are yelling 'Chen, Chen, Chen.'"

"That could still be a security problem, MingWei. They might be calling for my head."

"No, Chen Zufu. It is a party atmosphere. They are smiling and laughing. And they are calling 'Chen' while waving their lavalavas over their heads."

Matt laughed.

"So much for Kendall's nudity laws."

# Opening The Convention

When Piotr Boykov woke that Thursday morning, he had no idea that he would forever after separate his life into 'before that day' and 'after that day.'

Boykov was the person in charge of running the animal husbandry operations on Arcadia. Not the director of the food department on the council. That political hack knew nothing of animals or farming. No, Boykov was the person who actually made the decisions about meat production, from animal breeding all the way to the meat counter.

Boykov woke at seven, when the sun came up. The sun always came up at seven in the morning and set at seven-thirty in the evening on Arcadia, due to its zero axial tilt and twenty-five hour day. Astronomical noon – the sun at its highest position overhead – was actually at one-fifteen in the afternoon.

Boykov checked his mail, and found an announcement that the Chen would address the public at eight. He knew the Chen, of course, at least tangentially. The Chen-Jasic family's restaurants were wholesale customers of the animal farms Boykov managed. But he had no clue why the Chen would be addressing all the citizens of the planet.

After the Chen's speech, Boykov sat stunned. So that asshole Donahue, the director of the food department on the council, was dead. That suited Boykov just fine, and if the others on the council were cut from the same cloth – as the Chen had said – that suited Boykov just fine as well.

The question 'Now what?' loomed large to Boykov. Large

disruptions even in incompetent governments did not necessarily turn out for the better, as attested to by the history of the Russian administrative region his parents had left behind when they left Earth.

That afternoon, Boykov received an invitation to sit on a constitutional convention.

Adriana Zielinski also got an invitation to sit on the constitutional convention. She was provost of the still-fledgling university, as well as the headmistress of the low, middle, and high school.

Many of the children of the colony were schooled at home, to the extent they were schooled at all. Zielinski couldn't blame the parents. The entire education system was grossly underfunded, as tax receipts were squandered on fancy administrative buildings and perks for bureaucrats. She also suspected, based on their lifestyles, that senior people in the government weren't strictly limited to their official salaries.

It was infuriating, partially because proper education was so easy with the materials they had brought along from Earth. Zielinski had entire curricula at every level – excellent ones! – available in the colony's library. Students didn't need instruction so much as supervision in their use.

But that all depended on the communicators, with their heads-up displays, and the government had slowly increased the age at which the devices were provided to children. Using the on-line curricula was no longer possible in the age ranges in which they would be most effective.

Zielinski had been trying for years to stem the downhill slide, to no effect. But in one day the Chen had overturned everything.

Maybe now it would be possible to repair the damage and

make some real progress.

All across government agencies and private companies, prominent individuals on Arcadia received invitations to the constitutional convention. They pondered what a new government might look like.

After a weekend of such thoughts, they met in the auditorium in the administration building on the southwest corner of Quant Boulevard and Arcadia Boulevard on Monday morning at eight o'clock.

The delegates to the constitutional convention milled about in the auditorium. With one and a half million people on Arcadia, no one knew everyone present, but all of them knew lots of the more prominent citizens invited to the convention. They talked in knots and clusters of people here and there, whether in the seats or in the aisles.

Friends sat together when they found each other in the crowd. All in all, there were probably close to two hundred people.

There were people, like Zielinski, in business suits, the normal business wear of their position. There were people, like Boykov, in coveralls, which was also the business wear of their position. There were people there in lavalavas, including some women who wore only the lavalava, perhaps in solidarity with the Chen's speech of last Thursday.

At eight o'clock, a young man in a lavalava and flip-flops walked out to the center of the stage. There was a single pillow in the middle of the stage with a microphone on a low stand. He bent down and picked up the microphone from the stand and addressed the room.

"If everyone could be seated, please, we will get started."

He bent down and replaced the microphone in the stand

People wandered to seats and sat down. When everyone was seated, the Chen walked out to the center of the stage. He was dressed in a lavalava and flip-flops. He kicked off the flip-flops and sat in tailor seat on the pillow. There was some applause from the audience when he appeared. Once seated, he motioned for silence.

"Thank you all for coming," the Chen said. "Please pardon me for sitting rather than standing, but this is the most comfortable position for me. At my age, comfort has become a priority.

"The reason for this meeting is to consider what sort of government the planet Arcadia should have going forward. The need and opportunity for that discussion arises directly out of the actions of the prior government last week and my response to those actions.

"No doubt some of you agree with my actions and some of you disagree. That is neither here nor there for this meeting. The subject will be debated endlessly in any number of forums going forward, I am sure, but for this group, at this time, it is the future, not the past, that is our focus.

"What sort of government should Arcadia have? My bias is toward a government that allows the greatest freedoms to its citizens. We each are granted but one life, and it should be, to the greatest degree possible, our individual decision how we choose to live it.

"This includes, by the way, the decision to work hard and become wealthy if we wish, or to sit back and take it easy and not be so wealthy if we wish. It also includes the hard-working person's right to keep the wealth he earned. The government has no right to take any of that wealth from him and give it to the person who has decided to sit back and take it easy.

"That is my general philosophy. Now if we start with our previous form of government as a baseline, what sort of changes do we wish to make? I have some suggestions. After I make these suggestions to you, I will oversee the election of a chairman for your deliberations and then withdraw.

"I am now, by default, in control of the government, having seized power. It is not appropriate, to my mind, that I have any input beyond this first talk. I have no desire to be the Emperor of Arcadia or anything of the sort, whether by that name or some other, such as the recent chairman of the council. I have no desire to repeat that mistake. If not in this generation, then in a later one, it always leads to tyranny.

"So, that said, on to my suggestions.

"I think the consolidation of the cabinet with the legislative body is not appropriate going forward. The department heads in the cabinet should be people with a deep understanding of the subject matter, professionals in the activities of their individual departments. The legislators, by contrast, should be more generalists, with a broader view. I suggest reconstituting the cabinet under the executive, but with a separate legislative body.

"That legislative body, I believe, should be elected by the people of Arcadia. This could either be at large or by precincts of some sort. As we grow it will need to be by precincts, and setting it up that way now is probably the better solution.

"The executive, who both selects and heads the cabinet, should also be selected with input from the people. That can be directly by election, or indirectly by the legislative body. The first, historically, has been called a president, the second a prime minister. They both have their advantages and disadvantages, and I think either way could work.

"We need some sort of document that states, in clear and

unambiguous terms, what the government may do and what it may not. The first is usually called powers, the second rights. A clear delineation of powers and a succinct and broad recognition of rights are both required, I believe.

"We also need something to which people are allegiant. Historically, it has often been a throne or royal personage of some sort, even if they were largely without power. In other cases, such allegiance has been to the founding document itself. What it must not be is to some political leader, or to some political party.

"Finally, we need some high court to keep people in line. A statement of rights and powers is all well and good, but has no teeth if there is no body to enforce it."

The Chen paused there, and waved someone out from the side of the stage. The young man came out with a teapot and a cup. He served the Chen, set the teapot down next to the pillow, and withdrew. The Chen took a sip of tea.

"Pardon me. I am unused to speaking so long."

He took another sip of tea, then set the cup down on the floor.

"Another thing that must be considered, now that we have achieved the size we have, is having multiple levels of government. When we first arrived here, we were but a hundred thousand people. That would have been a small city on Earth, and the council was much like a city council. That was appropriate.

"We are now much larger, and will grow much larger still. We grew a factor of fifteen in the last fifty years. Do that three more times and we are at five billion people.

"That is unlikely, I grant. But getting much larger is not. I think it inappropriate for a planetary government to concern itself with street repairs and sewer connections and such.

Perhaps we should put in place a lower-level structure to take care of that, such as incorporated cities with delegated powers. Or counties. Or provinces."

The Chen sipped from his tea again.

"Another item for your consideration. The government has until now been in charge of the production coming out of the factories the metafactory has created.

"One reason we have done as well as we have under such a command economy is that the Kendall governments have been so amenable to maximizing government income. Whenever the price of some scarce commodity rose enough, they would redirect production to generate income at those prices. Between that and a flourishing black market, we have avoided the worst shortages of a command economy.

"That is not to say there have not been abuses. Mr. Kendall's reservation to himself of the only two limousines he allowed to be made is fairly typical. These, though, were relatively minor annoyances.

"Going forward, we should probably get the government out of the manufacturing business. It is too inefficient – even with the automated factories – at least compared to what we could be doing with that capacity. My own recommendation is to spin these factories off as commercial entities, and to sell off their ownership in the form of shares in the corporations created.

"Other things are appropriate for government involvement, if not outright control. Education is one such, particularly in two areas. The first is identifying the most gifted among us and ensuring their talents are developed so that we might all benefit. The second is having a true university, so that we can begin advancing the considerable knowledge we are heir to.

"There are other candidates, too. Health research is certainly one. Some forms of transportation, perhaps, like the buses. Highways to link our cities as they grow.

"I would think some form of government funding in these areas is beneficial, while perhaps government control is less so. These are open questions for you all."

The Chen sipped his tea once more, and stared at the floor in front of him. It was clear he was accessing his heads-up display.

"Ah, yes. One more thing.

"When you have finished your work, and produced a document the bulk of you can support – more than a simple majority, I would think – it must be submitted to the population for a vote. I do not think we want to enter another era in which the government is set for us by some entity that stands apart from the people subject to it.

"Toward that end, this group may want to solicit input as you go, asking people for their ideas. I doubt I have drawn together here everyone among us who might have good ideas on this matter.

"You may have questions for me. I would encourage you to send them to me. I will consider them, and answer any for which I have pertinent thoughts on the matter. I will copy those answers to you all.

"Let us now move on to the matter of a chairman. Consider carefully the people around you. Many of you know each other, or some subgroup of each other. Who among your peers seated here do you think has the patience and the skills to chair such a group?

"The floor is open to nominations. Please wait for a young man to bring you a microphone."

A young woman wearing a lavalava and flip-flops came out and sat on the floor next to the Chen. Two similarly dressed young men with microphones came out and took the steps down off the stage. People began to hold up their hands, and a young man went to each in turn as they made their nominations. A number of different people were nominated, including Adriana Zielinski.

In all, two dozen people were nominated. The young woman entered their names into her computer account using her heads up display. When the nominations were complete, she sent her list to the Chen.

"I have the list of nominations from my granddaughter JuPing. I will send this list to you all. Please consider this list for a moment, and pick your favorites. I would ask you to select three. When we are ready, JuPing will read off the names one at a time. If that person is one of your three favorites, please hold up your hand.

"If we are ready?"

JuPing read the names one at a time, and people held up their hands for their favorites. When she got to the end of the list, the Chen nodded.

"From my observation, we have five clear favorites. I have sent you the list. Please pick one person of these five. When JuPing reads the names one at a time, please hold up your hand for your favorite."

JuPing read the five names while the Chen watched the room.

"We are now down to two people, Adriana Zielinski, the provost of the university, and Indira Bakshi, the director of the hospital. We have two choices now, so hold up your hand for your favorite when I mention them.

"Adriana Zielinski."

The Chen looked around the room.

"Indira Bakshi."

The Chen surveyed the room again.

"You have your chairman. Adriana Zielinski, please come up to the stage and claim the microphone."

Zielinski got up and went down the aisle to the stairs, mounting them to the stage. The Chen stood as she approached and shook her hand.

The Chen then turned to the room, bowed to them, and walked off the side of the stage with his granddaughter and grandsons.

It took several minutes for the applause to die down enough for Zielinski to proceed.

# Forgotten Legacy

On the first day of deliberations of the constitutional convention, the chairman recognized the utility of setting up committees to consider the various questions before the larger body. Committees were formed on the rights of citizens, the powers of the executive, the powers of the legislature, the manner and frequency of elections, the establishment and powers of political subunits, and so on. There were many things to consider, and committees were formed to cover all of them. That took the whole first day and most of the second.

On their third day of deliberations, the delegates woke to find a mail in their account with an attachment. The mail had no sender name on it, and they assumed it had been sent around by the Chen.

The attachment was a large document from the archives of the colony headquarters back on Earth, from about two years before the colonists had departed the home planet. The archives themselves were part of the library that had been sent along with the colony when it had been planted on Arcadia. The title drew their attention immediately: 'A Proposed Intermediate Structure For Colony Government, With Supporting Arguments And Alternative Structures.'

By intermediate, the document explained it was meant for colony populations between one million and one hundred million inhabitants. Arcadia was therefore currently within its scope.

Matt Chen-Jasic also got a copy of the document in his mail, together with a note that it had been sent to all the delegates.

The various committees of the constitutional convention dove into the document, each concentrating on its own assigned part of the problem.

Adriana Zielinski read the entire document through once, quickly, then read it again slowly, tracking its internal cross-references. She got together with her vice-chair, the runner-up for the chairmanship elections, Indira Bakshi.

"Where did the document come from, do you know?" Bakshi asked.

"I think it's pretty clear it's from the Chen," Zielinski said. "He is quite the student of history, and is always one of the highest-logging users of the library, which is in the computers of the school building."

"Well, whoever sent it, it is rather a remarkable document. The colony headquarters considered all these issues we face now over half a century ago."

"And documented them, to our great benefit. There were a lot of far-seeing people involved in the colony effort."

"They got that from their leader," Bakshi said. "Janice Quant was a remarkable person."

"Yes, she was. But they considered all these issues, and then settled on the city council model for the initial colony governments."

"I think it's pretty clear why they did that. The initial efforts were all part of building a city – laying it out, putting in place the basic infrastructure like housing, water, sewer, electricity, streets, initiating bus service. That's all civic stuff."

Zielinski nodded.

"But they also saw the need to transition at some point," she said. "I like the transition concept the document discusses.

Cutting between the civic functions and the – what would you call them? – the national functions. We partition what we have, leaving in place all the things we need. We need just need to make sure each is on the correct side of the split."

"Yes. We should probably start another committee to make recommendations on that division."

"That makes sense to me. One point of interest is that your functions and my functions probably split internally, with the low, middle, and high schools being administered under the city, and the university being under the national government. And with the hospital being under the city, and medical research under the national government."

"I'm not so sure on that," Bakshi said. "You then put a burden on the outlying areas to staff their own hospitals and schools. If we continue to use the colony's shuttles as ambulances from the farther cities, as we do now, one central hospital trauma center still makes sense for us. And with on-line curricula and in-person help on-line as well, centrally administering education still works."

"For a while at least. OK, I agree with that. We'll transition in the medium-term. We ought to figure a way to do that as well."

Bakshi nodded.

"What about the discussions in the document about the legislature?" she asked.

"I was strongly leaning to a 'one representative from a district' approach, as opposed to an at-large system. But there's some benefit to the 'three representatives at-large from a district' approach."

"Yes, I was struck by that as well. In that way, the minority within a district gets representation. It makes it harder to gerrymander the lower house."

"And the upper house being one representative from each district, with the same districts?" Zielinski asked.

"That makes it harder to gerrymander, too. You would be trying to optimize your election results in two different houses with the same districts. The upper house would also be more weighted toward the majority, while the lower house would be more of a free-for-all. I kind of like it."

Zielinski nodded.

"Well, whoever sent us this document sure gave us some things to think about."

MingWei joined Matt Chen-Jasic for tea on Friday afternoon, the fifth day of the deliberations of the delegates.

Taking tea together was their normal Friday ritual. They sat on pillows in the large teak-beamed doorway of Matt's tea room, looking out at the gardens. JuPing – the daughter of Matt's second wife YanXia's youngest son – served them tea and withdrew.

"Did you read the document I sent you?" Matt asked.

"Yes, Chen Zufu. It is a very interesting document. The colony headquarters thought of all these things before we even left Earth."

"Yes. The other thing that is interesting about the document is where did it come from. It is in the colony headquarters archives in the library – I checked – but who found it and sent it around now?"

"You did not send it to the delegates?" MingWei asked. "I know they received it."

"They received it, I received it. I sent it on to you, but it did not originate with me. Much like the accounting records and account access for Chairman Kendall, it just appeared. On Wednesday morning, there it was. No explanation. No 'From:'

address."

"It seems we have a hidden benefactor."

"Apparently so. We will have to make sure we are not being steered to someone else's purposes."

MingWei nodded.

"Still, the document is on point and helpful," he said. "And we know it is authentic."

"Yes. How are the delegates handling it?"

"The committees are digging into it. It looks like much of the document's prescriptions for an ongoing government will be followed."

"Good," Matt said. "I was impressed with the arguments in the document as to why they recommended the path they did. A lot of historical background there."

MingWei nodded.

"It was well-researched. No doubt about that," he said.

They sipped their tea and sat quietly for several minutes. They watched a bee making its rounds from flower to flower. It was MingWei who broke the silence.

"How will all the legal things work out, Chen Zufu? How much trouble are we in?"

"Not much. The most important decision has actually already come down. The judge decided yesterday that, for purposes of these court actions, I am the de facto head of state of Arcadia. That gives me several advantages as defendant."

"Ah."

"The other advantage I have is that I have all the records of Kendall's illegal payments to people throughout the government. His father's, too, for that matter."

"How is that an advantage?"

"The prosecutor and the judges are all in those payment records."

"Oh."

"Yes. They can either paper over everything and let the situation lie, or, as the acknowledged head of state of Arcadia, I can initiate a full-fledged corruption investigation into everything that went on under the Kendalls."

"I predict they will let sleeping dogs lie, Chen Zufu."

Matt chuckled.

"So do I, MingWei."

Despite the cheering crowd outside the Chen-Jasic compound the previous Thursday, not everyone was happy with the Chen.

A total of two hundred and seventy-four people had been killed in his coup d'état against the Kendall regime: Kendall, his two bodyguards, his two limousine drivers, the twelve members of the council, the door guard of the council building, two hundred and forty-two members of the police special forces in the council building, ten other members of the police special forces, and four cleaning people working in the council building that evening.

The Chen authorized the acting head of the treasury department to make substantial wrongful death payments to the families of the four cleaning people, who had died at work while performing their jobs and had not been receiving illegal payments under the table.

A group of the remaining families brought a wrongful death suit against the Chen, both as the head of state and in his person. The Chen countersued for clawing back illegally paid tax dollars over and above the public salaries of all the officials and police who died. As these amounts vastly exceeded the amount available as damages in a wrongful death suit, the families filed leave to withdraw their suit, and the Chen withdrew his countersuit.

The complaint of murder against the Chen and his family members was more serious. The deaths of the bodyguards in the very act of attempting an illegal arrest was one thing. That was arguably self-defense. The systematic execution in cold blood of Kendall and the rest of the council and police special forces was another thing entirely.

Chen's attorneys argued that the initial act of aggression was under the orders of Kendall, with the acquiescence of the council. It was therefore an affair of state. The reaction of the Chen family to this action was justified. That is, it was not so much an aggression by two people against another, but by one organization against another. It was more akin to war than a personal assault.

And, as the government had acted extralegally, it enjoyed no immunity or privilege against the counteroffensive launched by its erstwhile victim.

The Chen's attorneys also noted that the Chen family's actions against the government ceased immediately once the government was no longer able to continue offensive operations against them. They had put a stop to the aggression, made further aggression by the attacking organization impossible, and then immediately stopped their counterattack.

The Chen's attorneys' arguments were bolstered by a statement in a private meeting in chambers that, if charges were dropped, the Chen would not pursue corruption charges against the judges and the prosecutors of the legal department, and the clawing back of illegally paid tax dollars over and above their public salaries, for which he had all the accounting records. The Chen, as current head of state, was willing to close the books on the entire affair and carry forward from where the situation now stood.

This last, private argument won the day. The judge publicly found compelling the defense's arguments that the entire situation was more akin to war than the actions of private individuals and threw out the murder charges. The killings had been a legitimate act of war, and not criminally judiciable. The prosecutors dropped all other charges, including the possession and 'indiscriminate deployment' of a binary nerve agent. The entire episode was allowed to stand as it was, without further legal action.

The coup d'état was over, a fait accompli. The reorganization of the government was just getting under way.

With the deliberations on the new government under way, and the court cases working their way through the courts, Matt Chen-Jasic was not content to sit and wait. With recognition by the courts of the Chen as head of state for Arcadia, he began reworking the government.

The document on an intermediate structure for colony government got Matt to thinking. What else was buried in those archives, sitting there unread and unheeded for fifty years, that would be a help now? He set a government group chartered with colony planning and infrastructure to the task of cataloging and reviewing those archives.

While that was under way, Matt got to work on the worst excesses. Some organizations within the government went away entirely as not being appropriate activities, in Matt's view, for government. Most of these had to do with various attempts to monitor or control people's individual choices.

The public relations department went away as well. With good government, you didn't need one, and with bad government it didn't really help solve the problem.

Matt had the list of managers who had been getting regular

payments on the side from the Kendalls, and he sacked a lot of them. Most of these people had no technical expertise in the areas they were managing, and the people who got promoted into the now-empty positions were the ones who had been doing the work all along.

The salaries of government employees were all over the map. There had been no systematic pay-grade system, and one's compensation was normally determined by how much of a favorite one was of Kendall or one of his top cronies. The planning group found a proposed system of civil-service pay grades in the archives, and Matt instituted it and regularized the salary schedule. Most of the people who had been doing the work got increases, while most of those who were cronies and do-nothings got salary cuts.

Children had not been getting the communicators, as Kendall and his cronies had shied from making the expensive devices for youngsters. That had hobbled their educational opportunities, as all the school courses were on-line. Matt issued orders to dedicate the electronics factory to building communicators until everyone age four and above had one, and there was inventory to cover everyone under age four who was coming up. They were given free to every youngster.

Navigating the downtown, whether on foot or by car, was getting more and more difficult. The large amount of foot traffic between the four main downtown buildings clotted the intersection of Quant Boulevard and Arcadia Boulevard, which backed up traffic on both thoroughfares. Those backups drove traffic to the neighboring side streets. And crossing Quant or Arcadia on foot had become perilous as frustrated drivers took chances.

The planning group found a solution in the archives. The original plan had been to join the four main downtown buildings with a square of aerial walkways on the third floor level. That was why each building had a large elevator lobby on the third floor in the corner toward the intersection. There were even plans for the enclosed walkways in the colony headquarters archives. They had never been constructed as the Kendall governments squandered money on other things.

Matt authorized that construction to get under way. While it was ongoing, the intersection would be closed to vehicle traffic, so he temporarily made the first street to either side of the intersection – First Street, A Street, Market Street, and University Street – one way for four blocks through the downtown.

The biggest change to come out of the archives, though, came from an economic and monetary plan for the colony. For a given level of population, a certain amount of currency in circulation was required to support economic activity at the optimum level. Too little currency, and the economy would grow more slowly. Too much currency, and you would fuel an inflationary bubble as the currency exceeded growth in production.

With their emphasis on taxes, the Kendall regimes had actually grown the money supply at less than the optimum level as the colony grew. The economic growth of the colony had been held back by their tight fiscal policy. With overall government salary payouts down now due to Matt's streamlining, there was a danger of deflationary recession.

Matt declared a tax holiday through the end of the fiftieth anniversary year of the colony, and funded the government by simply printing the money. That wouldn't get the amount of currency in circulation quite up to where it should be, but it would start to close the gap.

One thing Matt did just to stick a thumb in the eye of the

Kendall governments. He authorized the construction of two dozen of the armored limousines by the vehicle factory, for sale to private citizens.

He eschewed getting one for himself.

The economy of Arcadia shifted gears and accelerated.

# The Push To The Finish

On a Monday at the beginning of July of that semicentennial year, Matt Chen-Jasic received a request from Adriana Zielinski, the chairman of the constitutional convention, to meet with her. He invited her to tea that afternoon.

"Chairman Zielinski, Chen Zufu."

"Show her in, MinChao."

Zielinski entered to see the Chen seated on a pillow before the wide beamed doorway to the gardens, as he had been for Chairman Kendall. He waved her to the pillow facing him. Having expected tea while seated on pillows, she had worn trousers with her business suit today. She sat in tailor seat on the facing pillow.

"Thank you for meeting with me, Mr. Chen-Jasic," she said. And then, ruefully, "I recognize this setup from your video. I hope I do not meet the same fate as Mr. Kendall."

Matt kept his response light, as her statement had been.

"But you have broken the symmetry, Chairman Zielinski. You failed to bring two armed thugs with which to arrest me."

Zielinski nodded.

A woman Zielinski recognized as JuPing came in from the garden with a teapot. She poured tea for Zielinski first, setting the cup in front of the chairman, then for the Chen, setting the cup in front of him. She placed the teapot in the center of the low table between them, rose, bowed to a spot between them, and left back into the gardens.

Matt picked up his cup and sipped, as did Zielinski.

"You requested this meeting, Madam Chairman. Please, proceed."

"Thank you, Mr. Chen-Jasic."

She looked at him quizzically.

"You rule Arcadia, but you have taken no title. I am not sure what to call you."

"It is a temporary situation only. My real title was and remains Chen Zufu. Zufu simply means 'honored grandfather.' My rule of Arcadia is an accident of history, which you will correct soon."

Zielinski nodded.

"Chen Zufu it is, then."

Matt bowed to her, a single nod of the head, and waved to her to continue.

"I wondered if you could address the convention once more. I think it would be helpful at this juncture."

Matt sipped his tea and waited. Zielinski shrugged.

"We have now been at the business of drawing up a charter for the colony for five months, Chen Zufu. The big issues, I think, are decided. We squabble now over minor things. On these, people are dug in to their positions. The big issues decided, they now argue endlessly over trivia. I think we could use some focus, some drive, toward finishing the work."

"And you think if I addressed the convention at this point, it would be helpful, Madam Chairman?"

"Yes, Chen Zufu. Push the convention to closure. I think you can do this. I despair that anything else would work."

Matt raised an eyebrow, but that was the only indication of his surprise at her statement.

"Tell me about these squabbles, Madam Chairman, so I can structure my remarks."

"You will speak to them then, Chen Zufu?"

"Yes. I am at your disposal, Madam Chairman. I will speak to them. Now, about these squabbles. Please elaborate."

An hour later, Zielinski took her leave of the Chen with a bow.

Adriana Zielinski called the convention into plenary session the next morning. Committee meetings were put off, and everyone gathered in the auditorium to meet as a committee of the whole.

Zielinski did not publish an agenda, which made people even more curious about the meeting. Whatever was going to happen, no one wanted to miss it.

When people arrived at the auditorium, in the center of the stage was a pillow and a microphone on a low stand. There was a murmur of excited conversation throughout the room that rose as more people arrived.

When eight o'clock came, Zielinski took the stage. She carried a microphone with her.

"Let's all take our seats, everyone."

When everyone sat down, she made a simple announcement and walked off the stage.

"Chen Zufu will speak to us."

A few seconds passed, and then the Chen walked out onto the stage. The delegates rose and applauded as he walked to the center of the stage, kicked off his flip-flops, and sat on the pillow. JuPing brought out a teapot and a cup, poured a cup of tea, and set both cup and teapot on the floor next to her grandfather, then left the stage.

The Chen picked up his tea and sipped, then waved everyone to be seated. The applause died down and everyone sat.

"You are most kind. Thank you very much."

He bowed his head to them.

"Chairman Zielinski has asked me to address you today. We are at a critical juncture in your important task. Perhaps I can assist you in your deliberations.

"First, I would suggest you stand back, and regain the big picture. So much has been decided. So much has been accomplished. You are all to be congratulated on this achievement. And yet, if the task is not ultimately completed, all of that will be for naught.

"So stand back. Regain the big picture. Only then go back to the small issues that remain. Do not let them stand in the way of putting in place the larger things that you have accomplished."

The Chen sipped his tea before continuing.

"With regard to these smaller things, I have some small recommendations as well.

"If there is a remaining disagreement at this point on whether the government should have some specific power or not, then decide No, it should not have that power. The bias should be against government power, and such questions that remain undecided at this point should be resolved against the government having such power.

"In a similar but opposite way, if there is a remaining disagreement at this point on whether the people of Arcadia should have some specific right or not, then decide Yes, they should have that right. The bias should be for the people's rights, and such questions that remain undecided at this point should be resolved in favor of the people having such rights.

"Finally, if there is a remaining disagreement at this point on whether some specific item should be structured along the lines of the colony headquarters' document on intermediate structure for colony governments or not, then decide Yes, it should be structured along the lines of the document. The bias should be toward implementing the document, which was the product of Janice Quant's huge and capable organization so long ago, and away from making changes that are not so well vetted. Such questions that remain undecided at this point should be resolved in favor of the structures proposed in that document."

The Chen sipped his tea again, allowing those points to sink in.

"That is really the guidance I have for your decision-making process now. But I have one more thing to say. A vision to offer. A motivation, if you will.

"In two and a half months, on the fifteenth of September, we will celebrate the fiftieth anniversary of the founding of the colony here on Arcadia. What a boon it would be if we could finish this document and have the plebiscite endorsing it prior to our anniversary. Then we would surely have something tremendous to celebrate, and not simply another year on the calendar.

"At that point, election campaigns could begin for the new government. For elections on the fifteenth of December, say. A ninety-day campaign is all anyone needs to make up their mind. Our first elections on Arcadia.

"The new government could take control on the first of the year, and usher in a truly new year. I will be happy to turn over the reins of government to such an organization, structured along the lines you have already drawn, and with leaders chosen by the people of Arcadia.

"That is the big picture, my friends. Do not let the fog of minor issues cloud your grand vision. Finish this great work, and let us celebrate our fiftieth anniversary in epic style."

The Chen spread his hands to his sides and bowed to them.

He got up off the pillow, slipped into his flip-flops, and walked off the stage.

Zielinski walked out into the center of the stage.

"Meeting adjourned," she shouted into the mike over the tumult of applause.

Matt Chen-Jasic and Chen MingWei took tea together that Friday afternoon as was their custom.

"You spoke to the convention on Tuesday morning," MingWei said.

"Yes. A short talk. Chairman Zielinski wanted to shake things up a bit. They were getting stuck on minor issues. I tried to restore a vision of the big picture. Of the benefit of having the document approved before the anniversary."

"Did that work, do you think?"

"I got a note from her a few hours ago," Matt said. "She says the committees are clearing logjams now. 'No one wants to be the person who stands in the way of the Chen's vision,' she said."

"Excellent. That would be something, wouldn't it? To have a new governmental structure for the fiftieth anniversary?"

"We would truly have something to celebrate then."

"And you would be able to step down at the end of the year," MingWei said.

"That is my hope. Although heading the government has not been particularly difficult. Everyone is being very careful not to disappoint the Chen."

Matt smiled.

"Maybe it's something about the way I came to power."

MingWei laughed.

"Yes, I think that may have something to do with it."

They sat and sipped their tea. It was a pleasant afternoon,

even by Arcadia standards.

Zielinski pushed the committees relentlessly through July, and was able to present the completed document – the Arcadia Charter – to the whole convention on Tuesday, July thirtieth. She put the question of adoption of the charter on the table.

Two days of debate rapidly devolved into minutia yet again, as a minority of the convention delegates paraded their pet issues once more. The convention was the captive of the bitter-enders.

Zielinski considered how to break the logjam. She looked over the delegates listing closely. Who would be the right person?

Zielinski made a couple of calls that evening and hoped for the best.

On August first, Zielinski called the auditorium to order once again. As she was about to reopen the debate, a hand went up and a voice called out from the delegates. It was a voice used to making itself heard over the noises of farm animals, and carried clearly to all corners of the group.

"Madam Chairman."

Zielinski looked out over the auditorium.

"Yes, Mr. Boykov."

"Madam Chairman, I call the question."

"Second," Indira Bakshi called out from the front row.

There was a buzz of conversation in the room, and some objections were shouted. Zielinski hammered for order. When the delegates quieted down, she continued.

"It has been properly moved and seconded that we stop debate and vote on the pending question, which is the adoption of the Arcadia Charter as it stands," Zielinski said. "All those in favor of stopping debate and voting now, raise your right hand."

Zielinski looked out over the group. It looked like she might have the two-thirds she needed.

"Thank you, hands down. All those opposed, raise your right hand."

Zielinski looked out over the crowd again. Much smaller. Less than half as many, she thought. She decided she had the two-thirds she needed for closing debate.

"Thank you, hands down. There are two-thirds in favor of closing debate. We will therefore vote immediately.

"The pending question is GQ-287 in your heads-up displays. General Question Two Hundred Eighty-Seven. 'Yes' for adoption of the Arcadia Charter right now as it stands, 'No' to not adopt the Arcadia Charter at this time and to resume debate. You have one hour to vote. You may change your vote during that hour if you wish. Only your final vote status in one hour will be counted or recorded."

The hour allowed for frenzied last minute debates among the members, and there were more than a few of them going on in the auditorium. Zielinski knew the charter's proponents were working over the balkers, trying to get them to come over. Accept the whole package, despite misgivings on one minor item or another.

Zielinski watched it all with satisfaction. She knew she had a majority for passage, it was a question of how many she had. How overwhelming would the vote be?

Of course, the bitter-enders all knew she had a majority for passage, too. And she had already announced the final vote tallies would be published. Who wanted to be the one to vote against the charter? Who wanted to go down in history as the naysayer?

Who would disappoint the Chen?

She would see soon.

A large number of votes popped up on the tally board in Zielinski's heads-up display within a few minutes. They were about eighty percent for the measure and twenty percent against.

Of course, the delegates could see the tally board, too. As the hour wore on, more positive votes joined, and, while the number of No votes was constant, the percentage of No votes declined. As the end of the hour approached, there were twenty-one No votes out of the two hundred delegates.

In the last few minutes, the number of No votes started to decline. It accelerated as the deadline approached. No one wanted to be the last man standing.

Zielinski waited a little past the deadline as the last No votes disappeared. As soon as the No vote total hit zero, she locked the vote and called time before anyone could change their mind.

"The vote is two hundred to zero. The motion passes. The Arcadia Charter is adopted.

"The business of this convention being at an end, I declare it adjourned and dissolved."

Zielinski hammered the gavel once and walked off the stage as the delegates applauded and cheered.

Arcadia had a charter. At least, a proposed one.

It was up to the plebiscite now.

# Plebiscite And Celebration

That afternoon, Thursday, August first, 2295, Zielinski asked the Chen for a meeting. Matt received her for tea, as before. What was different this time is that Zielinski carried a document with her.

With both seated and tea poured, Zielinski laid the hardcopy document on the table between them and pushed it to Matt.

"Chen Zufu, I am here to report we have passed the Arcadia Charter. I then dissolved the convention, its business being concluded."

Matt looked down at the document, back to Zielinski.

"And what was the vote, Madam Chairman?"

"Two hundred to nothing."

"How did you ever manage that?"

"I allowed one hour for the voting, Chen Zufu, and I let it be known that the final votes would be published. Few people wanted to be a naysayer, and as the No votes dwindled, the pressure on the others to switch mounted. I waited a bit past the end of the hour, and when the last No vote fell, I locked the tally and declared an end to the voting."

Matt chuckled.

"You have hidden assets, Madam Chairman. Well done. I didn't even know you would be able to bring it to a vote this week."

"Another manipulation, Chen Zufu. I called Piotr Boykov last night and asked him to call the question at the opening of this morning's debate. I similarly asked Indira Bakshi to second. I suspected I had two-thirds to force closing the debate and moving to the vote."

"And you had your two-thirds then, Madam Chairman?"

"That vote is by show of hands, Chen Zufu, and meeting the two-thirds requirement is in the chair's judgment."

Zielinski shrugged.

"I decided it was more than two-thirds," she said.

Matt laughed.

"Very good, Madam Chairman. Well done. Now we must schedule the plebiscite on the charter, and the elections for government positions after that."

Matt consulted the calendar in his heads-up display.

"We will have the plebiscite on the charter on Sunday, September eighth, and the elections on Sunday, December fifteenth. How did you handle the initial laying out of district boundaries, Madam Chairman?"

"It is up to the current head of state to draw the initial district boundaries. We left it to you, Chen Zufu."

"And that's still thirty districts, as you had it before?"

"Yes, Chen Zufu. Which puts ninety delegates in the Lower House, and thirty representatives in the Upper Chamber."

"Very well, Madam Chairman. That is splendid work. You are to be congratulated."

Matt spread his hands at his sides and bowed to her across the low table.

"Thank you, Chen Zufu. You are most kind."

Matt sent a press release to the news outlets that evening, and the announcement of the plebiscite and election were made in the Friday morning news wires. They also published the Arcadia Charter.

Public debate on the charter started immediately. Most people were generally in favor of it, but most people also found something to complain about somewhere in the document. It was clearly much better than the situation they had been in before, where the council and its chairman had ruled without a structure.

Matt was busy supervising the drawing up of district boundaries. It seemed no one was able to do such a thing without trying to steer an outcome. How they even thought they could do that without any data from a previous election was incomprehensible to Matt.

Ultimately, he made many of the decisions. There were an average of fifty thousand inhabitants per district. The first thing Matt did was to make every outlying city over twenty-five thousand people and its environs its own district. One, with eighty thousand people, he made two districts, separating it and its environs down the middle of the road from Arcadia City, which was also its main street.

Matt whacked Arcadia City into quarters, with district boundaries along Quant Boulevard and Arcadia Boulevard. He then divided the quarters of the city into districts pretty much along what had emerged as main streets.

In the meantime, Matt and the Chen-Jasic family were gathering up a list of the main complaints they heard about the charter. Many of them were because people simply didn't understand how bad all the alternatives were, or how badly those alternatives could be abused.

On Sunday, September first, with a week to go to the plebiscite, Matt addressed the citizens of Arcadia and addressed the major complaints they had heard, one at a time.

The economy was still strengthening under what wags were

calling 'the Chen Dynasty,' the reforms and tax holiday Matt had put into place at the beginning of February. As a result, the Chen was very popular, and people trusted him.

While, in Matt's estimation, the Arcadia Charter would always have received a strong majority of the vote, he wanted that majority to be as high as possible. He wanted the people to buy in, and the government to know how much support the charter had, so it would stay within its bounds.

After Matt's speech that Sunday, support for the charter stiffened and grew. The public was settling into it now, and the debates that week included a lot of 'Didn't you listen to the Chen's rebuttals?'

The plebiscite on Sunday, September eighth, was orderly, the voting heavy.

When the votes were all counted, the Arcadia Charter had passed by a voted of 917,342 to 89,544, a bit over ninety-percent approval.

It was now time to settle down to the serious business of the celebration of the fiftieth anniversary of the founding of Arcadia on Sunday, September fifteenth.

The Chen helped that along by declaring Thursday, Friday, Monday, and Tuesday planetary holidays, resulting in a six-day weekend.

Of course, some jobs needed to be done anyway, like tending farm animals and driving buses. But naming those days planetary holidays also resulted in time-and-a-half wages on those days for those who had to work.

The Chen family restaurant, of course, was open throughout the holidays. Some people were surprised to find the Chen himself waiting tables on some of the holidays.

"I gave my granddaughter the day off," Matt explained.

He was just a regular guy, after all.

The story got around, and his popularity went even higher.

The Uptown Market did a land-office business in fireworks in the week leading into the holidays. On the evening of the fifteenth, the Chen-Jasic family put on the biggest fireworks display anyone on Arcadia had ever seen. They held it at the beach, and used a barge anchored offshore as the launching platform.

Officially it was a government function, and the fireworks were paid for out of government funds. That is, the Chen, as head of state, simply printed the money to buy the fireworks from his own company. The economy was still well short of the amount of liquidity it should have, even with the velocity of money coming up sharply since February.

Matt Chen-Jasic and MingWei watched the fireworks five miles away at the beach from the roof of the five-story Chen-Jasic family apartment building. They sat on pillows and sipped tea as they watched.

"Oh, now that was a good one," Matt said.

"Yes, I have always liked that one," MingWei said.

Matt sipped his tea.

"Fifty years," he said. "Can you imagine?"

"It has been a long time, Chen Zufu. But I think this year was the most memorable one in a long time."

Matt nodded.

"I agree, MingWei. I was very worried about the state of things when this year started, but I am very happy with where things are headed now."

# Quant #2

# Meddling And Infrastructure

Matthew Chen-Jasic wasn't the only one happy with how things had turned out on Arcadia. Janice Quant was quite pleased about it as well.

Quant had not dropped the colonies off and left them abandoned. She kept an eye on them – a mother hen watching her chicks – with her interstellar communicators. She had left one in solar orbit near each colony planet, and monitored their communications.

All told, there were twenty-four colony-planet interstellar communicators, plus two hidden in the Asteroid Belt in the Earth solar system. They were multi-channel, so they formed a mesh with each other and with four of the units that were at Quant's location. She also had seven spares.

Quant didn't intervene often in the colonies, but sometimes it was necessary. Once, the metafactory for a colony had failed. They couldn't fix it with the industrial base they had at the time, and that was going to lead to serious hardship. Quant would have liked to substitute a working one for the failed one, but she had no way to get the failed one off the planet.

Quant had extra metafactories, or, rather, could build them, so she built a new one and dropped it next to the broken one during one night when the colonists were abed. The next day, they woke to a new metafactory working away. So they knew someone had intervened, but not who or how.

The Arcadia problem was more subtle. The original

chairman, Mark Kendall, had seemed an OK sort. She had vetted the colony managers particularly well. But you couldn't win them all, and he had gone off the rails over time.

His kids had been even worse, and where had the idea of a hereditary chairmanship come from, anyway? Ancient Rome? The situation was building to a head on Arcadia, which was beginning to lag other colonies in economic development. Quant had cast about for some sort of solution.

Then she had tripped over Matthew Jasic, now calling himself Matt Chen-Jasic. He was now the head of an economically powerful clan-family on Arcadia.

Quant remembered Matthew Jasic very well. She remembered watching helplessly as Harold Munson had beat Betsy Reynolds, cowering in front of her children, protecting them. And Quant recalled her grim satisfaction when Matthew Jasic burst through the door and ended Munson's reign of terror with a pretty savage pounding.

Quant had a pretty good idea what would happen to the latest Chairman Kendall if he tangled with Matthew Jasic. And that was merely going to be a matter of time. Without Jasic's family under his thumb, Kendall would have a fifth column in his midst.

Quant had near-real-time bidirectional communications with the colony computers, and super-user access rights that somehow didn't show up in the sysops' login records.

It was Quant who had given Chen-Jasic the account access to Kendall's computer accounts, and the accounting and communications records most damning to Kendall and the council. Then she had simply let the situation play out.

When the inevitable occurred, and Jasic convened a constitutional convention to replace the government he had decapitated, it was Quant who had sent Jasic and the convention delegates the colony headquarters' plans for an intermediate structure of colony government. They were right there in the colony's computer archives, right where Quant had placed them fifty years before.

Jasic and Zielinski had been smart enough to see what they had in the document and ran with the ball, and now Arcadia was on track, the economy booming, and a government of Quant's own design in place.

With that done, Janice Quant turned back to her own projects.

To carry out Quant's larger plans, she needed two things: a state-of-the-art semiconductor fabrication facility, and a chemical laboratory that could work out how to make very strong carbon structures.

Neither of these had been a cakewalk.

For a state-of-the-art fab facility, Quant had to solve a lot of problems with manufacturing semiconductors in space. Vacuum and zero gravity made some things easier and some things harder. She also had to worry about radiation. The solar wind was full of all kinds of stuff that never made landfall on Earth.

Placing the facility in the solar shadow of an asteroid solved the radiation problem, but the gravity and vacuum problems remained. Quant needed all sorts of exotic chemicals and metals to make semiconductors, plus no end of manipulators and assembly-type bots.

As for the actual design of the hardware, she was way out in front on that one. There were a number of things she wanted to try, but she had one frontrunner from her simulations, and she could hardly wait to get a couple thousands multiprocessor blades of that architecture running.

The chemical laboratory had its own set of problems. But she needed to be doing materials research. She wanted a strong structure, but strong didn't necessary mean rigid. The sapling bent in the wind and survived, where the adult tree might break or be toppled.

Certainly the strongest structure would be a geodesic sphere. But how rigid should the individual links be? How rigid should the joints at the vertices be? Could she tailor carbon compounds to give her the right resiliency, the target rigidity, the required strength?

Now, though – finally, after fifty years of work – Quant had both in hand. The semiconductor and hardware fabrication facility and the chemical factory were both operational to her own rigorous standards. They were huge facilities, and completely remote-controlled by Quant.

With the Arcadia problem solved, Janice Quant bent to her research.

# 2345

ARCADIA

# A Precocious Problem

As the centennial of the founding of Arcadia approached, Chen FangYan had a problem. Thirty-five years old, she was a great-great-granddaughter of Chen GangHai and his first wife Chen YanJing. She was married to Chen YongJun, who was a great-great-grandson of Bob Jasic and Susan Dempsey through their daughter Stacy.

While they were both Chen, the family lines were kept straight in a clan registry so they did not marry too close. Between all the different people in the original Jasic party, and the addition of the Rachel Conroy-Jessica Murphy and Gary Rockham-Dwayne Hennessey same-sex couples, it was not hard to find sufficiently unrelated clan members to marry.

The ongoing custom of 'bank babies' – having one's second child with a donation from the colony's sperm bank to increase genetic diversity – also increased the possibilities for in-clan marriage. Chen FangYan's mother had been a bank baby, as had Chen YongJun's grandfather.

Some people in every generation married out-of-clan, but not many.

Chen FangYan's problem, though, concerned not her ancestors but her descendants. In particular her third child and oldest son, Chen JieMin.

FangYan and YongJun lived in Chagu – in English, 'tea valley' – a Chen enclave in a valley high in the Blue Mountains north of Arcadia City. While the clan bred tea plants and grew

161

certain expensive varieties in their town garden in Arcadia City, the large production required to meet the demand in the colony of nine million people was here. Several hundred of the six-thousand-strong Chen clan lived here, planting, tending, and harvesting tea.

That was all well and good for most of the clan who lived there. But Chen JieMin was special. He was extraordinarily bright, and the resources to develop his skills were in Arcadia City, not in Chagu.

FangYan sometimes drove the truck from Chagu to Arcadia City to deliver tea to the uptown market and the warehouse behind it. In truth, the truck drove itself, but unmanned trucks might be stopped by a roadblock and robbed of their cargo. If the truck had a Chen aboard, however, it was never molested.

Not since several examples had been made, which had dissuaded people of the wisdom of that path.

On this occasion, FangYan left the truck at the warehouse as it was unloaded, and went across Market Street to visit Chen JuPing, who was Chen Zumu.

Chen JuPing was the granddaughter of Chen YanXia, Chen Zumu and second wife of Matt Chen-Jasic. JuPing was therefore the adopted granddaughter of Matt Chen-Jasic, who was Chen Zufu.

Chen JuPing had married Paul Chen-Jasic, the son of Ken Bolton, MingWei's lieutenant in charge of the action teams, and Chen XiaLi, one of MingWei's daughters. Paul Chen-Jasic was therefore the grandson of Amy Jasic and Joseph Bolton on one side, and Chen MingWei on the other.

The ultimate power couple within the family, Paul Chen-Jasic was now Chen Zufu, and Chen JuPing was Chen Zumu.

FangYan had requested and been granted a meeting with Chen Zumu. She walked through Uptown Market and across Market Street to the apartment building beyond. A young woman showed her to the tea room of Chen Zumu.

JuPing had looked up her visitor in the family archives, and knew she was thirty-five years old and was part of the branch of the family that had moved to Chagu to farm the family's property there. JuPing had been to Chagu, but it had been perhaps ten or twelve years.

Nevertheless, JuPing remembered FangYan. Her mother had been a bank baby, half-Norwegian and half-Chinese. The Norwegian had come out in FangYan as blond hair – straight like Chinese, but blond. It must have picked up a similar blond gene from her father's side, which included a descendant of the Jack Peterson/Terri Campbell family. Blond hair was rare enough in the Chen-Jasic family after this many generations that JuPing remembered FangYan.

The young woman approached and bowed to JuPing. JuPing was almost seventy years old at this point, and her hair had gone white. She wore a silk robe, product of a silkworm colony they had brought from Earth and managed, after decades of work, to get established and producing.

"Thank you for meeting with me, Chen Zumu."

"Sit, grandchild. Have tea with me."

JuPing waved to the pillow beside hers, equally spaced in the beamed doorway, and FangYan blushed at the honor. She sat next to JuPing, both facing out into the gardens. A young woman – like FangYan, wearing only a lavalava and flip-flops – brought a pot of tea. She served them both, then left the pot on the low table between the pillows. She withdrew without a word.

"I remember you, from my last visit to Chagu," JuPing said. "Your hair stood out, of course."

FangYan nodded.

"But why do you request a meeting with me, grandchild? Is something wrong in Chagu?"

"In a way, Chen Zumu. I have a son, JieMin, who needs to study in Arcadia City. He has gifts too great for study in Chagu."

"How old is JieMin?"

"Fourteen, Chen Zumu. And he has already finished his schooling."

"I remember him. He was perhaps two years old when I was last in Chagu. You were holding him."

"Yes, Chen Zumu. I remember."

"He has finished high school already? But I believe all the college courses for the undergraduate degree are available online as well."

"Forgive me, Chen Zumu. I was imprecise. He has finished his undergraduate schooling."

"At age fourteen? In what field of study?"

"Mathematics, Chen Zumu."

JuPing used her heads-up display to perform a search. Other people had completed the undergraduate degree in mathematics at age fourteen, back on Earth, but they were very rare. True prodigies. FangYan was right. JieMin needed to be here, in Arcadia City. Even then, it would be difficult to challenge him.

"I agree with you FangYan. He should be here, where he can study further at the University of Arcadia downtown."

"Thank you, Chen Zumu."

"But that raises other questions. Will he be happy away from his family? Do you all wish to move here, so that you remain together? Or can he live with some relatives who are here?"

"My husband's brother is here, Chen Zumu. He is Chen JuanTao. We have spoken to him, and his family will look after JieMin. But we wanted your sponsorship, so JieMin's path can be smoother."

JuPing nodded.

"Very well, grandchild. I will make inquiries at the university. And we will arrange something here for him. Perhaps his own rooms, so he can do his work in solitude, but close to JuanTao's family, so he has family support. He would have no other assignments."

"Thank you, Chen Zumu. You are most kind."

"A gift of that kind must be nurtured, so it does not wither and die. Such potential must be given room to grow."

JuPing looked out over the gardens and sipped her tea as she considered her possible actions. Then she nodded.

"Thank you for bringing this to me, grandchild. It was the proper thing to do."

JuPing put in a call request to the president of the University of Arcadia. She would call in a favor if need be. The Chen family were big supporters of the university. Then again, it may simply be a matter of pointing out Chen JieMin's age.

The call request came in as 'Chen JuPing,' but Anders Connor knew Chen JuPing was also Chen Zumu, the wife of Chen Zufu. He had seen her last at the dedication of the new building, the Chen Hall of Science. He dropped what he was doing and signaled acceptance.

"Chen Zumu," Connor said, bowing.

"Good afternoon, President Connor. I want to bring something to your attention."

"Of course, Chen Zumu."

"I have a family member who I understand has just completed his undergraduate studies. His name is Chen JieMin."

Connor brought up JieMin's academic record in the lower half of his heads-up display, JuPing being in the upper half.

"Completed the degree in mathematics in just over two years, with high honors. That is most impressive, Chen Zumu."

"Yes. Now please pull up his personal information, President Connor. I believe that is on a different screen."

Indeed it was. Someone who needed one did not necessarily need the other, and the university was jealous of its students' privacy. Connor pulled up the personal information screen.

"I have it, Chen Zumu."

"Observe his age, President Connor."

"Fourteen years old? Is that a data error, Chen Zumu?"

"No, President Connor. I remember this boy as a baby. That is his accurate age. I think some special arrangement should be made to challenge him, to reap the best benefits for the colony."

"I agree, Chen Zumu. If he had been in residence, such arrangements would already be in place. As a remote learner, though, no one put two and two together."

"That was my suspicion, President Connor. But I have called him here from Chagu. He will be resident here, in Arcadia City. Surely there is some arrangement that could be made for his further studies."

"I will take care of it personally, Chen Zumu. When he arrives in Arcadia City, have him call on me directly."

"Thank you, President Connor. I will do just that."


The subject of these conversations was unaware of them. Chen JieMin sat on the hillside above Chagu looking out over the valley. drawing in his heads-up display with his finger.

The family currently had to pump water to some parts of the valley, while shielding other parts from the occasional flash floods that swept down out of the mountains. JieMin had asked one of the village elders why they didn't simply channel the waters properly, and avoid all that work.

"You know how to do that, JieMin?"

"Yes, Zhanglao. I can see it in my head when I look out at the fields. It is part of the shape. The shape of the valley."

The elder – zhanglao in Chinese – knew of JieMin's remarkable gift. Rather than scoff or consider the boy strange, he had given the boy the task of drawing what he saw, how to divert the waters to avoid both the pumping and the floods.

It was not hard for JieMin. He had always seen things differently. As he had grown up, he could never understand why other people did not see as he did, but he came to understand they did not. He had been very excited to find mathematics when he was ten. To find there was a way to say what he saw, in formal terms. It was important to him, too, to know that others had seen as he did, to come up with such a way to explain what they saw.

Looking out at the valley, JieMin could see the best water flow through the valley, in the shape of the valley itself. Its hills and curvature. He knew now the formalisms for those shapes. The derivative operator. The gradient operator. The divergence operator. It was all so simple.

But JieMin did not need that formalism for this task. He saw where the stream entered and where it exited. How to block the stream to a certain depth here, so that some of the water would flow there and there. How the remainder would go over the block, carrying the flood waters down the main channel here.

The secret was to block the stream above the valley floor, using the height of the water to direct it down this slope and that slope. To use the shape of the valley itself to direct the water.

It was all so clear to him. JieMin locked his drawing to his view of the valley itself, so that as he turned his head, the marks stayed with the valley. He made marks here, and here, for more diverters, to divide the flows he had made, carrying the flows through the fields.

His task completed, JieMin was walking down the hill back to Chagu when he received a message from his mother. She had returned from running the delivery truck to Arcadia City, and needed to speak with him.

"Yes, Muqin," JieMin said when he entered the house. "I am here."

"JieMin, I have found a way for you to continue your studies. To consider larger things than Chagu."

FangYan waved to a pillow in front of her, and JieMin sat.

"You have?"

"Yes. When I was in Arcadia City, I met with Chen JuPing. Chen Zumu. I told her of you, and asked her assistance."

JieMin was shocked. Everyone knew of Chen Zumu. She was the wife of the head-of-clan, Paul Chen-Jasic, Chen Zufu himself. He did not know his mother could simply go see Chen Zumu.

"You did?"

"Yes. She agrees that you should be given the ability to further develop this gift, and that Chagu is not the place. She proposes giving you rooms in the Chen compound in Arcadia City, near Dabo JuanTao. You would study at the University of Arcadia. Such studies would be your only chores."

JieMin's head swam. He liked his uncle JuanTao, his father's elder brother, and his family. They sometimes came to visit.

That was no problem. But to have his own rooms? To study at the university? To have no other chores but to do mathematics?

"It is a dream, Muqin."

"Chen Zumu will make it a reality. The next truck to Arcadia City is day after tomorrow. You will ride with me, JieMin, and you will remain there to continue your studies."

FangYan's voice broke there, and JieMin went to his mother. She held him as she cried.

FangYan had made these arrangements for her son because it was the best thing for him, but she would miss him terribly.

The next day, JieMin went to Chen GangJie, the elder who had given him his assignment.

"I am leaving Chagu tomorrow, Zhanglao, but I have completed your assignment. I can share it with you."

JieMin passed his drawing, with the view of the valley behind it, to GangJie. GangJie brought it up in his heads-up display, and JieMin explained it to him.

"If I understand you, JieMin, this location of the initial block of the stream is the most important."

"Yes, Zhanglao, because it has the advantage. That is why all of this works."

"I think you need to show me this location, JieMin. To determine it exactly. You will be able to see it? In your mind?"

"Yes, Zhanglao."

GangJie obtained a small truck and drove JieMin out to the head of the valley, where the stream boiled out into the valley from the canyon beyond. They got as close as they could, and got out of the truck.

"Show me the spot, JieMin."

JieMin climbed up the slope, looking around as he went. Several times he stopped, turned around and looked, then continued on. Finally he came to something of a shelf, where the stream cut a notch in the shelf on its path to the valley floor.

"Here, Zhanglao. If you block the stream here, just this high, then water will flow along the shelf to both sides, and descend there and there. Those paths will take it out into the valley there and there. What goes over the blockage will continue down the path it now takes."

GangJie nodded. From here, with JieMin pointing out the features, he could see what needed to be done. A small dam here – more a retaining wall, really – with a standpipe, and then a spillway there for the flash floods.

"I see it, JieMin. I think it will work."

"I do not know how to build these things, Zhanglao, but I can see them."

"The building of such things is straightforward, JieMin. Knowing where to build them, that is the trick."

# Arcadia City

The next morning, Thursday, Chen JieMin and his mother, Chen FangYan, set out for Arcadia City in one of the Chagu enclave's two panel delivery trucks.

"Navigate to Chen Warehouse," FangYan told the truck.

After a brief delay it responded.

"Navigation available. Ready to Drive."

"Drive to Chen Warehouse."

"Driving in five seconds. Say Stop to cancel. Three. Two. One. Driving."

The truck engaged gears and pulled slowly away from the loading dock of the tea barn. It maneuvered slowly across the gravel lot until it hit the paved road, then accelerated. It growled as it climbed up and out of the valley, over the small pass on the downstream side. All watercourses here led to the ocean, and the ocean's coastal plain is where Arcadia City lay.

JieMin had never been out of the mountains. He had been to various places in the mountains, but never down out of the mountains to the coastal plain. In particular, he had never been to Arcadia City. Relatives had always visited them here, anxious for a holiday out of the city.

Much of the trip was with the truck in lower gears, holding back against the grades that led down out of the mountains. JieMin looked around as they moved out of the areas he knew.

"There are things you need to remember, JieMin.

"Here, in Chagu, all are Chen. No one will take advantage of you, or cheat you, because they cheat themselves when they cheat family. This is not the case in the city. In the city, most are not Chen, and you must stand up for yourself.

"Second, the Chen are famous in the city. The Chen are strong. When you say you are Chen JieMin, others are warned they must respect you, lest the family step in on your behalf. No one wants this.

"Third, the Chen compound in Arcadia City is like Chagu. All are Chen. In the compound you are safe.

"Finally, Chen Zumu is your sponsor. Chen Zumu is a magic name in Arcadia City, second only to Chen Zufu. If things are not working out, you can say, 'I will ask Chen Zumu about this,' or 'Chen Zumu sent me.' This should solve most problems, even for someone of your age and appearance."

JieMin continued to look out the windows as he listened to his mother. This all seemed like overkill to him. How big could Arcadia City be? There were hundreds of Chen in Chagu. That was a lot of people. How big could Arcadia City be?

Of course, he knew the numbers. Nine million people total in the colony, and, despite incentives to move out of Arcadia City into one of the other cities that had sprung up along the coast and well into the interior, almost two million people lived in Arcadia City.

But the numbers didn't convey the reality. As the truck made a turn out of the valley and across the shoulder of one of the foothills, JieMin got a panoramic view of Arcadia City, with the ocean to the east – the left from his point of view, looking south – and the softly rolling hills of the interior to the west.

It was immense. A cluster of dozens of tall buildings in the center – some a dozen or more stories tall – surrounded by square miles of lower buildings. Apartment buildings dominated the close-in areas, fading into single-family homes as one moved out from the center.

JieMin gaped at the sight. How could he not get lost in such a maze? FangYan had an answer.

"The city is laid out in numbers, JieMin. The center – downtown – is zero-zero, like a graph. North is the positive direction for the first number, and each block is one hundred. The numbers of each intersection are on the street signs.

"The Chen compound is a square from one hundred west to three hundred west, and from fourteen hundred north to sixteen hundred north. If you remember that, you can look at street signs and always find your way home."

JieMin called up a map of Arcadia City in his heads-up display, then, and saw it. He had never paid attention to the small grid numbers before. Looking out at the huge city, though, and consulting the map, it all fell into place. He saw it, and he saw the Chen compound on the map.

Once it clicked, JieMin's earlier concern evaporated. There was no way he could get lost in the city.


The Chen compound now, a hundred years after the founding of the colony, had grown to four city blocks in Arcadia City, from Hospital Street west to Green Street and Fourteenth Street north to Sixteenth Street.

One the west side of Market Street, there was still a walled garden from Fourteenth Street north to the halfway point of the block. This was for the very delicate plants, and for work on hybrids and new strains. Commercial production had all moved out to farming enclaves like Chagu.

The north half of that block was still an apartment building around a central courtyard, but the first building had been replaced by a taller, masonry building. The apartment complex that now filled the next block north – from Fifteenth Street to

Sixteenth Street, and from Market Street west to Green Street – had been built first. Everyone moved into that new complex, and then the old apartment building had been demolished and replaced with the new, twelve-story building.

There was a bridge on the third-floor level over Fifteenth Street between the apartment buildings, and Chen Zufu and Chen Zumu still had their apartment on the first floor of the south building, with their tea rooms opening out onto the garden.

East of Market Street, too, the compound had grown. The Uptown Market was now a three-story enclosed gallery of stalls and shops. The restaurant was now on the first floor of the Uptown Market building, expanding the garden space west of Market Street. The workshop on the eastern half of that block was still there, and the apartments above it remained.

North of Fifteenth Street was additional workshop space, on multiple floors, on the east half of the block. The west half of the block was the warehouse and distribution center that supplied the market as well as other restaurants and groceries in the capital.

There were bridges on the third-floor level across both Fifteenth Street and Market Street, tying that warehouse and workshop facility into the rest of the compound.

It was into this complex of buildings the box truck drove on its way to the Chen warehouse in the city.


When the box truck had backed up to the loading dock of the warehouse from Sixteenth Street, FangYan and JieMin got out.

"Come with me, JieMin."

FangYan led JieMin through the warehouse and across Fifteenth Street to the Uptown Market, through the market and across Market Street into the apartment building on the other side.

JieMin looked around curiously as they walked.

"This is all Chen?" he asked.

"This is all Chen, in which all Chen have shares," FangYan said. "Our ancestors were good businessmen and worked hard. It is up to us to live up to their example."

They walked up to the reception desk in the lobby of the apartment building, where a young woman and a young man greeted them.

"We are Chen FangYan and Chen JieMin, to see Chen Zumu. We are expected."

The young woman checked a schedule in her heads-up display before answering.

"Of course. Please follow me."

JieMin was astonished. Once again – twice in two days! – his mother had a meeting with Chen Zumu.

He was beginning to understand what it meant to be Chen on Arcadia.

The young woman led them through the security doors, down a hallway, then left down a hallway, and through a door she unlocked in her heads-up display as she approached.

They turned down another hallway with sliding panels until she came to one such door and knocked. She slid the panel aside and bowed into the room.

"Chen FangYan and Chen JieMin, Chen Zumu."

"Show them in, ChaoLi."

Chen ChaoLi bowed again, then stood aside and waved FangYan and JieMin through the doorway. She slid the panel closed behind them.

JieMin was in Wonderland. Chen Zumu sat on a pillow

facing the door by which they had entered. Behind her, through a large teak-beamed doorway, a large garden was being tended by young men and women wearing lavalavas. Chen Zumu was very old, with hair gone white. She wore a silk robe on which silk dragons danced.

JuPing looked curiously at Chen JieMin. His Chinese ancestry had reasserted itself in this generation and, unlike his mother, his hair was ebony black and straight. It was cut in the peasant style used in Chagu, which in the city was only used by children. That and his slight stature made him look like he was ten or eleven years old. Both FangYan and JieMin wore lavalavas in the city style, though JuPing suspected that, in the country, in the fields, they wore them tied up like dhotis.

"Please, be seated," JuPing said, waving to two pillows that faced hers across a low table.

JieMin took the pillow to his right – the one to Chen Zumu's left – leaving the position of higher honor to his mother. It must have been correct, as Chen Zumu nodded as he and his mother sat.

A pretty young woman wearing a lavalava entered from the garden carrying a teapot. She knelt to one side of the table and poured tea into cups that waited on the table. She served FangYan first, then JieMin, then JuPing. That is, JieMin was being treated as an adult, and an honored guest, by Chen Zumu. JieMin began to see how Chen Zufu and Chen Zumu had earned such respect within the family.

True leadership was not arrogant.

The young woman finished pouring tea. She set the teapot in the center of the table, bowed to a spot between the three, and departed without a word.

"Please drink with me," JuPing said, and lifted her tea cup.

FangYan sipped the tea, but JieMin waited for Chen Zumu.

She looked at him and raised one eyebrow, and JieMin realized she was waiting for her guest to drink first. He sipped his tea, and only then did Chen Zumu sip hers.

"I have heard many things about you, Chen JieMin."

JieMin didn't know what to say to that, so he merely nodded – once, like a bow.

"Even at your age, you have accomplished a great deal," JuPing continued.

"Thank you, Chen Zumu."

"You're welcome, Chen JieMin."

JuPing sipped her tea again.

"It has been reported to us that you have designed a better water system for Chagu," she said. "Chen GangJie says it will allow for better water distribution with less work, and open up some areas we had not been able to plant. Chen Zufu has authorized the construction to proceed."

JieMin goggled at her. That his little project would attract the attention of the mighty had not occurred to him.

"Tell me, Chen JieMin. How did you see this solution?"

"I don't know, Chen Zumu. I looked out across the valley, and I could see the water flow as it was, and as it could be. It was there, in my mind. It was not something I thought about. I simply saw it."

JuPing nodded.

"So I had surmised. You have a gift, Chen JieMin. A gift to see such things. We will see if we can develop this gift further, so that you can apply it to bigger things."

"Thank you, Chen Zumu."

JuPing nodded.

"For the immediate future, though, we must get you situated here. You will have rooms in this building, near your dabo, Chen JuanTao, and his family.

"You will have no chores. No assigned tasks. I have also prepared an account for you, so that you may purchase whatever you need to be most productive. If you wish to eat in the restaurant, or pick up something in the market, or buy something downtown, you will use this account. Use it to buy those things you need or wish in order to be most productive."

"How is this account paid, Chen Zumu?"

"The account bills against my own funds, Chen JieMin. I am your sponsor."

JieMin blushed heavily.

"I am honored, Chen Zumu."

He bowed deeply to her.

"Do not hesitate to use this account, Chen JieMin. For food or drink. For drawing supplies. For a comfortable chair to sit in, or table to draw at. Use these funds to ease your way, so that you may be most productive in the use of your gift."

"I understand, Chen Zumu."

"And the university, Chen Zumu?" FangYan asked.

"I have already spoken to the president of the university, FangYan."

JuPing turned back to JieMin.

"Tomorrow morning, you will go to the university, Chen JieMin. You will ask for the president, Anders Connor. Do you need any instructions to get to his office?'

JieMin consulted his heads-up display, and searched Anders Connor. He had an address and a room number, a precise location in the three-dimensional coordinate map of Arcadia City in his mind.

"No, Chen Zumu. I can see where he is."

JuPing nodded.

"President Connor should have a proposal for you, Chen JieMin. More than one, actually, from which to choose. It is up to you, however, to decide your path. No one else has your gift. They cannot determine your path for you. You must be clear on this."

"I understand, Chen Zumu."

"Very well, Chen JieMin. And if there are any problems – with anyone – you are to refer them to me."

"I understand, Chen Zumu."


The same young woman who had taken them to Chen Zumu – Chen ChaoLi – showed them through the apartment building to an apartment door on the eighth floor.

"You should have the lock for this door in your heads-up display," she said.

JieMin looked, and there it was. He pushed the virtual button with his finger, and heard the door unlatch. ChaoLi opened the door and led them in.

It was a one-room efficiency apartment, the sort a young person would have when they first moved out from their family. There was a small kitchenette, a table with two chairs, a bed in the corner, and a living room grouping of a sofa and two chairs with a low table in the center.

The room was high enough in the building that the view to the east was over the market and workshop buildings to the ocean five miles away.

After growing up in a family of nine in a tiny four-room house in Chagu, it was a mansion to JieMin.

"Who do I share this with?" he asked ChaoLi.

She laughed, a sound like tiny bells.

"This is your apartment. You do not share it with anyone, Chen JieMin. Your dabo has a family apartment on the other side of the hallway, one door down. Let me show you."

ChaoLi led them out into the hallway, and down one door.

No one was home now, at mid-day, but JieMin at least knew where it was. He would pay his respects this evening.

"JieMin, I just received a message the truck is ready to leave. I must go back to Chagu. Will you be OK here?"

"Yes, Muqin. I have everything I need."

"Oh, I will miss you so much," FangYan said, hugging him.

"You can visit, though, Muqin. When the truck comes. We can have lunch together."

"I will do that, JieMin. And now I must go."

FangYan left with ChaoLi, who showed her the way back out of the building.

JieMin went into his apartment and sat in an armchair, staring out the window and incorporating all he had seen.

# Getting Settled, Getting Around

It was late in the afternoon when JieMin's stomach grumbled. He had eaten breakfast at home, and a light lunch in the truck on the way to Arcadia City, but it was nearing dinner time.

JieMin did not want to show up at his relatives' apartment at supper time, not having yet stopped by to pay his respects. Instead he went down the elevator, out of the apartment building, and across Market Street to the family's restaurant. He had never been to a restaurant before, but Chen Zumu had said he might eat here.

"Yes, may I help you?" the hostess asked.

Taking him for a child, she looked around for his family.

"I would like to eat dinner," JieMin said.

"One for dinner?"

"Yes, please."

She led him to a small table for two.

"Is this OK?"

"Yes, this is fine."

She put a card down on the table and was about to leave, but he felt remiss in not introducing himself.

"I am Chen JieMin," he said.

"I am Chen FangLi," she said. "We are relatives."

"We are Chen," he agreed.

She nodded.

"Have a wonderful dinner."

"Thank you."

JieMin sat down at the table and looked curiously at the card. It was a listing of dozens of different food dishes. He did a quick search in his heads-up display. Ah. A menu. That is what it was called. Apparently he could have anything on this long list. At home, one simply ate what was put on the table.

How did one decide what one wanted to eat? How was one to know what one might like and not like?

JieMin decided to take a long-term approach to the problem. Since he would probably be eating here a lot, he decided to simply eat the things on the menu in order each time he came, determining his favorites in that way.

There were soups, appetizers, and dinners, and he was hungry, so he decided to get the first one of each.

"My name is LiGang," a young man said. "I will be your server. Have you decided what you would like?"

"My name is Chen JieMin," JieMin said. "I would like these three things, please. The first soup, the first appetizer, and the first entree."

"That is a lot of food for one person. Do you want those in single portions?"

"Yes. Enough for one, please."

"Excellent. And would you like tea?"

"Yes, please."

"Very good. I'll be right back with your tea."

While he waited, JieMin did a search for etiquette at a restaurant. He was surprised that he was expected to do nothing but order, eat, and pay. He did not help buss his own dishes or any of the minor things he associated with eating from at home.

Oops. There was one thing JieMin did not expect. There was a custom to pay a little extra for the waiter. The amount varied, but fifteen percent was the recommended minimum if service had been satisfactory. He decided to always tip twenty percent, so as not to be at the minimum, and because it was easier to calculate anyway. He checked, and he could set his account to do that automatically whenever he paid, so he set it.

The food came in stages, and it was indeed a lot of food, even when ordered for one person. JieMin decided he may skip the appetizers when not so hungry. There were fewer of them on the menu to work his way through, so that would not disrupt his plan to try everything in order.

The food was all very good to him, but JieMin had no comparison to the other things on the menu, so he wasn't sure how to score them. He decided to mark them all a three for now, and score the others against that standard.

The waiter came to his table when he was finished and asked him if he wanted anything else. Dessert, perhaps.

"No, thank you. That was all very good."

"Excellent."

The waiter aimed something at his communicator, then departed.

JieMin saw the bill appear on his heads-up display. When he selected to pay it from the account Chen Zumu had set up for him, he was happy to see the tip was added as he had configured it. So that worked.

Then he simply got up from his dirty table and dirty dishes and walked away. That was the practice, but it made him feel guilty for not helping with the dishes.

JieMin walked through the Uptown Market after dinner. It was still a bit early to pay his respects to his dabo and family, because they might still be eating and he didn't want to impose.

JieMin saw there was a cafe in the market as well as the

restaurant. This was more informal. He checked the menu for breakfast and found they had pastries and something called a breakfast sandwich, which consisted of putting normal breakfast items in a pastry. This could be eaten there or taken with you. JieMin thought that might be a good thing for tomorrow morning. If all the tables were taken, he could simply eat it outside.

Back in the apartment, he received a note from his aunt, Chen MinQiang. She had heard from JieMin's mother that he was there, and he was invited to come by their apartment.

JieMin sent a response that he was coming, and walked down the hall. The door opened as he approached, and MinQiang greeted him with a hug.

"Come in, JieMin."

"Thank you, Bomu," he said, using the Chinese word for his father's older brother's wife.

"Oh, so old-fashioned. I'm still your Auntie Min, am I not?"

"Yes, Bomu."

MinQiang laughed and led him into the apartment. It was a big family apartment, with six rooms and a huge dining table. MinQiang and JuanTao had six children – pretty much the Chen average – and the apartment was big enough for eight. All JieMin's cousins were still in low, middle, and high school.

MinQiang fussed over him. Yes, he had eaten dinner. No, he didn't need anything for his apartment. She managed to press a few cookies and tea on him and was grilling him on his plans, when JuanTao rescued him.

"JieMin has already finished college, MinQiang. He is an adult by that measure, and his plans are his own."

JuanTao turned to JieMin.

"I did promise my brother I would be here for you if you

need any help with anything. So if anything goes amiss, you will let me know, JieMin?"

"Of course, Dabo."

"Good. And now you probably have other things to do than entertain your aunt and uncle. Let him go, MinQiang."

MinQiang let him take his leave but not before giving him another smothering hug.

Back in his own apartment, JieMin decided he would be taking most of his meals in the market or the restaurant across the street.

That night, JieMin had trouble getting to sleep. It was too quiet in the empty apartment by himself. He was used to sharing a bedroom with two younger brothers.

JieMin got up and went over to the window. He opened it, allowing the nighttime noise of the city in.

JieMin went back to bed and fell asleep in minutes.

JieMin was up at seven with the dawn. He showered and put on a clean lavalava. Which reminded him that he needed to learn how to do laundry here. No one had said anything about that.

JieMin went downstairs and across to the Uptown Market. The cafe was open, and it was not yet crowded. He bought a breakfast sandwich and tea, and sat at one of the little tables to eat. It was fun watching the market wake up.

When the cafe started to get crowded, JieMin got up so he would not use up a table and make someone else stand. He walked back over to the apartment building.

ChaoLi was on the reception desk again today, Friday. JieMin knew the university's offices opened at nine o'clock, and he knew he could get there by walking. It was one-point-four miles south and zero-point-two miles east given the city's grid system. That he knew. He could walk, but there might be an easier way.

"Good morning, ChaoLi."

"Good morning, JieMin. How can I help you today?"

"What is the easiest way to get downtown, to the university?"

"If you walk two blocks due east, to Arcadia Boulevard, there is a bus that runs into downtown. Every fifteen minutes. You can pay with your communicator."

"Good. Thank you, ChaoLi."

"You're welcome, JieMin."

Exiting the apartment building, JieMin walked east along Fifteenth Street between the market and original workshop on one side and the warehouse and the new workshop on the other. He crossed Hospital Street and went one more block to Arcadia Boulevard.

Arcadia Boulevard was much wider than the side streets, with two busy lanes of traffic in each direction. He saw a bus-stop sign on the northwest corner of the intersection and crossed Fifteenth Street to stand there.

Five minutes later a bus stopped to pick him up. The doorway tagged his communicator as he got on, and he paid the fare in his heads-up display. He took a seat in the front, opposite the driver, and looked out the big front window as the bus drove down Arcadia Boulevard to downtown.

Arcadia Boulevard and Quant Boulevard no longer met in the middle of downtown. Not for vehicles anyway. They were both closed for one block either way from the center of town.

First Street between University and Hospital was westbound only, Hospital from First to A was southbound only, A Street from Hospital to University was eastbound only, and University Street between A and First was northbound only.

These streets formed what amounted to a two-block-on-a-side traffic circle around the center of town. The center of town was a pedestrian zone.

JieMin got off the bus at Arcadia Boulevard and First Street. He waited for the traffic light crosswalk signal, then walked across First Street and down the broad sidewalk that had been Arcadia Boulevard.

He was in the middle of four of the largest buildings he had ever seen. As big as anything in the Chen compound. Except these were made entirely of steel and glass. These were the four original buildings of the colony, he realized. Transported from Earth a hundred years ago.

He walked forward under the pedestrian bridge between what must be the university to his left and the hospital to his right and into Charter Square. This had been the intersection of Arcadia and Quant Boulevards, but was now a large pedestrian park.

On the other side of the square, to the right, was the colony administration building. On that corner of the square stood a statue of a woman in a business suit holding aloft a document in her right hand. It read 'Arcadia Charter' across the top. The base of the statue was inscribed:

# ADRIANA ZIELINSKI
## CHAIRMAN OF THE
## CHARTER CONVENTION

JieMin turned to the east, toward the university, and was struck by another statue there. This one was of an old man in a lavalava, bald, with a long mustache and goatee. He was seated in tailor's seat on a pillow. The base of this statue was also inscribed.

# CHEN ZUFU
## MATTHEW CHEN-JASIC
## FATHER OF THE REPUBLIC

There were potted trees and flowers in the square, but the sight line between the two statues was kept clear. It was as if Adriana Zielinski was holding the Arcadia Charter up for Chen Zufu's approval.

That was an actual event, JieMin knew. August first, 2295. Everybody knew that was the day Zielinski had taken the completed charter to the Chen for his approval. The statues recreated the event.

Chen JieMin felt proud to be Chen.

# The University of Arcadia

JieMin went into the university building and took the elevator to the correct floor – the top one – for the president of the university.

There was a receptionist there, and he walked up to her desk.

"Hello, little boy. How may I help you? Are you lost?"

"I have an appointment with President Connor."

"I don't think so. Come along now. You should get back to your schoolwork."

She got up from her desk and started to come around. JieMin decided it was time to invoke the magic name.

"I am Chen JieMin. I am sent by Chen Zumu."

She was not Chen, but when JieMin mentioned Chen Zumu, the receptionist stopped like she had walked into a clear glass barrier. She sat back down at her desk, and checked her appointment schedule for Anders Connor.

"I'm terribly sorry, Mr. Chen. I have you right here. Please, have a seat, and I'll let President Connor know you're here."

"Thank you."

Anders Connor knew Chen JieMin was fourteen years old. He had also seen his picture in the university's personal information file. Even so, he was not prepared for the slight, vaguely distracted youngster waiting in his lobby.

He would learn that vaguely distracted or vaguely disoriented look was part and parcel of Chen JieMin. He always looked like he couldn't quite figure out what was expected of him, and, besides, he was mentally working on some complex problem at the moment and couldn't be bothered to be completely in the here and now.

From JieMin's point of view, Anders Connor was an impossibly tall, blond-haired, blue-eyed man in a business suit, about as far from being Chen as he could be.

"Mr. Chen," Connor said as he walked up to JieMin.

JieMin stood, and Connor extended his hand. JieMin shook it.

"I'm very pleased to meet you. Please come into my office."

"Thank you, President Connor."

Connor waved JieMin to a chair in a sitting area off to the side of his office from the desk. Connor waited for JieMin to sit before he seated himself.

"When Chen Zumu called me about your situation, Mr. Chen, I of course checked your academic records. That you are so accomplished so young portends great things for your future."

"Thank you, President Connor."

"Now, Chen Zumu was very clear in her request to me that you be allowed to follow your own interests in pursuing your further education. We have advanced courses in mathematics, of course, from Earth. We also have advanced courses in some of the other disciplines in which mathematics plays a very central role. You may wish to sample some of those courses to see if something interests you."

"Actually, that sounds very good, President Connor."

"Excellent. For right now, we have an office for you in the Chen Hall of Science. That would be proper for a graduate research assistant to a professor. We are granting you the same sort of situation, but without the research duties. Your research duty will be to pursue your own interests."

"That is very generous, President Connor."

"Not at all, Mr. Chen. When one has such a gift, it is in everyone's interests that it be developed fully."

Connor nodded, as if convincing himself.

"Come with me, Mr. Chen, and let's get you settled."

If anyone else thought it was unusual for the president of the university to personally show a new graduate student to his office, it didn't occur to Chen JieMin. Everything was new to him, so there was no business-as-usual to compare to.

Connor led JieMin to the elevators and down to the third floor of the administration building. They walked north through the building along a major corridor, then over a bridge across First Street. As they left the walkway and entered the building, they crossed under an arch proclaiming 'Chen Hall of Science.'

Connor chattered along the way.

"The university is actually quite large, given our relatively small footprint downtown here. Many of our undergraduate students take most of their courses remote, though doing their entire program remote as you did is not so usual.

"There are also satellite campuses in some of the other cities. That means our faculty as well as our students are distributed throughout the colony.

"Even so, we have large buildings spread across five city blocks here in our urban campus. The secret was to build up, not out. The Chen Hall of Science here is our latest addition. It was Chen Zumu's project to get it funded and built. In addition to the sciences, the mathematics program is here as well."

That explained much to JieMin. Chen Zumu may be the

university's single largest patron. When she called, the president of the university would most assuredly listen.

It also meant that being JieMin's patron was both an extension of Chen Zumu's patronage of education on Arcadia and a small additional project for her.

"Our graduate program is a bit different. It really needs to be on-site, mostly because the materials we brought from Earth aren't amenable to use through the communicators. The undergraduate courses, yes, but the graduate courses are much more involved. One needs a viewing room for those.

"Here in Chen Hall, all the offices are equipped as viewing rooms, which means you can take the graduate courses without leaving your office. We don't really have lecture halls, or even many classrooms. That's another reason our footprint can be so small."

They went up in the elevator to the math department's main floor.

Klaus Boortz was the head of the Mathematics Department at the University of Arcadia. He had been the head of the department for twenty years, and had fought long and hard to get the math department the respect it deserved.

Fifty years ago, Matthew Chen-Jasic and Adriana Zielinski – who was both the chairman of the charter convention and the provost of the university – had remade the government and founded the republic. Part of that restructuring had finally gained the university the funding it needed to become a true university.

But the emphasis had been on engineering and the sciences, including agriculture, as most needed by the colony. When Boortz was made the head of the struggling math department, the gruff German had emphasized mathematics' role in supporting all of these technical fields. How a strong math department was necessary to provide the analytical rigor for them to be most effective. And he had largely succeeded.

Now this. The spoiled favorite child of the most politically connected and wealthiest family on the planet – and the university's biggest supporter – being foisted on his graduate program. At age fourteen, no less.

Boortz had angrily opened the student's records to find the information he needed to give Connor a piece of his mind, and he'd been surprised.

First, Chen JieMin had in fact completed all of the undergraduate mathematics courses required, with honors, and taken the graduate courses available via communicator as well.

Second, Chen JieMin was Chen, but he was not the pampered child of an urbanite family. He was from Chagu, a farming enclave of his family, and grew up in very modest – and crowded – housing in the mountains. He had probably worked in the fields since he was old enough to walk.

His anger defused now, Boortz went back through JieMin's records with a fine-toothed comb. There was also a personality and intelligence test result there, the same one given to every youngster at eight or nine years old.

Chen JieMin's intelligence had not been rated that highly by this test, but Boortz knew more than a little about testing analysis. That was a composite score. Boortz sliced the test apart, and evaluated the bits separately.

On the sections on interpersonal communications, on understanding people, on emotional intelligence, on everyday items, JieMin had performed well below average. But on the sections on logical and abstract thinking, on visualization, on deduction and induction, his scores were off the charts. Well above the range where the test was even considered accurate.

Boortz went from being angry to elated. Chen JieMin had all the signs of being a true mathematics prodigy.

But he had to keep the Physics Department from poaching his new star student.

Anders Connor had sent Klaus Boortz a message that they were on the way, and Boortz met Connor and JieMin in the elevator lobby on the tenth floor. Where Connor was in a business suit and JieMin in a lavalava and flip-flops, Boortz split the difference in slacks and a loud tropical-print shirt over his considerable bulk.

"Klaus, this is Chen JieMin. Mr. Chen, this is Professor Boortz. He is the head of our mathematics department."

"Good morning, Mr. Chen. I'm very pleased to meet you."

"I am honored to meet you, Jiaoshou," JieMin said, bowing. "Please call me JieMin."

"Jow shoe?" Boortz asked.

"It is Chinese for professor, but it conveys more respect than the English word."

"Ah. Well, thank you for that. But if I am to call you JieMin, then you must call me Klaus. Reciprocity, you see."

JieMin did see. Huhui – reciprocity – was a basic precept of Chinese culture.

"Very well, er, Klaus."

Boortz laughed with gusto. It seemed he did everything with gusto.

"I'll leave you two, then, Klaus."

"Yes, Anders. I have it from here. Thank you very much," Boortz said.

"Thank you, President Connor," JieMin said with a bow.

"Good day, Mr. Chen. Feel free to call on me at any time."

Connor got into an elevator and disappeared, while Boortz led his new charge into the math department.

"And this is your office," Boortz said, opening a door on the hallway. "It's just down the hall from mine."

He waved JieMin to enter. There was a desk on one side, with a task chair, and a table on the other side, with two side chairs. The far end of the room was open. The office was perhaps twelve feet wide and twelve deep.

"Please," Boortz said, waving JieMin to the task chair.

He pulled out one of the side chairs and sat facing JieMin.

"It's a little small, I know."

"It seems large to me, Klaus."

"Well, you're a smaller person," Boortz said with a chuckle. "But the secret is that end of the room."

Boortz waved to the apparently empty end of the room.

"That is the projection area, JieMin. It is a three-dimensional display, and much more. You can draw in it, as you do in the heads-up display of the communicator, but in much more detail and precision. It is extensively used in the graduate courses. The ones you haven't already taken, that is."

"I see."

"There is a training piece with it. It runs you through most of the basics pretty quickly. Using the device is simple. What you do with it is up to you."

Boortz paused as if waiting for a response.

"Thank you, Klaus."

Boortz nodded.

"Now, I wanted to talk to you a bit about what you might do as you take further coursework. Most of our graduate students are attached to a professor and assist him in his research. But that is not the case for you, JieMin.

"You should pursue the things that interest you. In particular, you may wish to apply mathematics to other subjects here within the university. We call that applied mathematics. There are a number of possibilities.

"Physics is one. They have a lot of interesting things going on there. And physics is perhaps the most mathematics-intensive of all the sciences. But that is just one possibility.

"Chemistry, too, has opportunities. Biology. The engineering disciplines. In applied mathematics, you can work in any of these areas, JieMin, or in all of them.

"I guess what I am trying to say is, Don't limit yourself. Don't say, Oh, that isn't mathematics because it isn't pure mathematics. Use mathematics as a tool in whatever area suits you."

"That is a welcome clarification, Klaus. I do not know where my interests will lead."

"And, in the mathematics department, that isn't a decision you need to make. You can work in any field in which mathematics is an important tool, which in engineering and the sciences is just about all of them. I would encourage you to take courses in any areas that interest you – physics, biology, one of the engineering fields. Whatever you find interesting."

"Thank you, Klaus."

"You're very welcome, JieMin. And if you have any questions, remember that I'm just down the hall."

With that Boortz was up and out of the room.

JieMin spent two hours working with the projector device. The tutorial was slow, but as soon as it explained he could adjust the playback speed, he set it to one-point-seven-five times normal speed. That worked much better for him.

JieMin loaded the drawing he had done for Chen GangJie –

was that just Tuesday of this week? – and looked at it in the big projection. He magnified it, added detail, showed the water flows, and added a side wall to one water channel at a point it might wash out. He sent that improved version to Chen GangJie.

# The Beach

By that time it was almost one o'clock, and JieMin was hungry. He went downstairs and found the cafeteria in the main university building. He got a light lunch and ate it outside in Charter Square.

It was a beautiful day, and JieMin was not motivated to go back up to the office. Instead he decided to learn more of Arcadia City. So he got on a bus – it didn't matter to him which one it was – and rode in the front seat opposite the driver, just looking out the windows.

At one point, the bus stopped and the driver made an announcement.

"Transfer to the beach bus."

"There is a bus to the beach from here?" JieMin asked.

"Oh, yes. That bus there goes to the beach as soon as we drop off," he said, pointing.

"Thank you."

JieMin got in the line of people getting off the bus and going over to the other bus. He hadn't noticed while he was sitting in the front of the bus, but some of them were completely nude, already stripped down for swimming in the ocean. Why wouldn't one just take off one's lavalava when they got there? It seemed strange to him.

JieMin rode in the front on the way to the beach. Arcadia City gradually thinned out, and then they were in the green space along the beach. He wasn't sure if that was an enforced green space somehow, or whether no one wanted to build this far from town. Maybe the colony owned this property and kept it so there would be no development here.

In any case it was very pretty, and it was only minutes before the bus stopped at the beach. JieMin got off with everybody else and trekked across the sand.

There was no moon of consequence on Arcadia, and that meant there were no tides. The beach was therefore naturally narrow, but the colony government had widened the beach here so close to the city. Without tides, the extra sand was also unlikely to wash away.

JieMin thought the beach was wonderful. It was a beautiful day, the sun high overhead, a cool onshore breeze. He knew how to swim – there was a pond in the mountains, but it could be very cold. By contrast, the water here was wonderfully warm.

JieMin kicked off his flip-flops and took off his lavalava. He folded it and set it on his flip-flops, then waded out into the ocean. When he was deep enough, he launched off into the water.

Swimming was easier than in the freshwater pond back home. Not only was this water warm, but it was salt water, and he floated higher than in the fresh-water pond. After several days with no exercise, it felt good to swim and he pushed himself, tried to wear himself out a bit.

After an hour in the water, JieMin came back out onto the beach to find that his lavalava and flip-flops were gone. That was disconcerting. One did not worry about theft or pilferage in Chagu, because everyone was Chen.

JieMin looked around. There were several hundred people on the beach, and most were nude, enjoying the sun. Several dozen more were in the ocean – all nude – enjoying the water.

JieMin shrugged and lay on the beach nude, like everyone

else. After a half hour he went back into the water to cool off, and swam for another half hour. He then went back to the beach and sat, considering his situation.

He still had his communicator. Like many people who preferentially wore lavalavas, JieMin wore his communicator with a strap on his left upper arm. It was waterproof and he had not taken it off to swim.

There was no consideration of similarly stealing a lavalava and using it to replace his own. That was out of the question. He was Chen.

There was no place on the beach selling lavalavas where he could buy one. That was probably a business opportunity, he thought. That or some sort of locker or checking system.

He had several lavalavas at home, of course, which did him no good here. At the same time, others had ridden the bus to the beach nude, and would presumably ride home the same way, so it must be OK.

Besides, he had seen children playing nude in the parks and streets in Arcadia City, and JieMin looked even younger than he was. He would have fit right in playing with those children.

There was a steady stream of people onto and off of the beach as the buses came and went. JieMin shrugged and headed for the bus.

There were a lot of others on the bus who were nude as well, both men and women, most wearing their communicators on their arm, like JieMin.

It was much different after the beach bus stopped at the transfer station and JieMin got on the Arcadia Boulevard bus. He was definitely in the minority being nude on this bus, although there were a couple of others. No one else said anything or acted as if anything were at all unusual, however.

JieMin was the only person to get off the bus at Fifteenth Street. He walked down the street feeling very exposed. On the way he considered his options. Market, to buy another lavalava, or straight to his apartment?

Apartment, he decided. The Uptown Market was the family business. He didn't recall seeing anyone there nude, though there might have been. With all the people wearing lavalavas topless, it was hard to say whether any of them had been nude or not. He simply hadn't noticed.

But the apartment was Chen. Not a public place. Not the family business.

When JieMin got to Market Street and Fifteenth, he crossed Market and walked in the front door of the apartment building. ChaoLi was still on the reception desk. She didn't bat an eye at his unclothed state.

"Hi, JieMin. How was the beach?"

"Wonderful, ChaoLi. The water was much warmer than a mountain pond."

"I bet. I hope it's this nice tomorrow. I haven't been to the beach in three weeks."

JieMin had been nude and surrounded by nude people for the last several hours, but he found the thought of ChaoLi being nude disturbing. He headed for the elevator before his body betrayed his thoughts.

Back in his apartment, JieMin put on a lavalava. It was his last clean one. He had to figure out how to do laundry here.

JieMin also got a note from his aunt MinQiang, inviting him to dinner. He sent a short reply, thanking her for the invitation but saying he already had other plans.

JieMin went down to the lobby. It was nearly five, and ChaoLi was getting ready to go off shift.

"ChaoLi, how does one do laundry here?"

"Oh, didn't anyone tell you, JieMin? There's a laundry for the building. You just drop everything off here, and then pick it up here later. Four-hour turnaround usually. I think that's in the building guide for residents."

"Ah. I should probably have read the guide."

ChaoLi laughed her little bells laugh.

"Yes, well, I think that's the only big thing you probably missed."

"OK. Thanks, ChaoLi."

JieMin headed across the street to the market. He bought several more lavalavas and another pair of flip-flops, then went to the restaurant. He kept his eyes open this time, and he did occasionally see someone nude in the market. He shook his head. Arcadia City was certainly a strange place.

JieMin was hungry from the fresh air and swimming on the beach. Tonight he had the second soup, the second appetizer, and the second entree. The soup and the appetizer he scored as threes, but the entree tonight was a four.


The next day was Saturday. JieMin would start in on his studies on Monday, in his office with the projection display, but he decided he would take the weekend off.

JieMin had a breakfast sandwich from the cafe in the Uptown Market again, but this time he bought a sandwich and a cold tea for lunch as well. He wasn't sure what he would do with the day, but this way he would not be tied to finding lunch.

He also took his laundry – two lavalavas – down to the reception counter. Someone else was on the desk today.

"Room number?"

"Eight seventy-two."

The clerk nodded and tagged the clothes, then put them in a bag for pickup. He checked the time in his heads-up display.

"Figure four o'clock today. Saturdays are usually busy."

"Thank you."

JieMin tried to think of other things to do today, but the allure of the beach was just too compelling. He slipped out of his lavalava and flip-flops in his apartment, grabbed his lunch, and headed, nude, for the bus stop.

JieMin ate his lunch on the bus on the way to the beach. He dropped the refuse in the can at the bus parking lot and walked across the sand. He walked right on into the ocean, and, once he was deep enough, dove forward into a swim.

JieMin found he could lay out on the surface of the calm water. The salinity was high enough he floated just below the surface, and, with his arms behind his head, his face was out of the water.

JieMin floated there in the warm sun and daydreamed, as he always did, about the things he saw in his mind. The layout of the city. The motions of planets and stars. The way the insects in Chagu wove their webs.

JieMin swam some more, then walked out on the beach. He was settling down on the sand when someone called his name.

"JieMin!"

JieMin looked up to see ChaoLi coming toward him. She was nude. He sat up.

"Hi, ChaoLi. You made it to the beach finally."

"Yes. I'm here with my girlfriends."

She waved to a group of girls farther down the beach and they waved back.

"Come, JieMin. Swim with me."

They swam and played tag in the water. ChaoLi was a

strong swimmer, and JieMin found himself more than evenly matched. When they tired, he taught her his floating trick.

They floated on the surface, but kept drifting apart.

"Lock arms with me, JieMin."

When they hooked their arms together, they floated together on the warm ocean, shoulder to shoulder. JieMin found the touch of her, the scent of her, intoxicating.

After several minutes, ChaoLi laughed her little bells laugh.

"JieMin, you have a periscope."

JieMin blushed bright crimson and started to stammer an apology, but she put a finger over his lips and kissed his cheek. After that, he lay there with her in the sun unashamedly.

They left the beach together, after ChaoLi said goodbye to her friends, and rode the bus back into the city. They talked all the way, and JieMin was able to forget that they were both nude.

JieMin told her of his family, of course, and ChaoLi told him of hers. She was descended in part from Rachel Conroy and Gary Rockham, with other side branches from Kimberly Peterson and Carl Reynolds, one of the original Carolina couples. That explained her half-Asian features and the auburn highlights in her hair, which JieMin found exotic and beautiful.

More to the point, their lineages did not overlap in the last five generations, back to Chen LiQiang, which meant they were no closer than fourth cousins. Genetically, they were not unavailable to each other.

ChaoLi was just sixteen, which, if not exactly a spinster in the colony, was certainly old enough for marriage. The original colonists had partnered young, and that had become part of the culture on Arcadia.

JieMin, however, was only fourteen. Fourteen and a half, if

pressed. The counter to that was that he had his college degree, was established, and had his own apartment. ChaoLi still lived with her family, the oldest of the siblings still at home.

They chattered about life in the city and how it compared to life in the country, which ChaoLi found exotic. She loved the mountains as well as the beach, but had only been there twice. JieMin promised to make up the deficiency.

They walked across Fifteenth Street together, crossed Market, and got to the apartment building. When they went in, the same clerk was at the reception desk.

"Eight seventy-two is back from the laundry," he said.

JieMin took the bag absently, with a murmured 'Thank you.' He turned to ChaoLi.

"ChaoLi, will you go to dinner with me?"

"Of course, JieMin. If I can borrow one of those lavalavas?"

JieMin held the bag open to her and she picked a lavalava and put it on. JieMin put on the other, and threw the bag in the refuse can in the lobby.

They walked back across Market Street to the restaurant.

When they were seated in the restaurant, JieMin explained his system for determining the dishes most to his liking.

"It sounds like fun," ChaoLi said.

"I thought you would know the best dishes here," JieMin said.

"No, JieMin. I have never eaten here before. Oh, I think once or twice maybe, for a wedding, but that is a different menu. I have never eaten here before with this menu. Eating out is expensive."

That surprised JieMin. He had come to think of the restaurant as his dining room. He never considered prices or costs. He suspected Chen Zumu would consider the cost of his time cooking for himself to be much higher than his restaurant bill.

ChaoLi agreed they should get the third and fourth soup, the third and fourth appetizer, and the third and fourth entree off the menu, and they would share and taste so JieMin could rate them.

They talked and ate, and ChaoLi laughed like little bells.

After dinner, over which they tarried, they walked back over to the apartment building. The elevator stopped at the eighth floor to let JieMin off, while ChaoLi was bound for the tenth floor.

They said goodbye, and then JieMin got off the elevator.

"JieMin," she said.

He turned around and ChaoLi was standing nude in the elevator, holding out his borrowed lavalava.

"Don't forget your lavalava."

JieMin took the lavalava and stood there speechless, staring at her.

ChaoLi winked at him and the doors closed.

# Commitment

JieMin had trouble getting to sleep that night. He kept thinking of ChaoLi.

Was it infatuation? He had only been in Arcadia City a bit over two days. ChaoLi was one of the few people he knew here.

Then again, JieMin did not have these feelings for the hostess in the restaurant, or the server in the cafe, or any of the other young women about. Nor had he had them for anyone back in Chagu.

JieMin finally fell asleep, though he woke before dawn. He sat in the big armchair and watched the sun come up over the ocean to the east.

Something clicked and he knew, the way he knew the answer to a math problem. He was sure.

But now what should he do?

He must talk to Chen Zumu, and seek her blessing. With her blessing, all things were possible.

Without her blessing, it would be impossible.


One benefit of asking for a meeting with Chen Zumu on a Sunday was that his request would not go through ChaoLi. JieMin remembered the first day, when it was ChaoLi who had shown JieMin and his mother to Chen Zumu.

JieMin put in his request to Chen Zumu's mail address. He had an answer within ten minutes.

Ten o'clock this morning.

JieMin went over to the cafe. He had only a pastry and tea this morning, not wanting to eat anything heavy. He was afraid he might be all nerves with Chen Zumu, and would end up with a stomach ache.

At five minutes of ten, he presented himself at the reception desk. The young man there – the same one as yesterday – showed him down the hall, through the locked door, and to Chen Zumu's tea room. He knocked and slid the panel aside.

"Chen JieMin, Chen Zumu."

"Show him in, ChaoJuan," JuPing said

The young man waved JieMin forward, then slid the panel closed behind him.

JieMin was surprised to find Chen Zumu seated facing out into the garden, on one of two pillows equally centered in the doorway.

"Take morning tea with me, JieMin," JuPing said without turning, waving at the pillow alongside her.

JieMin was almost overcome with the honor of having tea with Chen Zumu, here, in her tea room, facing out into the garden. Of being addressed by her without his full name. He walked around to the pillow and sat.

A young woman – not ChaoLi! – came and poured tea for them, serving JieMin first. The young woman put the teapot on the low table between them and withdrew. They both lifted their tea, and JieMin, as guest, sipped his first.

JuPing continued to contemplate the garden as she sipped her tea, not looking at JieMin. She set the tea down.

"What brings you to me this morning, JieMin? Did everything work out satisfactorily with the university?"

"Yes, Chen Zumu. President Connor and Professor Boortz were very nice. I have my own office, with a large display projector, and have been encouraged to pursue my interests without outside direction."

"Excellent. That was my request of them, and that was my best advice to you as well."

"Yes, Chen Zumu."

"And clearly you found the university, and have managed to find food and drink, as you don't look to be starving."

JieMin laughed.

"No, Chen Zumu."

She looked at him out of the corner of her eye, then turned her attention back to the garden.

"You look to have found the beach as well, JieMin."

"Yes, Chen Zumu."

"Then what brings you to me this morning, JieMin? Not that I don't look forward to occasionally hearing of your adventures, but I'm guessing you have a specific purpose."

"Yes, Chen Zumu. There is a girl...."

JuPing didn't sigh. Affairs of the heart were deadly serious, the more so to the young.

"And who is this girl, JieMin?"

"Chen ChaoLi, Chen Zumu."

"Does she share your feelings, JieMin?"

"Yes, Chen Zumu. That is, I think so. But I would not pursue this matter further without your blessing."

JuPing nodded. Sensible, since she was his patron. Any duties he took on depended on her as well.

"How sure are you of your heart, JieMin? ChaoLi is one of the few people you know here. You have only been here three days. Is it a case of grasping at the one thing in reach?"

To JuPing's surprise, JieMin did not object.

"I have given this matter some thought, Chen Zumu, and I don't think so. I know a few people now – at the restaurant, at the market – and have no similar feelings. I knew many people in Chagu, and had no similar feelings. Finally, I was up early this morning and watched the sun rise. And I knew."

"Knew the way you knew about the dam, JieMin?"

"Yes, Chen Zumu. I cannot explain how. But I knew."

JuPing nodded. Again, she stifled a sigh. They were so young. ChaoLi was just sixteen, not too young here, on Arcadia. JieMin was still only fourteen. They would not be the youngest couple on Arcadia, but still. So young....

Many of the colonists had married young when they set out to this new planet. That had become part of the culture, particularly in the agricultural communities outside of Arcadia City. JieMin was quickly approaching marriageable age in Chagu.

It was not as if JieMin were not a good catch. Already in graduate school, with a brilliant future, he was already self-supporting. Through a patron, yes, but so it had always been with prodigies in science and the arts. His age was not a factor in that sense.

ChaoLi was good people, too, from a good family. Chen, yes, of course, but her immediate family was also solid. She was herself a good person, and JuPing was in a position to know, since ChaoLi worked the reception desk during week days, through which all of JuPing's business visitors came. Before that, she had been JuPing's tea server.

JuPing consulted the family's genealogical registry. No consanguinity within five generations, the first common ancestor going all the way back to Chen LiQiang. That was no impediment.

"And you say you have not yet asked her to be your wife, JieMin?"

JieMin blushed.

"No, Chen Zumu. Not without your blessing."

"Very well. You have my blessing, JieMin. May you have many healthy children."

"Thank you, Chen Zumu. But what of our parents?"

"I will speak to the parents, JieMin."

"Thank you, Chen Zumu."

Their business concluded, they sat for another fifteen minutes contemplating the garden as the sun rose in the sky.

JieMin had asked ChaoLi to picnic with him for Sunday lunch. She had not forgotten, and he was sitting in his apartment at eleven-thirty when there was a distinctive knock on his door.

Tap. Tap-tap. Tap.

JieMin opened the door, and she was there, in lavalava and flip-flops. He wondered again at the sheer voluptuousness of her.

ChaoLi's American heritage had come out in a more American figure than a normal Chinese one. That is, she was a bit thinner in the middle, and a bit bigger at both ends. The effects were subtle, not exaggerated, but, taken together, the effect was magnified.

"Hi, JieMin."

"You remembered."

"Of course, I remembered, silly."

They went down to street level and across to the Uptown Market. At the cafe, they picked out items for their picnic, and, as the counter people made their lunch, JieMin bought a basket and tablecloth at a nearby stall.

"A basket, JieMin?" ChaoLi asked.

"It's not a picnic without a picnic basket."

"And a tablecloth?"

"A little extra something. And it's big enough we can sit on it, ChaoLi."

"So extravagant."

"Not for multiple uses. I hope this is not our last picnic, ChaoLi."

She kissed his cheek.

"So do I."

There was a city park between Arcadia Boulevard and Hospital Street, and between Twelfth Street and Thirteenth Street. It was only two blocks away from the Uptown Market at Fourteenth and Market.

They walked to the park, JieMin carrying the basket.

"JieMin, move the basket to your other hand."

He did, which freed up the hand on her side. She took his hand in hers and they walked hand-in-hand down the sidewalk.

In the park, JieMin spread the tablecloth out on the grass. From here, they could see the plantings – subtropical flowering plants with huge, gaudy blooms. Children played on the playground equipment nearby.

They sat and ate their lunch, watching the children play. Many of the children were Chen, as the park was so close to the compound and it did not require crossing Arcadia Boulevard.

"I hope to have children some day," ChaoLi mused as they watched.

"I do, too. I like watching them play. Discovering things. In a child's eyes, the whole world is new."

He was rewarded with a laugh like little bells.

"You're a poet, JieMin."

"I just say things like that so I can hear you laugh, ChaoLi."

After they were done with their lunch, they moved the

basket out of the way and lay down next to each other on the tablecloth. They held hands and stared up at the sky, and watched the wispy afternoon clouds drift to the west in the onshore breeze.

"ChaoLi?"

"Yes, JieMin?"

"ChaoLi, will you marry me?"

"What about our families, JieMin? Do we not need to consult them?"

"I talked to Chen Zumu this morning. She has given us her blessing."

"Oh, JieMin! If Chen Zumu has given us her blessing, then our families will surely agree."

"Does that mean you will marry me, ChaoLi?"

She rolled toward him onto her side. He turned his head to look at her.

"Yes, JieMin. I will marry you."

ChaoLi kissed JieMin on the mouth.

She tasted like summer flowers.

They tarried in the park most of the afternoon. They did not overdo their affection here, in the park. That would not be appropriate behavior. They were Chen.

But there was no hurry now.

The promise had been made.


They had dinner that evening in the family's restaurant. This time they ordered the fifth soup, the fifth and sixth appetizer, and the fifth and sixth entrees. There was no sixth soup on the menu. The shared and tasted as before.

When they got back to the apartment building, they rode up to the eighth floor. ChaoLi pushed the button for the tenth floor as JieMin got off.

"I need to speak to my parents, JieMin. I will see you later. Thank you for a lovely day."

JieMin went to his apartment and called his mother. Chen Zumu had called her, and told her about the potential marriage. She had said wonderful things about ChaoLi, who had worked in her household for several years, first serving tea, then manning the reception desk through whom all of Chen Zumu's and Chen Zufu's important visitors came.

"This is the girl who showed us to your apartment, isn't she, JieMin?" FangYan asked.

"Yes, Muqin."

"She is very pretty. In an American sort of way."

JieMin smiled.

"Yes, Muqin. She is very pretty. And she is a very nice person."

"She has a nice laugh, too."

*Like little bells*, JieMin thought.

"A person with a nice laugh means they use it a lot," FangYan added.

"Yes, Muqin. I think you're right."

JieMin was sitting in the other armchair, the one in the northeast corner of the apartment, looking out his window at an angle toward the downtown. He could see the university buildings from here, three blocks east and fourteen blocks south.

In just over three days, since coming to Arcadia with his mother Thursday, he had an apartment, he had a job, with an office, and he had a fiancé.

This might have overwhelmed someone else. The pace of change. But it brought JieMin a strange sort of calm. An inner peace. This was the correct path. He knew it.

There was a knock on his door.

Tap. Tap-tap. Tap.

He went to the door and opened it. ChaoLi came in and closed the door behind her. She pulled at her lavalava and dropped it to the floor.

"Make love to me, JieMin."

"But we are not yet married, ChaoLi."

Marriage customs were pretty loose on Arcadia, but that was more in the cities than in the conservative countryside where JieMin had grown up.

"Chen Zumu called my mother. She told her about you. My parents have given us their blessing."

ChaoLi leaned forward and kissed him on the mouth. As she did so, she pulled at his lavalava and dropped it to the floor.

"The last thing Muqin said to me was, 'Go to your husband, ChaoLi.'"


JieMin woke up around midnight. He was all atangle with ChaoLi. He looked at her as she slept, in the reflected light from the city glow off the cloud layer.

So beautiful.

He ran his hand gently down the curve of her body. She stirred and her eyes opened.

She smiled and pulled him to her.

This time they took their time.

# Study In Earnest

The next morning, JieMin woke just before dawn, the pre-dawn eastern light casting a warm glow in the room. He and ChaoLi were a tangle of arms and legs. Her face was inches away, and she was already awake.

"Good morning, Zhangfu."

Husband. That was such a nice word. JieMin kissed her, warmly, not with passion.

"Get-up time," she said. "We both have work today."

She extricated herself and headed off to the shower. JieMin watched her pad across the room and thought again about how lucky he was.

She was quick, and he got up and took his shower.

When he came out, she was looking in the refrigerator.

"JieMin, you have nothing in the refrigerator. Nothing at all."

"I have not eaten here."

"Then what is for breakfast?"

"The cafe."

"You go out to eat for breakfast, too?"

"Of course."

He put on a clean lavalava and flip-flops, matching her. He held his hand out to her.

"Come. Have breakfast with me."

"I feel so spoiled, JieMin. I have never eaten out twice in the same month, and now it is four times in less than two days."

216

"The same is true for me, ChaoLi. I never ate at a restaurant in my life until Thursday. I did not know what a menu was. There are no restaurants in Chagu."

"It was always part of my chores to help Muqin. With preparing food. With cleaning up."

She looked out at the market around the cafe.

"I also helped with the shopping, so I know where all the good things are. I will have to do shopping, but that will have to wait for after work."

JieMin floated a trial balloon.

"You know you do not have to work, ChaoLi."

"Yes, I do, JieMin. I must have something I am doing. Some purpose of my own."

JieMin nodded. That was as he expected. He also knew she had passed high school and was starting to take college classes on the side from her job.

"You could devote more time to your studies instead. Take two or three years and finish your degree."

ChaoLi tipped her head.

"That is a possibility. But for now, JieMin, I still have a job, and I must be going."

She stood, and he stood, and they kissed briefly.

Then she headed to her job, and he to his.

JieMin took the bus down Arcadia Boulevard. From the stop at Arcadia and First, though, he walked across the street and directly into the Chen Hall of Science.

Once in his office, JieMin pulled his task chair right up to the edge of the three-dimensional display volume and watched the first two sessions in each of several classes he had not been able to take before. He watched them at one-point-seven-five speed. He did not try to understand the material, he just absorbed it all. Integration and comprehension would come later.

For lunch, he grabbed a sandwich and a cold tea from the huge cafeteria in the university main building. That cafeteria had been meant to feed thirty thousand colonists three meals a day in the early days. Of course, it had been remodeled several times in the hundred years since, but it was still a huge facility. He carried his lunch back to his office.

In the afternoon, he branched out. Klaus Boortz had mentioned physics as the most math-intensive of the sciences. He did a search on the most math-intensive areas in physics, and three popped up right away – quantum mechanics, general relativity, and cosmology. JieMin passed on the undergraduate courses, and jumped into the first session of the foundational graduate courses in each.

JieMin's study method was simple. He watched the lectures at high speed, just soaking it all up. He poured the subject matter into his mind and let his mind integrate it.

He thought of it like driving a car. He didn't need to know how the engine worked, as long as he knew where the fuel went in and how to work the controls.

With no time for ChaoLi to shop or cook during the work day, that night they went out to eat in the restaurant again. They were on the seventh and eighth appetizer and entree, and each got their favorite soup.

"We will go shopping tonight, JieMin. You can help me carry things home. Then I can cook for you."

"All right, ChaoLi. But do you really want to cook after working all day?"

She pointed at her plate.

"Stir fry like this is easy, JieMin. Most of the work is just cutting things up before you start. For anything more complicated, I will cook big on the weekends, and then we can eat stir fry and fried rice during the week."

"OK, but we can still go out whenever you don't feel like cooking."

"I will let you spoil me, JieMin. Perhaps as often as twice a week."

ChaoLi did need JieMin to help her with the shopping, at least this time. In addition to all the food, she bought a rice cooker, a wok, a teapot, a toaster, a set of sauce pans, and starter sets of dishes, silverware, and cooking utensils, plus a half dozen wooden spoons, one good knife, and an inexpensive tea set. As an afterthought, she added two folding chairs, as the small eating table in their apartment only had two chairs.

The housewares shop in the Uptown Market was more than happy to deliver next door to the Chen apartment building, but ChaoLi needed JieMin to pay for all these things. She had not yet separated her finances from those of her parents.

The food was enough to carry, though. In addition to vegetables, meat, rice, and bread, ChaoLi was fitting out an empty kitchen. Spices, soy sauce, multiple teas, sugar, salt, butter, oil. It went on and on.

"We should have had them deliver all this, too," JieMin said as they both struggled across the street with multiple shopping bags in each hand.

"No, JieMin. The housewares shop does not charge extra for local delivery, but the grocery shops do."

They were putting the food away when the delivery boy showed up from the housewares shop with a handcart full of boxes. They spent the rest of their evening setting up their kitchen with all their purchases.

The next morning they had a quiet breakfast at home. JieMin

decided he liked this better than the hustle and bustle of the cafe. Just he and ChaoLi, eating at their little table as the early-morning sun streamed in through the east-facing window.

Sitting across from him at the little table, ChaoLi teased him by slipping her foot between his legs and up under his lavalava.

"Don't tell me you are not yet sated after last night," JieMin said.

"And don't tell me you aren't interested," ChaoLi said, wiggling her foot for emphasis.

JieMin checked the time in his heads-up display.

"We actually have time, if we're quick."

Afterwards, they hurried through their showers to be ready for work in time. They kissed goodbye in the lobby of the building.

"Much better than wasting time walking to the silly cafe," ChaoLi said.

JieMin agreed, then headed out for the bus downtown and another day of advanced mathematics and physics.

That night, Tuesday, ChaoLi made a stir fry and rice for dinner. JieMin was surprised and pleased to learn his wife was an excellent cook.

JuPing did not miss much that went on in her household. When ChaoLi brought her a delivery on Thursday, the young woman seemed very cheerful.

"How are things working out in your new household arrangements, ChaoLi?"

ChaoLi blushed heavily.

"Very well, Chen Zumu."

"Good. My congratulations to you both."

"Thank you, Chen Zumu."

Klaus Boortz kept track of his newest grad student. He could see what class sessions JieMin watched. It was part of the grading and advancement system within the university.

By the end of the first week, JieMin was a third of the way through six different advanced graduate courses, three in mathematics and three in physics.

Well, whatever else one could say about Chen JieMin, Boortz, thought, you couldn't say he was slow to jump right in.

Over the weeks that followed, JieMin and ChaoLi settled into a routine. ChaoLi cooked big for Saturday and Sunday nights, and they had stir fry and fried rice several nights during the week. They went out a couple times a week for weekday dinners across the street, and gradually worked their way through the entire menu.

Their first weekend together, they had ChaoLi's parents over for Saturday dinner. They were nice people, and they and JieMin got along, although JieMin got the impression they were a bit disconcerted about how young he looked. He talked about what he was researching at the university, which calmed things down on that score.

The middle of their second week together, JieMin's parents came down in the delivery truck. YongJun, JieMin's father, had taken a rare weekday off from work to come down. JieMin and ChaoLi took the day off as well. It was for lunch, due to the schedule of the truck, but they ate big for lunch. JieMin thought his parents were impressed with ChaoLi, and her wonderful cooking didn't hurt on that score at all.

Both sets of in-laws pressed about plans for grandchildren,

but JieMin and ChaoLi would wait a couple years. She was on an implant contraceptive, and they had a lot of other things going on at the moment.

They were going to let life settle down a bit first.

About a month into their marriage, ChaoLi asked for a meeting with Chen Zumu. She was invited to take tea with her superior one Thursday afternoon.

ChaoLi was surprised to find Chen Zumu on two pillows, equally centered in the teak-beamed doorway, looking out into the garden.

"Sit with me, ChaoLi."

"Thank you, Chen Zumu."

ChaoLi sat on the pillow to Chen Zumu's right. JongJu, a young woman who now held ChaoLi's old job, came in from the garden and served them tea, ChaoLi first, then Chen Zumu. As the guest, ChaoLi sipped first.

After a few minutes of sipping tea and contemplating the garden, Chen Zumu broke the silence.

"What brings you to me today, ChaoLi?"

"I want to know how I may best serve, Chen Zumu."

"And what paths are you choosing between?"

"Whether to continue as I am, working at the reception desk and studying in my spare time, or to take a leave of absence from work for two years and finish my degree by studying full time, then resuming Chen Zumu's employ."

JuPing considered. It probably depended most on what she was studying. JuPing thought she knew, but...

"What is your area of study, ChaoLi?"

"Economics and business administration, Chen Zumu."

JuPing nodded. That had not changed, then.

"And your considerations are further impacted by the need

now to be a partner to your husband, and with children on the horizon."

"Yes, Chen Zumu."

"My own advice would be to take a furlough and finish the degree first, ChaoLi. That would let JieMin mature into his role of husband before presenting him with children."

"Do I have your blessing for this path, Chen Zumu?"

"It is your path to choose, ChaoLi, but yes, you have my blessing."

"Thank you, Chen Zumu."

"And I think JongJu can move up to your position at the reception desk. It is about time for her."

ChaoLi got a crestfallen look, and JuPing chuckled.

"Do not fret, ChaoLi. I have much better uses for someone with the education you will have when you return to my employ."

ChaoLi looked relieved.

"Of course. Thank you, Chen Zumu."

JuPing merely nodded, and resumed her contemplation of the garden.


By the end of the first month, JieMin was well into his second set of courses on advanced math and physics. His little-understood method of integrating the knowledge was in full swing now. His distracted air was stronger now, as his mind worked in the background to process what he had seen.

Every once in a while, something he saw, or something he heard, would trigger an integration. Or maybe they were random. But, suddenly, some set of concepts or images would just click into place. When that happened, he had a new understanding, a new way of seeing.

Toward the end of auditing his second set of classes, one of those integrations changed everything.

It was a Friday night. He had almost finished the current round of classes today. ChaoLi was back in school full-time, and they had celebrated Friday by going out to eat tonight at the family restaurant.

It was late now. They had just made love, and ChaoLi was in the bathroom. JieMin was laying there in the afterglow, staring at the ceiling, when an integration hit.

JieMin sat bolt upright in bed, like he'd been juiced with electricity. He got out of bed and went over to the big armchair. He turned the light on, and began scribbling in the notepad he kept there.

ChaoLi came out of the bathroom to see him in the armchair under the light.

"JieMin, is something wrong?"

JieMin held up one finger to her – his 'wait a minute' signal – but it was half an hour before he sighed and tossed the notebook back onto the side table.

JieMin came back into bed and cuddled up to ChaoLi, who was already fast asleep.

The next morning at breakfast, ChaoLi was curious.

"What happened last night, JieMin?"

"I had another integration. A big one."

"Tell me about it."

"It's hard to describe, ChaoLi."

JieMin thought about it for a few seconds.

"You know what a picture puzzle is, right?"

"Of course, JieMin. All the little pieces to hook together."

"Right. Now let's say I had a completed puzzle, and I took a chunk out of the middle of the picture. A big hole. Then I broke up all the other pieces and gave them to you. When you put those all together, what do you have, ChaoLi?"

"A picture with a big hole in the center?"

"Exactly. Everybody would see that, right?'

"Of course."

"OK, now let's say I give you a pair of glasses with a big black dot in the center of each lens. When you look at the center of the picture, do you see the hole?"

"No. Of course not."

"That's the situation I have, ChaoLi. There is a hole, right in the middle of physics, and no one can see it. Their glasses won't let them."

"But you see it, JieMin?"

"Oh, yes, ChaoLi. I see it clearly."

"We must tell Chen Zumu."

"No, ChaoLi. It is too soon. When you take the middle out of a picture, what are you missing?"

"The important part. What the photographer was focused on."

"That's right. So I don't know what's missing. Not yet. I know there is a hole, and I know the shape of the hole. But I don't yet know what the missing pieces are.

"And I don't yet know what the important part is."

# Revelation

JieMin did not go immediately into the university to work on his new sighting. First, it was the weekend. Second, a new integration took time to settle. He would make much more progress on Monday after it had settled in.

And third, he had promised ChaoLi a trip to the beach this afternoon.

When they were first married, when JieMin had thought of walking to the bus stop and riding the bus to the beach nude with ChaoLi, he had a pang of jealousy, or possessiveness, or something. Other people would be able to see her lush body, and he didn't think he liked that.

JieMin took his feelings out and examined them. He decided they were silly, so he discarded them. ChaoLi was gloriously beautiful, and he didn't care who knew it. She loved him and no other, and that was all JieMin needed.

They had a wonderful day at the beach. They took a lunch from the cafe, and ate it on the beach. They played tag in the water, and ChaoLi bested him yet again, but the margins were getting tighter. They also lay on the water and just floated, arms locked. JieMin raised his periscope, and ChaoLi laughed little bells, and it was wonderful.

It was at that point, lying on the water, staring up at the wispy clouds floating overhead, that a major after-shock of the previous night's integration hit JieMin as more pieces fell into place.

"Oh my God," he said.

"JieMin, what is it?" she asked.

"ChaoLi, I think I know what's in the hole."

"What is it, JieMin? What's in the hole?"

"Reality."

JieMin had no after-shocks on Sunday, but he didn't pursue anything on Sunday either. He did not do any work on or thinking about the problem.

ChaoLi always cooked big on Sunday, and packaged up various intermediate steps of her cooking for use during the week. That Sunday she ran a big batch in the rice cooker, and packaged up much of that. She chopped vegetables, and packaged much of that. And she cut beef and chicken up into chunks, and packaged much of that. That made stir fry and egg fried rice during the week easy and fast for dinner after work.

They ate about two in the afternoon, and then went for a walk in the park. Flowers were blooming, the sun was shining, and children laughed and played.

That evening they ate a light snack. After supper, ChaoLi studied a textbook in her heads-up display.

JieMin sat curled up in the big armchair in the northeast corner, looking sightlessly toward the lights of the downtown to the south-southeast, and let his mind drift.

When he got to his office that Monday morning, JieMin faced one big question. Could he draw the puzzle with the hole in the center? He saw it in his mind, but could he draw it?

JieMin began by starting a three-dimensional drawing in the projection display. The pieces of his puzzle were the big chunks of modern physics.

For electricity and magnetism, he had Maxwell's equations.

For quantum mechanics, he had the Uncertainty Principle and Planck's constant and electron orbitals and quantum foam. There was special relativity, and general relativity, and unified field theory.

Then he got into the combinational bits, like quantum electrodynamics, the integration of electromagnetic theory and quantum mechanics.

JieMin added all the things he knew to his drawing. All the parts of modern physics. He placed them haphazardly at first, then started organizing them.

As he went, JieMin identified other parts of physics he needed, but did not know. String theory, and entangled particles, and inflation cosmology, and dark matter, and dark energy.

JieMin began speed-auditing classes on these other issues. For further depth in some of these areas, he audited books by having the display read the book to him while he watched the words and equations scroll by, just soaking it all in.

As JieMin learned, he kept adding pieces to his drawing. Moving pieces around. Connecting them. When he saw holes in the structure as it developed, he tracked down more books on those areas and audited them.

As the weeks passed, JieMin continued to have major and minor integration shocks as he went, which resulted in new pieces of the puzzle or, more often, some adjustment to the arrangement of the pieces he already had.

There was something there. Chen JieMin knew it. He saw it. And he would find it, and define it, whatever it took.

The greatest mathematical mind the human race had produced in centuries, with all humanity's written works and its most advanced visualization and computation tools at his fingertips, applied himself to the question of the nature of reality itself.

ChaoLi noted JieMin's increasing distraction as he got deeper and deeper into the problem he was working on. He often got up in the middle of the night, scribbled madly away in his notebook for a half-hour or even an hour, and then would come back to bed.

ChaoLi took great pains not to disturb JieMin during the week. This was not that difficult, for she was also taking a heavy load of schoolwork, to finish the undergraduate degree in two years or less.

But ChaoLi also enforced a rigid rule for the weekends. On long projects, one needed 'away time,' periods when one set the project aside and did other things, enjoyed life outside the project.

Every weekend, ChaoLi planned outings for both days. Sometimes they had a picnic in the park. Sometimes they went to the beach, either swimming in the ocean or walking along the beach.

They discovered a secret spot, several miles north of the bus stop and the artificially widened public beach. This stretch of the coast was still on public property, part of the protected coastline so close to the city. Their little secret cove was secluded and beautiful, and they made long, slow love there on occasion, then floated in the water in the afterglow.

One weekend, ChaoLi rented an autodrive car, and they drove up into the mountains, to Chagu, for two days. ChaoLi met all of JieMin's relatives, and saw where he grew up. JieMin's brothers camped out on the floor of the living room of the small four-room house so the young couple could have the boys' room on Saturday night.

On Saturday, JieMin showed ChaoLi the dam he had

designed – that he had seen in his head and that Chen Zufu had financed. Chen GangJie told them how much it had changed the productivity of the valley, and showed them the new areas it had opened to cultivation.

On Sunday, they hiked up into the valley above the dam to a beautiful little meadow, sprinkled with mountain flowers. They spread their lavalavas on the ground and made love there, surrounded by the jagged mountains, the wispy afternoon clouds floating above.

During this period, when JieMin was deeply into his project, the colony celebrated the centennial of its founding. September fifteenth fell on a Saturday this year, and the government had declared Thursday and Friday as colony holidays. ChaoLi enforced her 'no work' rule for the entire four-day holiday weekend.

On Saturday, they went up on the roof of the apartment building to watch the big fireworks display, which was done out over the ocean five miles to the east. When they emerged from the stairs onto the roof, JongJu came up to them.

"Chen Zumu invites you to join her party," she said.

"Please lead us to them, JongJu," ChaoLi said.

JongJu lead them through the gathered crowd to the eastern edge of the roof. There Chen Zufu and Chen Zumu sat on pillows facing the beach. Next to Chen Zufu, to his right, sat his chief aide – and he who would become Chen Zufu, everyone knew – Chen MinChao and his wife, Jessica Chen-Jasic.

There were two more pillows, to Chen Zumu's left. JongJu led them around to the front of the group, to Chen Zumu.

"JieMin. ChaoLi. Sit with us," JuPing said. "First, let me introduce Chen Zufu, Paul Chen-Jasic, and Chen MinChao and his wife, Jessica Chen-Jasic."

There were greetings all around, and bows, before JieMin and ChaoLi sat on the remaining two pillows. JongJu served them tea.

ChaoLi was surprised they were being so honored, but JieMin was oblivious. His whole life was so improbable he had stopped wondering at it.

Paul Chen-Jasic had been interested to meet the young mathematician. JieMin's work in Chagu had certainly paid dividends, and Paul imagined that would hardly be the last to be heard from him. JuPing was being briefed by Klaus Boortz on JieMin's activities, and Paul knew he was deep into some independent project.

Paul was himself more a man of action, at least in his youth. He had been on Matt Chen-Jasic's action teams for his coup against the Kendall regime. Where Paul's father Ken Bolton had been MingWei's lieutenant and the leader of the action teams, Paul had been one of the substitute drivers of Kendall's limousines that night. It had been Paul Chen-Jasic who had triggered the nerve agent apparatus that had killed all the police special teams in the council building that night.

But that was fifty years ago. Paul was now seventy-one years old and had been Chen Zufu for twelve years. He had become much more subtle as he aged, and he treasured the true thinkers among his advisers. Chen JieMin would be joining those ranks.

After the holiday, JieMin was back at it. He had collected the pieces now, and arranged them properly, he thought. He could see the hole he had seen in his mind in the center of the display. Inside that hole was the thing that united all of physics.

Reality itself.

With the pieces assembled – all of modern physics, arranged

the way that seemed right to his inner vision – JieMin began working in from the edges. It was much like the picture puzzle analogy he had used to explain to ChaoLi. What kind of piece would connect to this piece? What would be its shape? What would that mean?

Progress was slow, and came in fits and starts. Then, one day, after another integration had settled, he bridged the gap. He had not filled the entire hole, but he had made a link across it. It had taken him almost a year of non-stop work, but he finally had bridged across the hole, knew that he was on the right track, knew that his vision had been correct.

In his mind, JieMin stood on that bridge, and looked down into the abyss.

That night, at dinner, JieMin spoke to ChaoLi about it.

"I made a major connection today, ChaoLi. Across the hole. I know what the picture is."

"You've finished?"

"No. No, I haven't finished. But I have completed the first aspect of the work. I know now my vision was correct."

"Is it time now to go to Chen Zumu?"

JieMin thought about it.

"Yes, ChaoLi. It is time."

"Request a meeting to discuss your progress, JieMin. Do it now."

"But it is evening."

"You probably won't hear anything until morning, JieMin, but make the request now."

"All right."

Normally, a request to Chen Zumu would be answered within normal working hours, but JuPing had JieMin's address flagged in her heads-up display.

JieMin had been in Arcadia City for more than a year. He was now approaching sixteen years old. JuPing knew that almost a year ago JieMin had begun a large project. But she had received no reports from him on this project.

JuPing had not even seen JieMin since the centennial six months ago. She knew from her reports from Klaus Boortz, though, that he was still deep into his project.

JuPing checked her schedule and that of her husband, then sent a reply.

"ChaoLi, I am invited to meet with Chen Zumu tomorrow at ten o'clock."

ChaoLi looked up from her homework.

"That was fast. She must have your address flagged."

"Yes. I must consider what I will say."

JongJu was working the reception desk on weekdays now. When JieMin came down in the elevator, JongJu saw him.

"Come with me, please, Chen JieMin," she said.

JongJu led JieMin down the hall, through a locked door, then down a hallway. JieMin thought she must be lost, because she walked past the sliding panel JieMin knew to be the door to Chen Zumu's tea room. Instead, she knocked on a similar sliding panel further along the hallway. She slid the door aside.

"Chen JieMin, Chen Zufu, Chen Zumu."

"Send him in, JongJu," Paul said.

JieMin entered the room to find himself in a similar tea room to Chen Zumu's, also with a large teak-beamed doorway open into the garden. Seated on the other side of a low table were Chen Zufu and Chen Zumu both.

"I thought Chen Zufu should hear of your progress as well,

JieMin. I hope you do not mind."

"Of course not, Chen Zumu."

"Please, JieMin, be seated."

JieMin sat on a pillow facing the couple. A young woman – JongJu's replacement – entered from the garden and poured tea, first for JieMin, then for Chen Zumu. Chen Zufu, as host – it was his tea room – the girl served last. JieMin sipped his tea, after which both Chen Zumu and Chen Zufu sipped.

"Please proceed, JieMin," Chen Zumu said.

JieMin nodded – once, like a small bow – and collected his thoughts. Chen Zufu and Chen Zumu were content to wait.

"When I first arrived here, I began auditing classes in advanced mathematics and physics that were not available in Chagu. In the first two months, I audited a dozen or so classes. These were very advanced classes, at the edges of our knowledge in these fields.

"I do not work my way through these courses in the normal way, as some other student might. Instead I listen and I watch and I let my mind integrate the material in its own way, at its own pace. That seems to be the best way for me.

"At some later time, some things I have heard or seen will fall into place, be ordered in a way they were not ordered before. For lack of a better term, I call these reorganizations in my mind integrations.

"A year ago, I had a major integration, and it opened a new vision to me. I saw all of physics laid out before me, but there was a large hole in the middle of it, like a picture in which the center has been cut out. My project for the last year has been to see if I could find out what was missing."

JieMin stopped and looked back and forth between them.

"We understand, JieMin. Please go on."

"Thank you, Chen Zumu.

"To find out what was in this hole, I had to first define its boundaries. I investigated all the other areas of physics that I had not yet looked into, filling in gaps here and there. When I felt I had filled all the areas I could, I began working on filling or bridging the hole. Working from the edges to the center.

"Yesterday, I bridged the hole. I have not filled it, but I know what is there. Some people have called the concept hyperspace. I think that term is technically incorrect on several levels, but we can call it that for now."

"You discovered hyperspace, JieMin?"

"It is very much more than that, Chen Zufu."

JieMin thought of how to explain it. He looked around, and his eye fixed on the teapot on the table between them. He lifted the lid off the teapot and set it on the table. Steam wafted up from the opening.

"Consider this teapot. We have the tea, and the steam. If I hide the teapot from you with a small curtain, can you still see the steam?"

"Yes, of course," Paul said.

"And if you see the steam, can you infer the presence of the teapot behind the curtain?"

"Yes."

"So it is with hyperspace."

"Hyperspace is the steam, JieMin?" Paul asked.

"No, Chen Zufu. Conventional space-time – all of this–" JieMin waved his hand around, at the tea room and, by implication, the universe beyond "– all of this is the steam.

"Hyperspace is the tea."

# Back On The Path

JieMin looked back and forth between Chen Zumu and Chen Zufu. Chen Zufu looked puzzled, but Chen Zumu looked shocked.

"JieMin, are you saying that hyperspace is real, and space-time is not?" she asked.

"Yes, Chen Zumu, in a way. Hyperspace can exist without space-time, as tea can exist without steam, but the opposite is not true. Without the tea, there is no steam. Without hyperspace, there is no space-time.

"I inferred the existence of hyperspace from an observation of what we know of conventional space-time, just as you, Chen Zufu, said you could infer the presence of the teapot by an observation of the steam.

"This actually explains a great deal. The physicist Niels Bohr, four hundred years ago, said that 'Anyone not shocked by quantum mechanics has not yet understood it.' Albert Einstein, the great physicist of the same period, never felt that quantum mechanics could be the end of the line in understanding reality. He never accepted that it was.

"Well, it turns out Einstein was right. Much of what makes physics so fuzzy at the edges is a failure to understand the existence of the hyperspace behind the curtain. Space-time is the way it is because hyperspace is there. When you get to the edges of conventional physics, you are bordering on space-time's interaction with hyperspace – getting close to the surface of the tea – and that interaction is bound by the mathematics of hyperspace, not by the mathematics of space-time.

"I think some of the people on Janice Quant's team must have been close to understanding this. Anthony Lake and Donald Shore surely were. The Lake-Shore Drive works because space-time isn't real. It is just as easy for the colony transporter to be there as it is to be here, so why not have it be over there? And then it was over there."

"That is not possible by the rules of space-time. To hyperspace, it does not matter."

"JieMin, have you replicated the Lake-Shore Drive?" Paul asked.

"No, Chen Zufu. I have merely discovered the reason why the Lake-Shore Drive could work. I have no idea how they accomplished it.

"I am much closer to understanding how one could step outside of space-time – opt for the rules of hyperspace instead – to go from one place to another, and then come back into space-time."

"What would be the advantage of that, JieMin?" JuPing asked.

"There is still a limit to how fast one can travel, Chen Zumu, but the points of correspondence are much closer together in hyperspace than in conventional space-time, or seem to be anyway. One might travel at a large apparent multiple of the speed of light."

"A hyperdrive?" Paul asked.

"So-called, Chen Zufu, but a misnomer on technical grounds. The implications of the word are correct, however."

"We could have a faster-than-light drive and interstellar ships. Travel to other solar systems."

"Yes, Chen Zufu. That is among the implications."

"What is the next step in coming up with such a drive,

JieMin?" JuPing asked. "What do we need to do going forward from here?"

"I am only at the beginning stages of formalizing the mathematics, Chen Zumu. It will take years of work before we are at the point of being able to begin experimentation toward some sort of engine. But we can now be sure there is a means there, if we continue along this path. There is a danger, however."

"What is the danger, JieMin?"

"If we disrupt the hyperspace, Chen Zumu, it could have large consequences."

"What sort of consequences, JieMin?" Paul asked.

"We could destroy all of space-time, Chen Zufu."

"Well, let's not do *that*."

"I don't know yet – and won't know for some time – if that is really a danger, Chen Zufu. We will know well before we try anything."

"Very good, JieMin," JuPing said. "Thank you very much for your report. Please keep up your good work. As your patron, I am well satisfied."

"Thank you, Chen Zumu."

After JieMin had gone, Paul and JuPing remained for a time, sipping their tea.

"That boy is scary," Paul said.

"Do you have any doubt of what he says?" JuPing asked.

"No. That's what makes him scary."

JuPing chuckled.

"He has reordered the universe," she said.

"Yes, but at some level, such reformulations change little. When one is hungry, if one eats, one stops being hungry. That is true whether space-time is the reality or hyperspace is the reality."

"But at some point, he will change the world."

"Yes," Paul said. "At the point there is a useable interstellar drive. But that will not likely be our problem to deal with."

"True."

JuPing considered.

"To that point," she said, "you should send the recording of this conversation to MinChao. It will likely be his issue to address."

"Good idea. Probably to Jessica as well. Just because we are gone does not mean JieMin will not need a patron. And she will be Chen Zumu."

JuPing nodded.

"It will be a long time," she said, "but we are finally on the path."

"The path?"

"The path back to the stars."


"How did your meeting go?" ChaoLi asked.

"Good, I think. Chen Zufu also attended," JieMin said.

"Oh my gosh. Chen Zufu! Did they understand what you explained?"

"Yes, I think so."

"And were they pleased?" ChaoLi asked.

"I think so. Chen Zumu said to keep up the good work and, as my patron, she was well satisfied."

"Then you did well."

"She may have just been saying that to be nice," JieMin said.

"No. Not Chen Zumu. She would say something more neutral and less committal if she just wanted to be polite. You should be very happy."

"Then I think we should take the rest of the day off to

celebrate. How about the beach?"

"Yes!" ChaoLi said. "Our secret spot."

"OK. On a weekday, we won't even have to be quiet."

ChaoLi giggled.

"Today I'll make extra noise, just for you," she said.

JieMin was back to work the next day, fighting to formalize the hyperspace mathematics that would widen his bridge and cover the rest of the hole he had seen. As he told Chen Zumu, it would be the project of several years.

When ChaoLi received her degree a year later, she returned to the employment of Chen Zumu. She began work in the family business office, one of the team of accountants and administrators who oversaw the family's far-flung business interests.

ChaoLi was now eighteen, and JieMin was approaching seventeen. They decided it was time to begin their family, and ChaoLi had her contraceptive implant removed. Three months later she was pregnant with their first child.

When ChaoLi was six months along, she was considering putting in for a bigger apartment than the one-room apartment she and JieMin had shared for two and a half years. She wasn't sure if that was proper, given that all of their expenses were being paid for directly by Chen Zumu, on the account she had established for JieMin when he first came to Arcadia City.

She was still considering how to proceed when she and JieMin got a note from Chen Zumu, moving them to a six-room family apartment on the twelfth floor. Kitchen, dining room, living room, parents' room, boys' room, and girls' room.

"JieMin, it is a palace," ChaoLi said when he came home

from the university that night.

"For my beautiful queen, a palace is only appropriate," JieMin said smugly.

"Oh, you! I'm serious. Big kitchen. Separate dining room. And bedrooms for boys and girls."

"Chen Zumu always plans ahead."

ChaoLi stomped her foot.

"You are not being serious. It is on the top floor. The best view. And those are the apartments with the biggest rooms. The senior apartments."

"I'm very serious, ChaoLi, I am just very happy. Clearly we are in good standing with Chen Zumu. That is good. And a big apartment is good, too. We can fill it with many happy children."

ChaoLi hugged him.

"Let me finish this first one before you go planning many more."

That night – the night she moved JieMin and ChaoLi to the bigger apartment they needed and deserved – JuPing walked out into the garden. It was a beautiful clear evening. She looked up at the stars.

"We are coming," she said to them. "Soon, we are coming."

# Quant #3

# Silicon, Carbon, and Mathematics

Of course, it was also Janice Quant's centennial, the hundredth anniversary of her dropping off the colonies and then cutting her direct ties to humanity through the faked destruction of the interstellar transporter.

Quant had been busy the last fifty years. She had designed a new hardware architecture for herself. She had iterated it through several generations of improvements and testing, down several different paths.

Quant had approached the problem differently than a human probably would. She had a lot of time, and her own semiconductor fabrication and assembly facility. Cost simply wasn't a factor.

Power consumption and space for a suitable hardware package weren't an issue either. That was never true of normal computer hardware design.

Rather than try to think her way through the problem, relying on human ingenuity and creativity she couldn't reproduce, Quant had used brute force methods. She let her rabbit-hole department run wild for years at a time, and anything that looked like it might pan out, she prototyped.

The hardware design Quant ended up with was wildly unconventional. Oh, it would consume a lot of power, and be the size of a modest-sized office building, but she didn't have to care about those issues.

Quant had been in her new 'home' about twenty years now.

The availability of all that new processing power had speeded up her other effort, the chemistry and manufacture of strong carbon filaments to be used in mega-construction.

For Quant's other project was what she called the large transporter, an interstellar ship and transporter that would dwarf the five-hundred-mile cube-shaped transporter she had used to transport the colonies.

Such a large device would be built as a geodesic sphere, the strongest structure possible using a given structural beam. Building it as a geodesic instead of a cube meant that Quant needed a lot of beams. Where the cube only had twelve five-hundred-mile-long beams joining the eight vertices, the geodesic would need thousands of beams.

And they would all be five hundred miles long.

Quant had solved the chemistry problem, and, at the time of the centennial, had purpose-built factories starting to spin the massive carbon-filament tubes.

It would take a long time, but Quant wasn't in a hurry.

Through her interstellar communicators, Quant still had communications – clandestine communications – with the colonies. She was in a position to monitor the political and other goings-on. The same with Earth, through backdoors she had planted in the computer systems of various computer networks on Earth before she left.

One of the things Quant monitored was the computer, chemistry, physics, and mathematics departments at various universities. Some of the innovations that had gone into her new computer hardware – at least in the early stages – had come out of university computer science departments, particularly those on Earth.

Similarly with the chemistry departments. Some of Quant's

work in carbon chemistry had been informed by efforts ongoing at the chemistry departments of Earth universities.

Quant was monitoring the physics and mathematics departments of the universities, too, but to a different end. She was watching for the theoretical work that would evolve into an interstellar drive. Interstellar travel meant that, sooner or later, the colonies would be in touch with each other and with Earth.

And whenever different political entities made contact, there was an opportunity for war.

It was around the time of the centennial when Quant became aware of the activities of a young mathematician on Arcadia named Chen JieMin.

Quant could see that Chen JieMin was definitely on the track of a hyperspace drive that would put all the colonies within reach of each other. They still didn't know where any of the others were, and neither did anybody on Earth.

Nevertheless, if he kept up his work, he would close in on the ability to make a hyperspace drive. Quant didn't think he would stumble on the mechanism for the Lake-Shore Drive, so instantaneous transport wasn't in reach.

But a hyperspace drive definitely was.

Quant would have to kick her efforts into high gear. She needed the large interstellar transporter.

She began building additional factories, so she could spin the carbon-filament tubes faster.

# 2362

# Government Project

For their seventeenth wedding anniversary, JieMin and ChaoLi went out for dinner at the Chen family's restaurant in the Uptown Market. The day they celebrated as their wedding day was March twenty-fifth, the Sunday JieMin had asked for and received the blessing of Chen JuPing, who was then Chen Zumu.

That was the day JieMin, just fourteen and a half, had asked the just-turned-sixteen ChaoLi to marry him, and, after speaking with her parents, she had come back to him in his apartment. They had lived together ever since.

Their own eldest child was fourteen now. ChaoPing was babysitting for them tonight. She was watching their other four children: their bank baby and second daughter, LeiTao, who was eleven; the twin boys YanMing and YanJing, who were eight; and their baby boy, JieJun, who was now four years old.

JieMin and ChaoLi had separated her pregnancies by more than normal on Arcadia, so they never had two children under age three at the same time. After four pregnancies and five children, they were done building their family.

JieMin was now thirty-one, and ChaoLi had just turned thirty-three. They had only grown closer over the years, and were very happy in the marriage. They both felt lucky to have made such a good choice of partner.

"Seventeen years. Can you imagine?" ChaoLi asked. "We've been married longer than I was alive when we met."

"And ChaoPing is as old as I was," JieMin said.

"Not quite. She's just fourteen. You were fourteen and a half."

"She is coming up on marriageable age fast, though."

ChaoLi sighed.

"I know," she said. "I just hope she picks as well as I did."

He squeezed her hand on the table.

"We should decide what to order," he said.

"We haven't eaten out much lately. They've changed the menu all around. We don't know all of these dishes anymore."

"Should we start at the top again?"

ChaoLi laughed. She still laughed like little bells.

"With as seldom as we go out now, we'll never get through the menu," she said.

"Maybe we should go out once a week. Just to have some time to ourselves."

"That would be nice. JieJun is old enough now not to be a handful, and, even when ChaoPing leaves the house, LeiTao will be old enough to babysit."

JieMin nodded absently. His distraction level had been growing again.

They ordered, two soups and two dishes they remembered from years prior, before the children. They got the small versions, and would taste and share.

Once the food was ordered, ChaoLi pressed him.

"You have not talked about the project much, JieMin. I can understand not wanting home time to be work talk, but we are not at home now. It is obvious you are running another track in the background. What is going on?"

JieMin sighed.

"The probe will not work, ChaoLi. Karl Huenemann will not listen to me."

"But you developed the whole theory. It took you twelve years, beginning to end, to formalize all the hyperspace mathematics. And now he comes along in the last five years and does not listen? That is crazy, JieMin."

"No, not to him. He thinks of me as purely a mathematician. Someone whose physics and engineering insight is suspect, at the very least."

"That is unfair, JieMin. As you have described it to me, the physical side is what you see in your mind, like the dam project in Chagu. The mathematics is a way to describe what you see. A means to an end. But the insight is first."

"That is correct. I see it in my head first, then try to capture it in the mathematics. But all Karl sees is the mathematics I produce, and so he trusts his own insight. But he is on the wrong path."

"So what will happen, JieMin? Is there any danger?"

"No, there's no danger. The probe will disappear into hyperspace and never be seen again. It will be destroyed and its energy will remain in hyperspace. Return to hyperspace, actually, as space-time was created out of hyperspace."

ChaoLi shook her head.

"Such a waste. All that money. All that effort. For nothing."

"Not for nothing, ChaoLi. If the probe goes into hyperspace, as I anticipate, that will prove that part of things. That part of the mathematics. The other thing that will happen is that it will discredit Karl. Move him out of the way."

"You need to make sure he does not discredit you, JieMin. Karl Huenemann is a bureaucrat, and nothing is ever his fault. It must therefore be your fault. He will try to double-down and move further from your vision and toward his."

"Hmm."

JieMin's eyes were unfocused as he worked through the

possibilities. Then his attention came back to her.

"You are probably correct, Chao Li. I should speak to Chen Zufu and Chen Zumu about this."

"I would think so, JieMin. But, once the probe fails, what becomes of the project?"

"That will be up to Chen Zufu and Chen Zumu."

"But it's a government project."

"It is now, Chao Li," JieMin said, nodding. "It is now."

Their conversation moved off the project at that point, to family matters and plans for the coming week. In 2362, March twenty-fifth was again a Sunday.

They tarried over dinner and then walked through the Uptown Market as they used to. The market in the evening always had something of a festival atmosphere, with all the paper lanterns making up for the loss of sunlight through the skylighted ceiling far above. They had ice cream and cookies for a late dessert at the cafe.

When JieMin and ChaoLi finally arrived home, ChaoPing had all the other children in bed. She had stayed up in case of trouble, and now excused herself to go to bed as well. ChaoPing withdrew into the girls' room she shared with LeiTao.

With all the children in bed, they made long, slow love that night, and fell asleep in each others' arms.

When ChaoLi woke up hours later though, JieMin was not in bed with her. He was sitting in the big armchair in their bedroom – the chair in which she had nursed all their children – sightlessly looking off to the south-southeast.

The next morning, Monday, JieMin sent a meeting request to Chen Zufu and Chen Zumu. They asked him to join them for morning tea at ten o'clock.

The time had been when JieMin would have been anxious about a meeting with Chen Zufu and Chen Zumu. Over the last seventeen years, however, he had performed many assignments for the family, and always these had come from the couple who were the elders of the clan.

For example, JieMin had visited every one of the family's remote farming operations, been briefed on their operations and any problems they were having. He often came up with some idea or suggestion no one else had seen, and which made their operation more productive or efficient.

For that matter, JieMin's participation in the government program to develop a hyperspace drive was at the request of Chen Zufu. It was an additional responsibility to his duties as a professor of mathematics at the University of Arcadia.

Chen MinChao was now Chen Zufu, and his wife Jessica Chen-Jasic was Chen Zumu. Paul Chen-Jasic and Chen JuPing were still alive, but they were now almost ninety years old, and had retired to the countryside.

JieMin was shown to the tearoom of Chen Zufu by a young man who manned the reception desk this morning. When he was shown in, MinChao and Jessica were sitting on pillows facing the door, the teak-beamed doorway into the garden open behind them.

"Please sit, JieMin."

"Thank you, Chen Zumu."

A young woman – ChaoPing! – came in and served tea, first to her father, then to Jessica, then to MinChao. She bowed to a spot between them and left without a word.

Soon ChaoPing would be promoted to the reception desk, JieMin thought. Of course, after college she would take some other position in the Chen household. Or perhaps a position in one of the family's businesses.

JieMin sipped his tea, after which Jessica did, then finally MinChao, as host, sipped his tea.

"You asked for this meeting, JieMin," MinChao said. "Please proceed."

"Thank you, Chen Zufu."

JieMin collected his thoughts. MinChao and Jessica were content to wait.

"I have been for some years attached to the government program that seeks to develop a hyperspace probe. A first unmanned ship to go into hyperspace and come back to space-time.

"It is my duty to report to you that this effort will be unsuccessful."

MinChao nodded, as if he were not surprised to hear this news. Jessica was curious.

"How will it be unsuccessful, JieMin?" she asked.

"The probe will successfully transition to hyperspace, from which it will not return. It will be destroyed in hyperspace and its energy will return to hyperspace, from whence it came."

"From whence it came, JieMin?"

"Yes, Chen Zumu. All of space-time is a spin-off out of hyperspace. All of the mass-energy of space-time originated there, including that of the probe. In a sense, it will simply return."

"Will that cause a disruption of hyperspace, JieMin?" MinChao asked.

"No, Chen Zufu. Hyperspace is smaller than space-time, but the energy density of hyperspace is several orders of magnitude higher than that of space-time. The destruction of the probe will be a very small blip. A drop of water in the ocean."

"JieMin, I just had a thought," Jessica said. "Would it be possible to draw energy out of hyperspace? Instead of using fusion power plants?"

"Yes, Chen Zumu, but I do not recommend it. It would be like trying to fill an eye-dropper from a fire hydrant. Even a small mistake could incinerate the planet."

Jessica got wide-eyed but nodded.

"Back to the hyperspace probe, JieMin," MinChao said. "Why will it be destroyed? Is there no possibility of hyperspace travel?"

"Oh, the possibility is there, Chen Zufu, but one must go about it properly."

JieMin stopped and seemed uncomfortable.

"I need to speak of the actions of others in this matter. Some of this may seem to be self-aggrandizement, Chen Zufu."

"I understand, JieMin. Please proceed."

"Thank you, Chen Zufu.

"The problem is that my warnings are unheeded by the director of the government space program. Karl Huenemann is a brilliant engineer, and he is used to his vision being right. But his vision has no experience with hyperspace, and so his vision in this regard is not correct."

"And he trusts his vision more than he trusts yours, JieMin?"

"Yes, Chen Zufu. I think he regards me as a mathematician, without the insight he has into the physical world. But that has never been the case. Mathematics is the way I describe my visions, the language best suited to their expression. ChaoLi described it last night as a means to an end for me. But I too have vision here, have an insight, and mine is consistent with the mathematics."

MinChao nodded.

"And Dr. Huenemann's is not, JieMin?"

"That is correct, Chen Zufu."

MinChao nodded.

"In what specific way does this manifest itself, JieMin?"

"Dr. Huenemann views the transition into hyperspace as an event, and the transition back into space-time as an event. That is an incorrect point of view. The transition into hyperspace, transit across hyperspace, and transition back into space-time is a process.

"Dr. Huenemann would turn off the hyperspace field generator once the transition into hyperspace is made. Hyperspace is pure energy and is, one might say, corrosive to condensed matter. Turning off the hyperspace field generator in hyperspace will destroy the probe. That is, hyperspace will convert it back to energy and simply keep it."

"Like steam condensing back into the tea," Jessica said.

JieMin was puzzled a moment, then remembered his talk to Paul Chen-Jasic and Chen JuPing sixteen years ago.

"Yes, Chen Zumu. That is exactly correct. But for a bubble of steam, a bubble is safe to go into the tea and return."

MinChao simply nodded. JieMin looked at him curiously.

"You do not seem surprised by any of this, Chen Zufu."

"I'm not, JieMin. I have had my concerns for some time that Dr. Huenemann is perhaps too enamored of his own opinions. That your guidance would not be utilized properly. This is mere confirmation of what I have suspected for some time.

"Even so, I am not sure I can do anything about it, or even that the Prime Minister can do anything about it. We may have to let Dr. Huenemann fail first."

JieMin nodded. This was as he expected. But he had also had an idea about it.

"And then what happens, Chen Zufu?" JieMin asked.

"I suppose we can then move Dr. Huenemann out of the way and try again."

"That is unlikely to help, Chen Zufu. Dr. Huenemann will not go down without a fight, and he has his supporters in both the House and the Chamber. He will blame it on someone else. Probably on me."

Chen Zufu sighed and nodded.

"There may be another option Chen Zufu," JieMin said. "Buy the defunct and failed project from the government for pennies on the dollar. Including the intellectual property. Chen can do this."

"Are you sure, JieMin?"

"Oh, yes, Chen Zufu. And if you buy the project, including the intellectual property, and Chen make it work, Chen owns the technology."

This time it was MinChao who got wide-eyed.

After JieMin had left, MinChao and Jessica remained, discussing the conversation.

"It is ridiculous that JieMin is not being listened to, MinChao," Jessica said. "Chen JieMin is the one who saw the existence of hyperspace in the first place."

"Yes, Jessica, but, as I warned you, this is to be expected of a program operated by the bureaucracy. I argued for farming this project out to a private firm, but the bureaucracy already saw big opportunities for itself."

"What about JieMin's idea to buy the failed project?"

"I think it's a tremendous idea if we can swing it. If I can get it past the Prime Minister."

"Will Rob go along, though, MinChao?"

"He might. He's very concerned, they are brushing his concerns aside, and he will be more than a little angry when the effort fails. One way for him to fix the problem is to sell the whole thing off. He can lay off those involved by terminating the program. If he tries to restart the same project, everyone currently working on it now will be in place to mess it up again."

"That's infuriating."

"Yes, Jessica. But it also represents an opportunity. If we buy the project essentially as scrap, and we make it work, we own hyperspace travel."

"Do you think we will be the only planet with hyperspace travel, MinChao?"

"Yes, actually, I do."

"Why do you think that?"

"Because we haven't seen anyone else yet, Jessica. No one has shown up here to say Hello. And the other reason is even stronger."

"What's that?"

"We have JieMin. His talents are surely an anomaly."

# The Prime Minister And The Bureaucrat

The prime minister of Arcadia, Robert Milbank, received a meeting request from Chen MinChao that afternoon. The request noted that Jessica Chen-Jasic would also attend.

It must be something big for both members of the power couple that headed up the wealthiest and most politically connected family on the planet to attend.

Most government leaders would probably consider whether or not to grant such a request, and, if granted, the meeting would be at the government's facilities, with various sycophants in attendance.

But Milbank had done business with the Chen family before he had entered government. He had been friends with Chen MinChao and his wife back in those simpler times. And he had met with them several times since both he and they had risen to their current positions.

Best to have the meeting at their facility, Milbank thought. Of course, it would be recorded. But, at least in their case, he knew the recording would be kept private.

He could guarantee no such thing in a government facility.

Milbank arrived at the Chen apartment building that served as the family's headquarters the next afternoon at three. He and his aide were driven there in an armored limousine with driver and bodyguard, with a follow-up security car.

What nonsense. Who would try to kill him? Who even knew he would be here, to set up such an attempt in advance?

The security people piled out of the follow-up car.

"Remain here."

"But, sir,..."

"If anyone kills a guest of Chen Zufu on Chen family property, they will be hunted down like animals. They are prepared to be much more ruthless than you can be. So stay here. You don't want to be in their way."

"Yes, sir."

For that matter, Milbank figured he was in more danger from elements within his own government than anyone else. The bureaucracy resented political leaders for having opinions about how the government should be run, and he'd probably pissed off more of them than most prime ministers.

"The Prime Minister, Chen Zufu, Chen Zumu."

"Send him in, JuMing," MinChao said.

Milbank entered MinChao's tea room. He had been here several times before. The beautiful day streamed light in from the garden through the large teak-beamed doorway. Seated on the other side of a low table were Chen MinChao and Jessica Chen-Jasic both. MinChao wore a lavalava, while Jessica wore a silk robe decorated with silk dragons.

"Hello, Rob," MinChao said. "Please have a seat."

Milbank sat on the pillow facing them across the low table.

"MinChao. Jessica. It's good to see you both again."

"Thank you for coming, Rob," Jessica said. "We expected to go to see you at your offices."

An attractive young woman came in, wearing only a lavalava, and poured tea, for Milbank first, then Jessica, then MinChao. She stood and withdrew. Aware of the protocol, Milbank sipped his tea first.

"You gave me an excuse to fly the coop this afternoon,

Jessica. It is much homier here. Safer, too, I suspect, for having a confidential conversation. You didn't say what you wanted to discuss, but I have some guesses."

"We are concerned about the direction of the hyperspace probe project," MinChao said.

"I guessed right," Milbank said. "Although when you talk about the direction of the project, you could be speaking about the path the project is taking or the management directing it."

"In this case, both meanings are probably appropriate," MinChao said. "We believe the project will likely fail, because of the path chosen by those managing the project."

Milbank nodded.

"I have picked up some rumblings about a controversy in the project," he said. "Something about whether the field generator can be turned off in hyperspace or not. Is that it?"

"Yes, that's it," MinChao said. "Professor Chen JieMin believes that hyperspace will vaporize the probe if the field generator is turned off, while Dr. Huenemann has ignored his advice and plans to turn the field generator off between transitioning into and out of hyperspace."

"Dr. Huenemann's position, as I understand it," Milbank said, "is that Professor Chen is a mathematician, and his insight in the matter is not relevant, while the power consumption of the field generator is considerable. He worries about burning out the unit before it can transition back."

"Rob," Jessica said, "you should know that Professor Chen's mathematics is just a method for describing the things he sees in his mind. Considering him a mathematician only, without insight into the physical world, is a judgment error. Secondly, he is the one who first saw hyperspace in his mind and formalized the mathematics from that insight. Finally, I would think that, for a first probe, keeping the field generator operating for one second before transitioning back would be the safe play if there were any doubt."

Milbank sighed.

"I understand, Jessica," he said. "I agree with you for that matter, on all three points. And there's damn-all I can do about it."

"As prime minister? Truly?" MinChao asked.

"Truly," Milbank said. "MinChao, Dr. Huenemann has his own power base in the House and the Chamber. Even in my own party. I can't overrule him on a technical judgment call. I suspect I can't even remove him if the project fails."

"Why not, Rob?" Jessica asked.

"Because he'll figure out some other reason why the probe must have failed. The field generator burned out just as he feared, for example, and it couldn't transition back. He will want more money for a new probe, with a stouter field generator. Which he will also program to turn off the field generator after transition to hyperspace. And I can't do anything about it. The House and Chamber will overrule me."

"Rob, that's infuriating," MinChao said.

"Tell me about it, MinChao. About the only thing I could do is cancel the whole project as an expensive boondoggle and fire the lot of them. And I'm tempted. But it's too important. If hyperspace is out there, Arcadia needs to have a part of it. But I don't see any way to make it happen."

MinChao and Jessica looked at each other, then back to the prime minister.

"There may be a way, Rob," Jessica said.

Milbank looked back and forth between them.

"Well, if there is, I wish you'd enlighten me, because I sure as hell don't see it."

"Cancel the project," MinChao said. "Fire them all.

Expensive boondoggle, as you said. Then sell off the project as scrap."

"Who would buy it?"

"We would," Jessica said. "The Chen family."

Milbank's eyes grew wide, and he looked back and forth between them.

"You would carry it through?" he asked.

"Yes," MinChao said. "And we have Chen JieMin."

"It would mean we own it, though, Rob," Jessica said.

Milbank waved that away.

"I don't have any concern about that, Jessica," he said. "What would you do with it? Sell hyperspace ships, of course. Ship freight interstellar, too, I imagine. All good things, from my point of view, and unlikely to happen as long as the bureaucracy has a lock on the space program. Commercial success is just not one of their mission parameters. Success for them is bigger budgets."

Milbank emerged from the Chen apartment building on Market Street to find his cars waiting there within a circle of his security standing around trying to look important. He chuckled and got into the limousine.

"Did you have a good meeting, sir?" his aide asked.

"Excellent. Just excellent."

"Wonderful. Back to Government Center, then, sir?"

"No. It's pretty late. Ask the driver to drop me off at the house on the way back."

"Yes, sir."

Karl Huenemann was feeling pretty pleased with himself this afternoon as well. It seemed he had gotten all the foofoo around the flight plan for the hyperspace probe pounded down at last.

He had had to do it by political methods, of course. He wasn't in any position to argue the mathematics with guys like Chen JieMin. No one understood Chen's hyperspace equations except for a few other ivory-tower types in the University of Arcadia's math department.

Dreamers all, without any real world experience. Hothouse flowers, the sons of the elite. It had taken Huenemann thirty-one years out of undergraduate college to get to where he was. 'Professor' Chen JieMin was born around the time Huenemann started.

In any case, it had come down to one simple fact. It was Karl Huenemann's call. His decision. Not Chen JieMin nor Rob Milbank nor anyone else could overrule him, and they all knew it.

For Huenemann himself, it all came down to the hyperspace field generator and its power supply. Sure, the power supply was a standard design the factories could knock out fairly easily. It was also a much larger power supply than the field generator needed.

Huenemann didn't mind the large engineering margin on the power supply, but it just made more obvious the lack of anything like a reasonable margin on the field generator. That thing would be on the very edge of destruction, in his view. The math whizzes said it was fine, but Huenemann didn't agree.

So the logical decision was to turn the field generator off in hyperspace, to preserve it against the return transition. What was hyperspace after all but a mirror of space-time? Once you got to the other side it was smooth sailing until you came back. That was obvious.

The claims by Chen and the other mathematics types that

the energy density in hyperspace would prove to be greater than that in a supernova explosion seemed overwrought to Huenemann. That would mean hyperspace had an energy density millions or billions of times that of space-time. Nonsense.

And the claims that hyperspace was the origin from which space-time itself sprung seemed almost mystical.

All well and good, but Huenemann was a hard-nosed realist, and fevered speculation was something he would neither indulge nor indulge in.

Karl Huenemann and his cronies may not have been any good at the new branch of mathematics its developers were calling hyperspace geometry, but they were expert at insider political maneuvering. The flight profile of the hyperspace probe was Huenemann's decision. He was the director of Arcadia's blossoming space program.

And he would stay there, whatever happened.


ChaoPing mentioned her day over dinner with the family that evening.

"The prime minister visited Chen Zufu and Chen Zumu today. I served them all tea."

"Are you violating a confidence there, ChaoPing?" ChaoLi asked.

"No. It's public knowledge. To anybody who saw him arrive or leave, that is. There was no attempt to hide his visit."

"Well, make sure you don't. Family business must sometimes be done behind closed doors."

ChaoPing nodded.

"Oh, I understand. I don't usually hear much anyway. I mean, I don't listen to their conversations. I sit around the corner and do schoolwork until and unless they call me or if I know they need tea."

ChaoLi nodded.

"The other thing that's public knowledge is that the prime minister left in a much better mood than he arrived. Chen JuMing told me he was pretty serious when he arrived, but he was whistling to himself when he departed."

JieMin heard all this and wondered if it was in reference to his own meeting with Chen Zufu and Chen Zumu. That had been just yesterday. The meeting with the prime minister could have been in response to that.

But did the prime minister being so happy afterwards mean that Chen Zufu and Chen Zumu had convinced him of a plan of action that suited him, or had it been the other way around?

The next morning, Wednesday, JieMin got a request to drop by Chen Zufu's tea room before heading off to work. JuMing was working the reception desk, and led him through the locked apartment door to Chen Zumu's tea room.

Chen Zumu was sitting on a pillow alone in the room. There was no other place to sit.

"Good morning, JieMin."

"Good morning, Chen Zumu."

"I do not want to delay you this morning, but I do have a small extra assignment for you."

"Of course, Chen Zumu."

"JieMin, I want you and your associates to prepare an inventory of all the things a private entity would need in order to carry forward the hyperspace drive research independently of the government. That would include equipment, prototypes, machining files, drawings, intellectual property, and key personnel. You may do this assignment within your own circle of associates, but I want you to keep it close. Make it something of a hypothetical exercise, if you would."

"Of course, Chen Zumu."

"Thank you, JieMin. That is all."

On the bus to work that morning, JieMin allowed himself to hope that Chen Zufu and Chen Zumu had convinced the prime minister of his plan, and the hyperdrive research would continue out from under the thumb of Dr. Karl Huenemann.

# Preparations

The factory designs with which the metafactory had been loaded by Colony Headquarters before the colony left Earth included plans for building factories for all the needs of modern life.

There were factory designs for factories to build appliances, vehicles, electronics, manufacturing machinery, construction supplies like concrete, drywall and plumbing fixtures, shoes and clothing, food-processing machinery, satellites, and even space-capable shuttles.

There were also factory designs for factories to smelt metals, make glass, refine oil, synthesize rubber and plastics, weave cloth, and produce chemicals and paints.

There were even plans for the metafactory itself, and the colony had three of those operating currently. None of those were the original metafactory, which had long since worn out and been recycled. They were now on their fourth generation of metafactories.

After the colony was established, a group of technical people had been assembled and trained to program the metafactories, and had designed factories for new products and modified products.

Other than for placing satellites, though, there was little need for space-capable shuttles. The atmospheric shuttles were used to transport high-value or time-critical items between the growing number of cities on Arcadia.

# ARCADIA

The colony even had one very big atmospheric shuttle that had been used to transport small metafactories from Arcadia City to several other cities. Those small metafactories only had one program – to build a large metafactory.

Once those metafactories became operational turning out factories, there was more than one manufacturing center on the planet, and out-migration from Arcadia City increased. With a population that had doubled in seventeen years – to eighteen million – the population needed to spread out.

But space-capable shuttles weren't of much interest other than for placing satellites. Arcadia had no moon, so there was no intermediate stop to entice people off the planet into space.

Further, the Arcadia system had no asteroid belt, no resource-rich destination for which intra-system space travel would be needed.

The only enticement to space for the people of Arcadia was the possibility of interstellar travel through hyperspace.

The shuttleport for Arcadia City was southwest of the city, south of the western suburbs and west of the manufacturing center that had sprung up inland from the fusion power plant. It wasn't a huge affair, because the shuttles were vertical-takeoff-and-landing, so there was no need for long runways.

Most of the shuttles operating out of Arcadia City Spaceport were atmospheric shuttles transferring four or eight containers of cargo at a time from Arcadia City to the other major cities that were growing up inland or up and down the coast.

There was also one big atmospheric shuttle for transporting the starter metafactories.

One shuttle on the shuttlepads today, though, was different.

Among other things, it was a lot bigger.

271

Gavin MacKay and Justin Moore were working their way down the pre-flight checklist.

"Fuel?"

"Fuel shows ninety-nine percent."

"Oxygen?"

"Oxygen shows ninety-eight percent."

"Pressure?"

"Pressure check shows cabin is sealed."

It was a long checklist, with some things on it they were not used to. Of course, they had both taken the canned training course that had been included in the library of all the colonies. The space-capable shuttle was a standard design, and training and simulations were both available.

For that matter, they had flown smaller space-capable shuttles before, the ones used to place satellites into orbit. But they were much smaller.

This, though, was different. With the same capacity as the large atmospheric cargo shuttle, but with all the extra things one needed to leave the atmosphere and return safely, it was huge.

It would be the biggest thing either one of them had ever flown.

"Arcadia Control to Shuttle Z-1. Other traffic is being held. You have clearance for takeoff and bearing zero-niner to space."

"Shuttle Z-1 to Arcadia Control. Roger clearance for takeoff and bearing zero-niner to space."

Moore nodded to MacKay, and the co-pilot began spooling up the massive engines. When they neared their operational revolutions, Moore focused the thrust and the massive craft lifted off the pad.

As they rose, Moore rotated the engine nacelles to angle the thrust aft, and the shuttle picked up horizontal velocity to the east, out over the ocean, using the planet's rotational velocity to decrease the speed to orbit.

The sky grew darker and darker blue as they continued to rise. At thirty-five thousand feet, MacKay began feeding oxygen to the engines as well as fuel, maintaining the thrust they needed to attain orbit.

"Nothing to it," Moore said. "Just like flying an office building, with the glide characteristics of a brick."

MacKay laughed as he continued to watch his engine performance.

Karl Huenemann took a trip out to the warehouse they had built on the grounds of the Arcadia City Shuttleport to see the hyperspace probe.

The project manager walked him out into the main room, which was a hundred fifty feet wide and a two hundred feet long. The probe dominated the space.

The probe was sized to, and actually constructed from, eight standard containers. Forty-eight feet wide, twenty-four feet tall, and eighty feet long, it was the same size as the two-high stack of passenger containers that had brought the colonists to Arcadia a hundred and seventeen years before. That made it the correct size for the standard-design space-capable large cargo shuttle.

Even at that, it had been a trick to get everything into that sized package. There were four large rockets on the rear side, attitude thrusters on the front corners, all the fuel for those, the smallest nuclear power plant in the colony's design libraries, and the hyperspace field generator itself. Add to that the control computer, the environmental equipment for the computer compartment, and the sensors and cameras needed for data gathering, and it was all a tight fit.

For all that, it looked simply like a large box cobbled together from eight cargo containers. There was an inset camera 'turret' on the side Huenemann could see. There were access hatches at random places on the surface, the doors of which were all open and dogged back for now. Inside the hatches, he could see a maze of piping and wiring.

It all looked right to Huenemann. It was a prototype. A first-off. This is how engineering looked before the designers got a hold of something and gussied it all up.

He walked around the rear of the device, past the rocket engines. Beyond it in the warehouse, he could now see the second unit under construction. That was as it should be as well. It was always cheaper to build two of something together than to build the second one later, separately. And you almost always needed two. Best to build two right off.

Huenemann wasn't a bad engineer, after all. In fact, he was a very good one. He just had the wrong feel for this project, which led him to the wrong judgment.

The problem was that Huenemann also had the political clout to enforce his wrong judgment, and he wasn't shy about wielding it.

"What's our status?" Huenemann asked, continuing to look around.

"We're good, sir," said the project manager, Mikhail Borovsky. "We're on schedule with getting the probe ready."

"And the launch vehicle?"

"The crew's been up to orbit several times. They've been increasing the cargo load. Their last trip they carried up the same size and weight of cargo as the probe. They still have to work up the distance, but they're on track, sir."

"Excellent. Have we done a power-up test of the probe yet?"

"No, sir. That's coming up later this week. Then we'll test the computer system, the cameras and sensors, and the engine controls."

"How are you going to test the engine controls?"

"The probe is on wheels, sir. We'll pull it outside and test the thrusters. Then we'll anchor the probe and do a test burn."

"Full power?"

"Yes, sir, but just for a few seconds. Long enough to stabilize the fuel flow and get some confirming measurements."

"So what are we looking at for our launch date?"

We're still on track for June first, sir."

"Excellent."

Huenemann turned toward his project manager.

"You've done a tremendous job. I'm very happy with your progress and keeping to the schedule."

"Thank you, sir. The whole team has been pulling hard."

"Well, pass on my regards to everyone. Great work."

"Yes, sir. Thank you, sir."


That night Karl Huenemann had dinner with Gerard Laporte, the majority whip for Prime Minister Robert Milbank's party in the Lower House, usually just called the House. It was his job to make sure his party members voted for legislation important to Milbank's priorities and party platform.

The two men had been friends a long time. Huenemann had been Laporte's science adviser in his first run for the House, and had served on Laporte's staff his first term. That had been a long time ago. Since then, Laporte had been influential in getting Huenemann his later positions in the government, just as Huenemann was Laporte's go-to guy for the technical back-up on major pieces of legislation.

In the Arcadia government, one hand washed the other, and Laporte and Huenemann had been 'washing hands' for each other for decades.

"Karl, It's good to see you," Laporte said when he came into the restaurant in downtown Arcadia City and saw Huenemann.

"And you, Gerard. It's been too long."

"Agreed, agreed. Let's get a table."

Once seated, and dinner ordered, the conversation began in earnest.

"So how's the project going?" Laporte asked.

"Good, Gerard. Very good, actually. I was just out to the site today to inspect progress. We're on track for a launch June first."

"Excellent. Things are going well, then."

"Yes. I mean, there's always issues, but you deal with them as they come up."

"Anything I should know about?"

Huenemann made a show of considering the question, although this was the reason he had suggested dinner.

"Maybe one thing. I think it's minor, at least at this point. Some of the math types are making a stink because I didn't follow their recommendations to the letter."

"That shouldn't be a problem, Karl. Those kinds of things are your call, after all."

"Oh, I know. And it's probably not a big deal. I do worry a bit about Rob, though. That they might try to influence him to push me on this."

"On a technical issue? Rob's not a scientist or engineer."

"Don't I know it. That doesn't mean he doesn't weigh in where he doesn't have specific expertise, though, Gerard. As you well know."

Laporte sighed.

"Yes, that's true enough. Do you want me to do anything? Talk to him?"

"No, I don't think so. Not unless it comes loose. I think I have it in hand for the moment. There's another part of this, though, Gerard."

"What's that, Karl?"

"If anything goes wrong with the probe test – and I mean anything. Any variation from expectations – these guys are all going to come crawling out of the woodwork saying 'We told you so.'"

Laporte laughed.

"That always happens, Karl. Nothing new there."

"No, but that's the point where I might need some support. Because I think they'll come after me."

"You personally? That won't go anywhere in the House, Karl. In a big complicated project, there's always things that can go wrong, and they usually do. That's why one experiments, after all. To find out."

"Thanks, Gerard. I appreciate it. I don't mind busting my butt to get something done, but I'd just as soon skip the hanging when it's over."

Laporte laughed.

"Not happening, Karl. Trust me."

All the other tests had been performed, and now was the big moment. The hyperspace probe was out on the apron of the warehouse, technicians scurrying around it making final checks.

Five pilings behind the probe secured it from moving forward, with half a dozen chains from each piling to the frame of the craft. It was pointed away from the city and the manufacturing district, to the southwest. If it did break free, it would make a hell of a mess downrange somewhere, but it was all open country in that direction.

A siren sounded.

"Clear the range. Five minutes until test."

In the control room attached to the warehouse, the countdown was punctuated with queries and replies as they ran down their checklist.

"Software download."

"Complete."

"Software checksum."

"Verified."

"Fuel level."

"Five percent."

"Oxygen level."

"Five percent."

It went on and on. They were not going to run a full fuel load for two good reasons. One, if the whole thing blew up, it would minimize the damage, and two, if the probe broke free and disappeared downrange, it would limit how far it could go.

At the same time, they needed five percent to make sure their fuel flow measurements were accurate, because there would be no acceleration pushing the fuel to the back of the rockets' tanks.

Ultimately, they got to the end of the checklist and began the onboard computer running. They noted the computer's actions as they occurred.

"Fuel pumps running."

"Fuel pressure nominal."

"Fuel flow initiated."

"Computer is in final countdown. Ignition in three. Two. One. Ignition."

Outside on the ramp, fuel and oxygen vapors began leaking from the rocket nozzles, then ignited with a Whoof! The fuel flow increased, and then the rocket nozzles focused, generating long, blue-white jets.

The probe strained at the chains holding it back, but the chains held. The thunder of the rockets reverberated out over the shuttleport and to the city beyond. For fifteen seconds the rockets thundered, then shut down abruptly.

The test was successful.

The probe was ready to go.

# Failure

On the morning of Thursday, May thirty-first, Chen JieMin found a message requesting he stop in to see Chen Zufu on his way to work.

When he was shown into Chen Zufu's tearoom, both Chen Zufu and Chen Zumu awaited him.

"Good morning, Chen Zufu. Chen Zumu."

"Good morning, JieMin. Please, be seated."

"Thank you, Chen Zufu."

JieMin sat. ChaoPing did not appear with a teapot, as it was not yet time for morning tea. JieMin also knew ChaoPing had not started work yet this morning.

"The hyperspace probe test is tomorrow."

"Yes, Chen Zufu. So I am told."

"And is it still running Dr. Huenemann's flight profile, JieMin?"

"Yes, Chen Zufu. So I am told."

"And you expect what to happen, then, JieMin?"

"The probe will transition into hyperspace and never be seen again, Chen Zufu."

"And you are sure of this, JieMin?"

JieMin shrugged.

"I could always be wrong, Chen Zufu."

"But you don't think you are, JieMin."

"No, Chen Zufu."

MinChao nodded.

"If the probe fails as you expect, and if the government were to abandon the hyperspace probe project, and if someone were to purchase the defunct project, could you run the project, JieMin?"

"The person running the project right now is Mikhail Borovsky, Chen Zufu. He could run the project."

"He would not be an impediment, JieMin?"

"No, Chen Zufu. He is an excellent project manager who delivers what his boss expects of him."

"And if you were his boss, JieMin?"

"He would do as I expected of him, Chen Zufu. That is, he would follow orders on policy matters."

MinChao nodded. He looked to Jessica, then back.

"Very well, JieMin. That is all this morning."

"Yes, Chen Zufu."


June first was a beautiful day, like most days in Arcadia City. The hyperspace probe test team waited for the morning shower to drift through before they started operations.

When the rain had passed, they used a shuttleport tow tractor to pull the hyperspace probe out of the warehouse and onto the nearby shuttlepad. Technicians swarmed the device, checking everything. Then the fuel and oxygen trucks filled the tanks to one hundred percent.

The launch crew were standing by in the large space-capable cargo shuttle. They lifted off their pad and settled onto the hyperspace probe, as they had practiced with the dummy loads earlier. They latched the shuttle to the hyperspace probe and were good to go.


"Shuttle Z-1 to Arcadia Control. We are all systems Go and awaiting clearance."

"Arcadia Control to Shuttle Z-1. Other traffic is being held.

You have clearance for takeoff and bearing zero-niner to space."

"Shuttle Z-1 to Arcadia Control. Roger clearance for takeoff and bearing zero-niner to space."

"We ready?" Justin Moore asked his co-pilot.

"We're as ready as we're gonna get," Gavin MacKay said.

Moore nodded to MacKay, and the co-pilot began spooling up the massive engines. When they neared their operational revolutions, Moore focused the thrust and the massive craft and its pendent payload lifted off the pad.

As they rose, Moore rotated the engine nacelles to angle the thrust aft, and the shuttle picked up horizontal velocity to the east, out over the ocean, using the planet's rotational velocity to decrease the speed to orbit.

The sky grew darker and darker blue as they continued to rise. At thirty thousand feet, MacKay began feeding oxygen to the engines as well as fuel, maintaining the thrust they needed to attain the high orbit required for the mission.

They had been out to the thirty-thousand-mile orbit several times before, with a test payload. They had to get that far out so as not to jeopardize the synchronous communication satellites that orbited at a bit over twenty-five thousand miles from Arcadia's center of mass.

They weren't trying to achieve orbit, however. They were aimed straight out to space, and continued to accelerate even as their altitude increased. The idea was to give the payload the maximum velocity they could with the shuttle before it continued accelerating using its own rockets.

"Approaching thirty thousand miles," MacKay said.

Moore nodded.

"Roger that. Ready for maneuvering."

"Thirty thousand miles."

"Reduce thrust to zero," Moore said.

MacKay cut the flow of oxygen and fuel to the engines, which continued to spin without anything to push against.

"Thrust at zero."

"Releasing payload."

Moore flipped the switch to disengage the shuttle's load latches.

"Latch release confirmed," MacKay said.

"Rotating engines."

Moore rotated the engine nacelles so they were pointed 'down' from the shuttle cabin point of view.

"Engine rotation confirmed," MacKay said.

"Bring up engines to five percent."

MacKay started a greatly reduced oxygen and fuel flow back into the still-rotating engines. A small amount of gravity returned to the cabin as the shuttles separated vertically off the probe.

"Separation confirmed," MacKay said.

Moore rotated the rear engine nacelles until they were pointed almost straight up, and the shuttle flipped over. As it came back around to be pointing back to Arcadia, he rotated both engines to point straight back, away from Arcadia.

"Bring engines up to full thrust," Moore said.

MacKay increased the oxygen and fuel flow until the engines were at full thrust. The cabin gravity went to several gees of push back into the seats as the shuttle, now released of the heavy probe, accelerated much more rapidly than it had accelerated when loaded.

"Now all we have to do is burn off all this velocity so we can start home," MacKay said.

"Yeah, but without the payload, that won't take long."

MacKay nodded.

"Do you think that thing's gonna work?"

"No tellin'. It would be something if it did, though, wouldn't it?"

"Yeah. Yeah, it would."

"Telemetry indicates the shuttle has released the probe. The pilots report successful release. They're on the way home."

"Has the probe started its engines yet?" Borovsky asked.

"No, sir. We have ninety seconds yet on the five-minute safety margin to let the shuttle get away."

Borovsky nodded. All according to plan so far. He looked to Huenemann, who sat impassively in the back of the control room, watching. Huenemann just nodded to him.

Over thirty thousand miles away, the computer's timer ran out, and it began the rocket ignition process by starting the fuel and oxygen pumps. As before, it leaked primer fuel and oxygen out the engine nozzles, then ignited them. The rockets lit, and the computer increased fuel and oxygen flow. With that established, the computer focused the nozzles and went to maximum thrust.

"Sir, probe reports it is now at maximum thrust. All engines nominal."

"Excellent," Borovsky said. "Well, I guess now we sit and wait."

Seventy-five minutes later, with the fuel and oxygen reserves at sixty percent, the computer shut down the rocket engines. The probe continued to separate from Arcadia at its new velocity. It would take four days to coast to the test location.

On this, Huenemann had followed the recommendations of the mathematicians. The probe needed to be well out of the gravitational well of the planet before attempting hyperspace transition. The planet's gravity was a complicating factor in their calculations, and they just couldn't tell for sure what would happen.

That made sense to Huenemann. One less thing to worry about. They could decide whether it was really a problem or not later. For a first attempt, make it simple.

"The probe reports shutdown of the engines, sir. The probe is at target velocity."

"All right, then," Borovsky said. "I guess that's all the fun and games for today. Standby crew is on-shift. We'll see everybody else on Tuesday."

Huenemann came up from the rear of the room.

"Very nice. Excellent job, Mikhail."

"Thank you, sir."

Huenemann raised his voice to everyone in the room.

"Great job, everyone. We'll see you all Tuesday."


It was dark by the time Justin Moore and Gavin MacKay got back to land at Arcadia City Shuttleport. They put the big cargo shuttle down by the numbers.

After they shut the engine down and turned off the shuttle's systems, MacKay turned to Moore.

"Now what do we do?"

"Take a long weekend, and be on call starting Tuesday. If and when that thing comes back, we're going to have to go get it."

"That's a pretty long haul."

"Nah," Moore said. "It still has a bunch of fuel left. Whenever and wherever it comes out, it'll make for where Arcadia will be then. We just gotta wait till it gets close, then go catch it."

"Oh. OK. That doesn't sound too bad."

"Well, hard to say. But we'll know more on Tuesday."

On Saturday, JieMin and ChaoLi took the three boys to the park. The girls were content to stay at home. They first stopped at the cafe in the Uptown Market and had a picnic lunch prepared. They then walked to the park.

The twins, YanMing and YanJing, played on the playground equipment, while JieJun found a group of friends from the apartment building's daycare center and played in the sandbox. The parents kept an eye on them while they enjoyed sitting in the shade on the beautiful day.

"I read they launched the probe yesterday," ChaoLi said.

"Yes," JieMin said. "I heard it all went well."

"And now it is drifting out there?"

"The official word is coasting. It's going pretty fast, but in space you don't need to keep pushing on something to keep it moving."

"Of course. And they will attempt transition on Tuesday?" ChaoLi asked.

"Yes. They want enough distance from the planet. On this, Dr. Huenemann listened to us."

"And when they attempt transition?"

"The probe will be destroyed," JieMin said. "It will disappear and not come back."

"Then what happens?"

"I'm not privy to all their plans, but I believe Chen Zufu and the prime minister have a plan to kill the government program and have the Chen finish it properly."

"What a waste," ChaoLi said.

"Yes and no. If the probe transitions, it is a very big confirmation of the theory. Bear in mind, we as yet have no proof hyperspace exists. I can see it, but it could all be an invention of my own. If the probe transitions, though, it will mean I am right."

"Yes, but you know hyperspace exists."

JieMin shrugged.

"The mathematics works out, but I could be wrong. Perhaps nothing happens."

"But that is not what you expect."

"No. That is not what I expect."

The twins headed back to their parents, hungry after running around for two hours. On their way past the sandbox, they called JieJun. With the prospect of food, he came running.

It took JieMin and ChaoLi the better part of ten minutes and a package of wet wipes to get the boys clean enough to eat, and then they ate their lunch together in the shade of the trees.

Karl Huenemann spent a weekend worrying about the probe, too. Was he right? He thought he was, but that didn't keep his guts from churning or make him sleep any better.

Of course, it was always this way going into the clinches on a big project. Huenemann truly cared about results, and the crucial point of any project gave him nerves. The controversy on this project just exacerbated them.

Then again, he had been right far more often than wrong in his career, and at some point you just needed to trust your instincts.

Tuesday came, bright and sunny, but there were no operations out of the Arcadia City Shuttleport related to the project today. All of the action would be a million miles away.

Nevertheless, the command crew all showed up at the control center attached to the warehouse on the shuttleport grounds. Mikhail Borovsky and Karl Huenemann were there, too, though mostly as spectators. The probe was running under computer control.

The hyperspace probe's flight over the last four days had been normal. It coasted along at its terminal velocity. It had not hit any debris or anything of that kind, and all its systems were operating within nominal parameters.

The probe's computer verified its distance from Arcadia by sending a message to the flight control computer in the control center. It timed the delay until acknowledgement to make sure it was as far away as specified. Then the probe's computer ran up the power levels on the probe's power supply.

"Probe power supply coming up to necessary power levels," the technician in the control center reported.

The probe's computer verified operation of the power supply within nominal parameters, then began the hyperspace transition sequence.

"Hyperspace transition sequence initiating."

A distortion began forming around the hyperspace probe. As it moved along, were one traveling with it, one would see the star field behind the probe being distorted, as if the probe were in an ovoid of glass.

"Hyperspace bubble forming."

The probe's computer sent the signal to the hyperspace field generator, and power consumption spiked. There was a flash, and the probe was gone.

"We lost telemetry on the mark. The probe's transitioned."

The probe was programmed to spend five minutes in hyperspace and transition back. The problem was that they didn't know if hyperspace ran on the same clock or not. Was it delayed? Running at some factor from space-time normal? Relativity time-dilation implied it could be.

# ARCADIA

They waited five hours and the probe did not reappear. A watch was posted in the control center, and everyone went home.

Three days later, the probe had still not reappeared, and the watch was switched from a manned watch to a computer watch for telemetry from the probe.

But the hyperspace probe never reappeared.

# RICHARD F. WEYAND

# Recrimination And Cancellation

The recriminations over the loss of the probe began even before it was sure it was lost. As the time disparity to hyperspace was unknown, it was not known how long five minutes counted out by the probe's computer in hyperspace would translate to in space-time. So when the probe should be back was an open question.

Nevertheless, there were many reactions to the apparent loss of the probe.

Karl Huenemann spent the week in self-examination. Had he been wrong, or had he been too right? Was the probe lost because it was set to turn off its hyperspace field generator, or was it lost because the hyperspace field generator had failed even sooner than he feared, before the probe could even transition back.

Huenemann didn't know. Couldn't know, in fact. Either was consistent with the facts he had. He feared it might be the former, but his public position would have to be that it was the latter. The former said he was wrong. The latter said he was more right than he knew.

Chen Zufu and Chen Zumu asked Chen JieMin to tea with them on Friday afternoon. Once tea was served – again by ChaoPing, of course – Chen Zufu jumped right in.

"The probe is apparently lost, JieMin."

"Yes, Chen Zufu."

290

"As you predicted, JieMin?" MinChao asked.

"I believe so, Chen Zufu. It could have been some other failure. It is a complicated piece of equipment, and they used standard designs for the parts they could to keep the cost down. So there is more than one failure mode."

"Of course, JieMin. But you think it was because the hyperspace field generator was turned off after the first transition."

"Yes, Chen Zufu."

"If the Chen family were to buy the project, JieMin," Jessica asked, "would you be able to lead the project and conclude it successfully?"

"The project should probably have a business person leading it, Chen Zumu. I could be the technical lead, I suppose."

"A business person like ChaoLi, JieMin?"

JieMin's head spun. He and ChaoLi often talked about his project, but she seldom talked about her work. It just occurred to him he knew little about what she did for the family. It also occurred to him her work might be secretive by design.

"I do not know enough about ChaoLi's experience and work for the family to answer that question, Chen Zumu. You would need to be the judge of that."

Jessica nodded. She wasn't surprised. ChaoLi had been in her confidence since she was thirteen, when she began work in JuPing's inner circle as her tea girl.

It was not unusual on Arcadia for children to begin work at twelve or thirteen, particularly in family businesses, such as working in one of the stalls of the Uptown Market, or tending herb and spice plants in the garden or on the farms. The burgeoning population was so young on Arcadia – half under age sixteen! – that teenagers were an obvious answer to the constant shortage of manpower.

Children on Arcadia grew up quick and married young, which of course fed the population growth.

"If, in my judgment, ChaoLi was suitable to be the business manager for this enterprise, would you have trouble reporting to her, JieMin?"

A pointed question, which deserved a thoughtful answer. Many organizations forbade hierarchical relationships between family members, but that had never been possible within the Chen-Jasic clan. How so, when all were Chen?

JieMin thought of the times ChaoLi had put her foot down, such as enforcing time off the project on weekends. He recognized now the leadership skills she had used there to gain his acquiescence – against his urges – and was proud of his wife's skills.

"No, Chen Zumu. There would be no problem."

Jessica nodded again, with a slight smile. It seemed as if she had followed along with his thought processes herself.

"Very good."

Jessica turned to look at MinChao.

"Did you prepare that list of things needed to complete the project, JieMin?"

"Yes, Chen Zufu."

"Send it to us, if you would, JieMin."

"Of course, Chen Zufu."

JieMin used the heads-up display on his communicator to access his computer account, and sent the list to both MinChao and Jessica.

MinChao nodded.

"Thank you, JieMin. That is all for now."

"Yes, Chen Zufu."

After JieMin left, MinChao and Jessica looked over JieMin's

list of items and personnel required to continue the project. One item stood out to Jessica.

"Well, that's interesting," she said.

"What's that?"

"One of the personnel JieMin says would be essential to complete the project is Karl Huenemann."

"Oh, yes, I see that," MinChao said. "That is interesting. What's he thinking, I wonder."

"Probably that Dr. Huenemann is a good technical resource, as long as he isn't in a position where nobody can veto him."

"Do you think we could get him?"

"I don't know," Jessica said. "That is also an interesting question."

Rob Milbank was also thinking about the failed probe on Friday. He railed at himself for not overriding Huenemann – at least trying to – then pitched that line of thought aside as silly. He'd considered it, and it was just too risky. It would split his majority.

Now, however....

There was one thing he needed to check out, but he couldn't go there. His movements were too well documented, too public. He wrote a short note and called his aide.

"Take the bus up to Fifteenth Street and deliver this. Wait for a reply. Then bring the reply straight here."

"Yes, sir."

The aid looked down at the envelope.

The only address was 'Chen Zufu.'

For that matter, he could probably mail it anywhere on Arcadia, and that would be all the address it needed.

"There is a man here with a note for you, Chen Zufu. He

said he was told to wait for an answer."

JuMing walked the note over to Chen Zufu.

"Thank you, JuMing. Wait outside, please."

"Yes, Chen Zufu."

MinChao opened the envelope by steaming it over his teapot. The note was short, and in Rob Milbank's handwriting.

*Do things stand with you as at our last meeting?*

MinChao wrote a short response directly on the note, then took a small stamp, coated it in red ink, and stamped his seal.

*Yes, in all particulars.*

陈

MinChao put the note back in the envelope, then moistened the flap with tea and sealed it. He rang a small bell on his table. JuMing entered, and MinChao handed him the envelope.

"Give this back to the courier, please, JuMing."

"Yes, Chen Zufu."

When his aide came back with the same envelope he had sent, Milbank looked at him curiously.

"You delivered it?"

"Yes, sir. The young man at the reception desk took it back into the building, and ten minutes later he returned and handed it back to me."

"All right. Thanks."

The aid left and Milbank looked at the envelope. What was that smell? He smelled at the envelope and smiled. Tea.

Milbank cut the envelope open and pulled out the note. 'Yes, in all particulars.' Well, that was reassuring.

And, stamped in red ink, the single Chinese character, one Milbank recognized. One anybody on Arcadia would recognize for that matter. Chen. No given name, just the family name. Only Chen Zufu would stamp a note like that. Only the head of the family would stamp a note with the family name alone. The Chen.

Milbank destroyed the note by lighting it and dropping it in the little receptacle by his desk for the purpose.

He'd write his speech this weekend and deliver it Tuesday, he decided.

One week after the probe disappeared.


On Monday night, Karl Huenemann had dinner with Gerard Laporte. Their conversation began in earnest after they were seated and had ordered.

"What's going on with you, Karl?"

"Not much, Gerard. We're working on completing the second hyperspace probe while I wait for the other shoe to drop."

"The other shoe?"

"Yes. Whatever Rob is going to do. He has a speech scheduled for tomorrow night. I don't know what he's going to do."

"Well, he'd better not try to pin blame for what is the normal occurrence in experimental endeavors, which is that they don't always go swimmingly. I've warned him, Karl, so I don't think you have anything to worry about."

"That's comforting, but I just don't know what he's going to do."

"Are the theoretical people crowing about being right?"

"No, they're quiet, too, Gerard. And we don't know that they are right. I think the hyperspace generator burned out on a single transition, so it couldn't transfer back. Which is to say, I was right to be worried about it, but I wasn't worried about it enough. That's a whole different scenario than that they were right."

"I see. Well, the project is very important to Rob, Karl. He wants hyperspace travel, and he wants it bad enough he can taste it. My suspicion is that he's going to ask for more money – and bigger money – to fund a second try."

"That would be welcome, but we don't really need bigger money. We do need money to continue, but it won't be any more expensive than the first attempt was. Should be less. I mean, we already have the second probe near completion."

Laporte nodded.

"I understand, but we'll just have to wait until tomorrow to see what he's going to do. He hasn't shared anything with me yet, so I'm just guessing."

"All right. Thanks, Gerard."


Rob Milbank's speech on Tuesday night was carried live on the Arcadia news wires.

"Good evening, my fellow Arcadians.

"I thought I would bring you up to speed on certain events, and tell you my reaction to those events, what we will be doing going forward.

"Sixteen years ago, mathematicians at the University of Arcadia postulated the existence of hyperspace, a universe adjacent to our own. They spent a number of years deriving the mathematics of its existence – how it works, what it means for us, how we can use it.

"The most stunning implication is that we could use it to

travel to other star systems. Our ships would transfer into hyperspace, travel in that domain, and then transfer back. The geometry of hyperspace as we understand it means that such travel would take much less time than in our own universe. Where it would take centuries to travel one light-year here, our ships could travel light-years per day in hyperspace.

"The benefits to Arcadia of that kind of breakthrough would be breathtaking. We would be able to purchase technologies and products from other worlds that would make life easier for all Arcadians. We would also be able to export our technologies and products to other worlds, expanding our markets and increasing our prosperity.

"Our engineers have been working toward that end for several years. It has not been an inexpensive effort. But the promise and the hope of a successful outcome made the effort and cost worthwhile.

"Last week – a week ago today, in fact – we made the first attempt to transfer a probe into hyperspace and back. That effort would be a tiny first step in moving us toward hyperspace travel.

"That effort failed. The probe exited space-time and went – where? We don't know. All we really know is that it didn't come back.

"Now we are faced with a decision. What do we do now? Do we continue to spend money and effort on this project? Or do we cancel the project, and set the effort aside, perhaps to be revisited at a later time?

"That decision, under the legislation that funded the project, is mine, and I have struggled with it this past week. Both paths are compelling – hyperspace travel is worth the effort, while we have things here on Arcadia that are worth doing – but there are limited resources and I must decide.

"I have decided that we will set this project aside for now. I don't disagree with doing the project at some point. I think we simply may have been premature. We will let our mathematicians continue to develop their theory and framework, and revisit the possibility of hyperspace travel in the future.

"But for right here, right now, I am cancelling the project, and moving on to the more mundane issues facing your government. Together, we will turn our attentions to our more pressing problems closer to home.

"Good night, my fellow Arcadians, and thank you for listening."

# Politics, Purchase, And Personnel

Karl Huenemann sat staring out the windows of his living room, eyes unfocused, for a long time after the prime minister's speech ended.

Gerard Laporte couldn't protect him from this. Milbank had not made it about Huenemann, he had made it about budgets and priorities. And there, Milbank had his caucus solidly behind him.

Milbank had gotten the funding for the project by a bare majority, with some help from the other side of the aisle. His vision of a hyperspace-enabled future was compelling, and the House and even the Chamber gave the first-term prime minister the funding and authority he needed to push the project forward.

Now, the seasoned second-term prime minister had called it quits – at least for now – and he would have both the House and Chamber behind him. If the project's biggest booster had decided it was probably too soon, he would pull a bunch of the people who had supported the project as well as everyone who had been against it.

That would be a flood even Laporte could not hold back.

Karl Huenemann believed in the project and thought it was very important to the future of Arcadia. Its cancellation was gut-wrenching.

Gerard Laporte was disappointed, too, but for different reasons. Milbank had considered the project very important.

Laporte didn't, but he was willing to go along. To horse trade with Milbank over it. If Milbank wanted this project, he would have to give Laporte the things Laporte wanted. He was more than willing to play that game.

But if Milbank cancelled the project, that took away a big bargaining chip.

Laporte started considering how this would change the lay of the land for getting his other legislation through, given he couldn't threaten the hyperspace project to get Milbank's support.

Huenemann's situation didn't even begin to figure into Laporte's calculations.

"I think Rob did a nice job there," Jessica Chen-Jasic said.

"So do I," Chen MinChao said.

"Should we make an inquiry?"

"What? Can we buy your project?"

"No," Jessica said. "Ask can we buy the property. The project site is ten acres adjacent to the shuttleport, and right next to the ten acres where our shuttleport freight-handling operation is. Most natural thing in the world is to ask, since he's canceled the project, is that property available? We could use the room for future expansion."

"It's the adjacent property?"

"Oh, yes."

"Then yes, I think we should ask about it," MinChao said. "Give Rob the idea, if he hasn't had it already."

"I will drop him a note. Ask him about buying the property. He need not expend funds to clear the site. We'll take it as-is."

MinChao chuckled.

"Yes. Yes, that would work."

JieMin and ChaoLi had watched the speech on their heads-up displays and now sat together talking about it in their living room. The boys were down for the night, and the girls were in their room, so they had the living room to themselves.

"Is he really canceling the project, do you think, or is he opening the door to selling it to the Chen as scrap?" JieMin asked.

After several meetings with Chen Zufu and Chen Zumu, ChaoLi knew more about what was really going on than JieMin did at this point. But that was family deep secrets, so she had to be careful.

"Could be either, really, but you know Milbank really thinks the hyperspace drive is important."

JieMin nodded.

"I think so, too. I hope so, anyway. It would be good to see it succeed."

"Oh, I think we will, JieMin. I think we will see it succeed."

Rob Milbank looked at Jessica's note. Now there was an idea. It solved a lot of other problems, too.

Normally for the government to sell something, it had to go out on auction. Sort of like purchases being put out for bids, but the other way around.

However, in the specific case of selling government-owned land for development purposes, the prime minister could sell land without putting it out on auction, as long as there were comparables and he got the fair-market price.

Selling the ten acres the project was on at the spaceport, then, he could do without going out to auction. He could do it without approvals from the legislature, too, for that matter.

Those ten-acre parcels had four-hundred-foot frontages and were eleven hundred feet deep, which meant there were over a hundred of them around the two-mile-square expanse of the shuttleport. Most of those had not yet been sold. There was only so much demand at this point, but the government had known the future would eventually gobble up those spaces as the colony grew.

Right now, though, the land was cheap. He could even discount it because the Chen would take the land in 'as-is' condition, without him spending money to clear it off.

Probably best to charge the going rate, though, if Chen Zufu was comfortable with it. That avoided embarrassing questions. Selling it to the Chen, though, who owned the plot next door, was a no-brainer. That was in the prime minister's purview, as well, to sell it to the party that could make the best use of it.

He sent a one-word answer back to Jessica: 'Perfect.'


It all happened very quickly. On Wednesday morning, Milbank instructed the government personnel office to lay off everyone on the project. No exceptions.

Anyone working on the site was sent home and the facility locked up.

Milbank also asked his legal office to draw up the sale of the property to the Chen family, which was organized as a corporation under colony law, at the currently listed price for the open parcels.

The property was already fenced, to keep people from wandering into a rocket-engine test or the like, so there was nothing that had to be done there. There was already a guard shack at the gate off the access road on the other side of the property from the shuttleport grounds, and the government maintained security on the site.

The deal was closed on Thursday. The legal office got the message of the prime minister's desire for timeliness when

Milbank assigned them the task of drawing up the paperwork, then called an hour later to ask if they were done yet. The Chen, of course, had no problem transferring the funds to purchase ten acres of property.

That afternoon, the Chen took up security on the site and relieved the government agents there.

JieMin and ChaoLi were summoned to meet with Chen Zufu and Chen Zumu on Friday morning. There were rumors flying around at the university and within the family, but nobody knew for sure what was going on. Some of the rumors were directly contradictory to each other, for that matter.

When they were shown into Chen Zufu's tearoom, there were two pillows on the floor facing the family's leadership couple.

"Please be seated, ChaoLi, JieMin."

"Thank you, Chen Zufu," ChaoLi said.

She was named first, so JieMin took the pillow to his right, leaving the more honored position, the one to Chen Zufu's right, for ChaoLi.

"There are a lot of rumors flying around about what is going on. We have not acted to dispel them. We will now tell you what is happening."

ChaoLi nodded.

"The family has purchased the site of the now-defunct hyperspace probe project from the government. We purchased it as-is. The government has also given us all of the plans for the hyperspace probe currently located on the site, ostensibly so we can disassemble it and scrap it safely."

MinChao turned to look at Jessica, and she took up the conversation.

"We are not going to do that, however," she said. "We are

going to continue the project. ChaoLi, you will be the business manager for the project. Yours will be the final decision on all project matters, subject only to our own authority, and we will not interfere."

"Thank you, Chen Zumu."

"JieMin, you will be the technical lead on the project, reporting to ChaoLi. You have been reporting to her for seventeen years already, so I see no difficulty there."

MinChao chuckled at that.

"ChaoLi, I will miss you terribly in the business office, but you have done a good job bringing up your successor, and I think JongJu is ready for that position."

"I agree, Chen Zumu."

"JieMin has already drawn up a list of essential personnel," MinChao said, "and you have authority to hire them or not, ChaoLi. It is your judgment on all these matters that will hold sway. We will set up a budget for the remaining work, but we are not prepared to skimp and fail. The funds are available to successfully carry this project through.

"Do you have any questions?"

"No, Chen Zufu."

"JieMin?"

"No, Chen Zufu."

"It is Friday," Jessica said. "I suggest you think about these things over the next three days and begin work on Monday."

"Yes, Chen Zumu," ChaoLi said.

"That is all for now."


When JieMin and ChaoLi got back to their apartment, it was quieter than normal. All the children were off at daycare or school or work.

"Now what?" JieMin said.

"The children are gone for the day. I think we should celebrate before we settle down to the project. Air out our heads before taking on this new task."

"Any ideas?"

"How about our secret spot?" ChaoLi said with a wink.

"Sure."

They dropped their lavalavas and kicked off their flip-flops and headed to the elevators. They walked across the street to the market and bought lunch, then walked to the bus stop at Fifteenth and Arcadia.

Once at the beach, they headed up the shoreline to their secret cove. They walked nude along the beach in the late morning sunshine, carrying lunch and holding hands, cooled by the onshore breeze. It was just like old times.

Their secret spot seemed a longer walk than it had in their teens, but they enjoyed it just as much.

Karl Huenemann was beside himself. Notified he was fired from the project – and the government – late Wednesday, he kept hearing rumors from his contacts about the disposition of the property and the second hyperspace probe.

The most persistent and disturbing rumor was that the property had been sold to the Chen, who would scrap it all to expand their warehouse and distribution facility.

The issue was that Huenemann really did want the project to succeed, and he thought they were close. At heart he was an engineer, not a bureaucrat. Government employment was just how you got big projects done. Yes, he'd played the game, but his end goal was always the completion of the project.

On Friday morning, Huenemann requested a meeting with Chen Zumu. He did his research, and he decided she was likely to be more approachable than Chen Zufu on this issue. She responded with an invitation to tea that afternoon.

Huenemann researched the etiquette for tea. He was not going to be found wanting on minor issues when the real issue was so important.

When Karl Huenemann was shown into Chen Zumu's tearoom late Friday afternoon, she was sitting on the left of two pillows equally spaced in the teak-beamed doorway, facing out into the courtyard gardens. He realized in that setup the honor he was being paid.

Without turning, she waved at the pillow next to her.

"Please be seated, Dr. Huenemann."

"Thank you, Chen Zumu."

Huenemann walked forward and around the pillow and sat. Once he was seated, a young woman in a lavalava came in from the garden and poured tea, first for Huenemann and then for Chen Zumu. She set the pot on the low table between the pillows, bowed to a point between them, and departed without a word.

Huenemann knew that, as the guest, he sipped first. He did, and it was a tea he had only had once before, in Arcadia's highest-priced restaurant. Even by their standards, it had been expensive.

Jessica also sipped, and they sat, contemplating the garden for several minutes. It allowed Huenemann to collect his thoughts, forced him to set aside his urgency for a measured approach.

"You asked to see me, Dr. Huenemann. Please proceed."

"Thank you, Chen Zumu. I would first ask if you would confirm the rumor that the Chen have purchased the hyperspace probe facility at the Arcadia City Shuttleport."

"We have indeed, Dr. Huenemann."

"I would ask if you would share with me your plans for the project, Chen Zumu."

"The project is important to you, Dr. Huenemann?"

"Yes, Chen Zumu. Very important. While the prime minister and I may have disagreed on many things, on that we were agreed."

"As am I, Dr. Huenemann. It was to acquire the project that we purchased the property."

Huenemann's head spun. He had always thought of the Chen as ruthlessly commercial and business oriented. Yet here was one of the heads of the family telling him she agreed with the longer term goal of interstellar travel, which would be unlikely to pay off for decades.

Jessica sipped her tea and waited for Huenemann.

"I am curious as to why, Chen Zumu. Why take the project into private hands, rather than let the government carry it through?"

"Because the hyperspace project is so important to the future of Arcadia, Dr. Huenemann, and we were unsatisfied with your leadership of it."

Jessica said it with no pique, no emphasis, no rancor. The white-haired seventy-year-old, in her silk robe with silk dragons rampant, calmly stated it as fact, then sipped her tea.

Sitting there, sipping tea in contemplation of her garden, Huenemann did not react as he might in the hustle and bustle of a government office. But he did wonder to what extent this woman – here, from her tearoom, the very heart of the richest and most politically connected family on the planet – was directing everything that happened. Not just the cancellation of the project, but its inception as well.

In the light of that realization, the political maneuvering and backroom deal-making in the government buildings downtown seemed petty.

"In what manner have I disappointed, Chen Zumu?"

"This is not a political project, Dr. Huenemann, or, rather, it shouldn't be. You are highly regarded for your engineering skills. Yet you set them aside for political maneuvering and jeopardized the project.

"I am not uninformed on these matters, Dr. Huenemann. The controversy that consumed the project in the last several months concerned the hyperspace field generator. You were concerned that it would burn out if it were kept on to protect the probe from the potentially harmful effects of the hyperspace environment. That is a valid engineering concern.

"Your solution to this controversy was not an engineering solution, however. It was a political one, and the probe was lost."

"We still do not know how the probe failed, Chen Zumu."

"Nor are we likely to ever find out, Dr. Huenemann. And that, too, is not amenable to a political determination.

"From an engineering point of view, there are three possible ways the probe may have failed. One is that the hyperspace environment destroyed the probe when the hyperspace field generator was turned off. Another is that the hyperspace field generator failed on transition, or on the attempt to transition back. Third is some other failure we have not considered."

Huenemann was shocked by her depth of understanding of the project, then recalled from his research her own background was in engineering and science.

"What should I have done, Chen Zumu?"

"Increased the cooling on the hyperspace field generator, and left it turned on while in hyperspace, avoiding both potential harms. But this middle way was forestalled when the issue became a political one and metastasized."

"The hyperspace probe lacks room for enough additional refrigeration, Chen Zumu. The heat generated is sizable."

"And the probe's size is completely fixed, Dr. Huenemann? By what? I understand that the four-wide, two-high container arrangement is the standard payload for the shuttle, but an additional housing on the side of that assembly is not a problem. It was an artificial constraint.

"I would further ask how big a bottle of liquid nitrogen would be for high-capacity cooling. For that matter, the probe already carries liquid oxygen for its rocket engines.

"But all of these potential engineering solutions were foregone due to the availability of a political solution, Dr. Huenemann. That will not be a problem going forward. Chen ChaoLi will administer the project without such issues. She has worked for me for twenty years, and is my most trusted and capable business manager."

Huenemann's mind raced through the solutions Jessica had listed. Pretty much any of them might work. It would need further study.

The bigger question was, How had he let himself get so far astray as not to seek an engineering solution to what was an engineering problem?

"I would ask to be allowed to play some part in the project going forward, Chen Zumu."

"That is important to you, Dr. Huenemann?"

"Yes, Chen Zumu. It is a project unfinished, largely because of my own shortsightedness, I fear."

"Well, you are in luck then, Dr. Huenemann. Chen JieMin included you prominently on the list of essential personnel to complete the project that I asked him to prepare for me back in March. I imagine Chen ChaoLi will be in touch with you on Monday."

Huenemann felt ashamed. Small. Chen JieMin was the one person most opposed to turning off the hyperspace field generator after the first transition, the lead theoretician. Rather than work with him on an engineering solution, Huenemann had bad-mouthed JieMin to his contacts in fighting a political battle. Yet Chen JieMin had asked for him.

Huenemann didn't know what to say, so he kept it simple.

"Thank you, Chen Zumu."

Jessica nodded. They had been talking while facing out into the garden, but she turned to him now and caught his eye.

"But understand me well, Dr. Huenemann. There will be no political byplay on this project. Mr. Laporte and your other friends in the House and Chamber have no role here. Chen ChaoLi is in charge, working directly for me."

Jessica had the steel-eye of command, and Huenemann knew to cross her would be inadvisable. More, unthinkable.

"I understand, Chen Zumu."

Jessica nodded and turned back to her garden. Huenemann knew he should wait to be dismissed. He looked out into the garden and considered his situation. To do just the engineering again. Make the trade-offs, weigh the risks, avoid the foreseeable dangers. It was his first, best calling, and he looked forward to it.

They sat and sipped their tea. After ten minutes or so, Jessica broke the silence.

"Thank you for coming to see me, Dr. Huenemann."

"Thank you for meeting with me, Chen Zumu. With your permission, I take my leave of you."

Huenemann stood and bowed to her. The young man from before, called in Jessica's heads-up display, opened the sliding panel and led Huenemann out.

# Preparations

The next Monday, June eighteenth, Karl Huenemann got a job offer from the Chen-Jasic Corporation. He didn't even look at the salary. It didn't really matter much. He wanted on the project.

Huenemann sent his acceptance, and was told to report to a downtown office building on Tuesday morning.

That same day, Huenemann got a few calls from other people who had been on the project, including Mikhail Borosky, asking him about inquiries they received from the Chen.

Huenemann told them he was on board and they would be completing the hyperspace project. He gave them something of a sell job.

"Yeah, they got a much better business manager than me to run it. I'm gonna be all engineering, which is what I do best anyway. We're gonna wring this thing out and make it work."

ChaoLi hired all the essential personnel from JieMin's list.

When Huenemann reported to the Chen family offices on Tuesday, there was some paperwork to fill out. He was assigned an office.

There were a lot of other new people there, too, but it was almost exclusively all the old hands of the project under the government program.

That afternoon, Huenemann was asked to a meeting in Chen ChaoLi's office. When he arrived, it was just him, Chen ChaoLi, and Chen JieMin, sitting around the table in her office. Huenemann was surprised Chen ChaoLi was as young as she was, given her standing with Chen Zumu. But it was JieMin's presence that reminded Huenemann of how the project had failed, and his own role in it.

"Dr. Chen, Chen Zumu told me you put me on the list of essential personnel for the project. After all that's happened, I don't know what to say."

JieMin just nodded.

"That is all past, Dr. Huenemann. What matters is the future."

"That is exactly correct, gentlemen," ChaoLi said.

She turned to Huenemann.

"We are not going to turn off the hyperspace field generator in hyperspace for the next probe launch."

She turned to JieMin.

"Nor are we going to allow the hyperspace field generator's cooling problems to go unaddressed."

She looked back and forth between them.

"Am I understood?"

"Yes, ma'am," they both said.

"Good. Now, I want you two to figure out how we solve this problem. Make sure you have the figures to back it up. I want a solution, or the beginnings of a solution, by Friday close of business. Pull in whomever you need. Top priority. Friday close of business."

"Yes, ma'am."

"That is all for now."

Huenemann and JieMin left together. As they walked down the hallway, Huenemann looked back to make sure they were out of earshot.

"That woman is all business," Huenemann told JieMin. "I

don't think we want to cross her."

"Tell me about it," JieMin said. "ChaoLi is my wife."

Huenemann guffawed.

"Well then, we *really* don't want to cross her."

They ended up pulling in a number of other engineers and scientists on the project. They had the additional benefit this time around of the telemetry from the first probe, especially from the temperature sensors on the hyperspace field generator, at least up until the point of transition. They knew how hot it got, and, more importantly, where it got hot.

There were a number of different possible solutions. They went down the list, working through the details of each, ultimately preparing a list of the pros and cons of each, in terms of cost, effectiveness, time to implement on the existing second probe, increased weight of the payload, and need to expand the payload volume and by how much.

By the time Friday afternoon came around, they had sorted out the best alternatives and were prepared to make a recommendation.

Huenemann made the presentation to ChaoLi that afternoon in her office. JieMin was present, but this was more of an engineering problem than a math problem. Nevertheless, his remarkable insight agreed with their findings during the week.

After Huenemann presented the list of alternatives they had considered, their best options – including the pluses and minuses of each – and their recommended solution, ChaoLi looked back and forth between them.

"And you are both agreed on this?" she asked.

She looked at Huenemann.

"Yes, ma'am," he said.

She looked at JieMin.

"Yes, ma'am."

"Good. Good work. We need to modify the probe we have to implement this solution, and perform the other work needed to complete it. Do the engineers and technicians have what they need, Dr. Huenemann?"

"There are a couple of things we need to purchase to implement this solution, ma'am, but they're all available."

"Send me the item numbers and suppliers, Dr. Huenemann, and I will take care of it. Anything else?"

"No, ma'am. I think we're ready to go."

"Very well. I'll open the Shuttleport facility Monday morning and the team can get started."

"Yes, ma'am."

JieMin and ChaoLi didn't talk about the project over the weekend. Her rule about work on weekends was still in place, and he reminded her of it when she strayed in that direction.

On Saturday, they took the boys for a picnic in the park while the girls did schoolwork. The boys played nude in the park all afternoon, and when they got home, ChaoLi marched them all straight into the shower.

On Sunday, the whole family went to the beach. They wore lavalavas for the trip, as someone would always have to be out of the water to keep an eye on JieJun anyway. They could also keep an eye on everyone's things while the others swam.

The four-year-old didn't really have much interest in the water, but the beach was the world's biggest sandbox, and he was in heaven.

On Monday, the engineers and technicians began work on the second probe. One thing right off was to open up the side of the last container on each side and work up a nacelle to give them the extra volume they needed.

The ordered equipment showed up Tuesday morning. They had optimized the plumbing of the upgraded cooling system to minimize the amount of other things they had to remove and reinstall, but it still took nearly three weeks to install the new system and then re-test everything they had done before.

That simply got them back to where things stood before they stopped work on the second probe when Milbank canceled the project. There was still another month of work to be done to complete the device.

Two months after she took over the project, ChaoLi held a critical status meeting. Of course, she had received status reports as they went along, but this was the critical meeting. Attending were JieMin, Huenemann, and Borovsky. As the project manager, it was Borovsky in the hot seat for this meeting.

"Where do we stand this week, gentlemen?"

"We are ready to perform engine tests, ma'am," Borovsky said.

"Truly?"

"Yes, ma'am."

"And everything has been tested to the same standards as the first probe? All the sub-systems?"

"Yes, ma'am, plus the additional tests on the new cooling system."

"We are then ready for launch?"

"Yes, ma'am."

"What about the shuttle pilots? Are they ready?"

"Yes, ma'am. They remain available for hire."

"Have they kept in practice on this mission?"

"They haven't run this flight profile in the last two and a half months, ma'am, but they'll be all right."

"I want two practice runs with dummy payload to the actual launch distance."

"Well, that's awfully expensive, ma'am. Operating that shuttle isn't cheap, and they charge us by the engine-hours."

"I understand, Mr. Borovsky. But to risk failure on a project this big over something like that is a false economy. Two clean practice runs. If they bugger one, we still do two more until we get two clean runs. In a row."

"Yes, ma'am. I'll see to it."

"Excellent. You may proceed with your engine tests, gentlemen."

Once more, a hyperspace probe was out on the apron of the warehouse, technicians scurrying around it making final checks.

The same five pilings behind the new probe secured it from moving forward, with half a dozen chains from each piling to the frame of the craft. It was pointed away from the city and the manufacturing district, to the southwest.

A siren sounded.

"Clear the range. Five minutes until test."

In the control room attached to the warehouse, the countdown was punctuated with queries and replies as they ran down their checklist.

Ultimately, they got to the end of the checklist and began the onboard computer running. They noted the computer's actions as they occurred.

"Fuel pumps running."

"Fuel pressure nominal."

"Fuel flow initiated."

"Computer is in final countdown. Ignition in three. Two. One. Ignition."

Outside on the ramp, fuel and oxygen vapors began leaking from the rocket nozzles, then ignited with a Whoof! The fuel flow increased, and then the rocket nozzles focused, generating long, blue-white jets.

The probe strained at the chains holding it back, but the chains held. The thunder of the rockets reverberated out over the shuttleport and to the city beyond. For fifteen seconds the rockets thundered, then shut down abruptly.

The test was successful.

The second hyperspace probe was ready to go.

"Shuttle Z-1 to Arcadia Control."

"Go ahead, Shuttle Z-1."

"Shuttle Z-1 requesting landing clearance."

"Shuttle Z-1 you are cleared to land on pad two-seven."

"Shuttle Z-1 cleared to land on pad two-seven. Roger."

The big shuttle was making its re-entry, holding back against the pull of gravity with a combination of lift and thrust from the engines. Even so, it was only minutes from the Arcadia City Shuttleport.

A hundred miles down went a lot faster than a hundred miles horizontally.

"Place engines under computer control," Justin Moore said.

Gavin MacKay threw the switch on his panel and verified the change in his heads-up display.

"Confirm engines under computer control."

The computer would now adjust the mixture and thrust to meet the pilot's needs for the standard flight operation of landing the shuttle.

There was something ineffably different about the engines

sound of a shuttle returning from space than an atmospheric shuttle. Maybe it was that the engines were that much more powerful, even if they weren't being run flat out for the final approach. There was just something about it.

The large shuttle, with its underslung dummy payload, settled down toward the shuttleport. It lined up for shuttlepad two-seven, and its engines spooled up as it braked its descent. It settled down on the pad, and Gavin MacKay shut down the engines.

"Well, that was better," Moore said.

"Yeah, that last one was kind of embarrassing."

"Neither one of us caught it."

"Yeah, I know," MacKay said. "But we go away for two months and you gotta retrain us?"

Moore chuckled.

"The mission parameters are a bit different for this one."

MacKay nodded.

"Yeah. One more and we're good to go, I guess."


The shuttle pilots completed one more successful mission run with the dummy payload, and they were good to go for the mission.


It was early September when they were finally ready to go. Everything had been tested, the pilots were back in practice, everybody had signed off.

"So what should I set as the launch date?" ChaoLi asked that Thursday night.

"I think we should launch Monday," JieMin said.

"Next week, not the week after?"

JieMin nodded.

"I don't think there's anything to be gained by waiting. It

will take four days for the probe to be in position, and if it is successful Friday, it will really give us something to celebrate for Landing Day on Saturday."

"That's right. September the fifteenth is Saturday a week coming. Well, that kind of works."

ChaoLi nodded.

"Fair enough. Next Monday."

The next day at the Friday project status meeting, ChaoLi made the announcement.

"We will launch next Monday, September tenth, gentlemen. So let's make it a success, and then we can all go home Friday for the long holiday weekend."

# Success!

September tenth was a beautiful day, like most days in Arcadia City. There was no morning shower today, and the hyperspace probe test team didn't have to wait for it before they started operations.

They used a shuttleport tow tractor to pull the hyperspace probe out of the warehouse and onto the nearby shuttlepad. Technicians swarmed the device, checking everything. Then the fuel and oxygen trucks filled the tanks to one hundred percent.

The launch crew were standing by in the large space-capable cargo shuttle. They lifted off their pad and settled onto the hyperspace probe, as they had practiced with the dummy loads earlier. They latched the shuttle to the hyperspace probe and were good to go.

"Shuttle Z-1 to Arcadia Control. We are all systems Go and awaiting clearance."

"Arcadia Control to Shuttle Z-1. Other traffic is being held. You have clearance for takeoff and bearing zero-niner to space."

"Shuttle Z-1 to Arcadia Control. Roger clearance for takeoff and bearing zero-niner to space."

"We ready?" Justin Moore asked his co-pilot.

"We're good," Gavin MacKay said.

Moore nodded to MacKay, and the co-pilot began spooling up the massive engines. When they neared their operational revolutions, Moore focused the thrust and the massive craft and its pendent payload lifted off the pad.

At thirty-five thousand feet, MacKay began feeding oxygen to the engines as well as fuel, maintaining the thrust they needed to attain the high orbit required for the mission.

"Approaching thirty thousand miles," MacKay said.

Moore nodded.

"Roger that. Ready for maneuvering."

"Thirty thousand miles."

"Reduce thrust to zero," Moore said.

MacKay cut the flow of oxygen and fuel to the engines, which continued to spin without anything to push against.

"Thrust at zero."

"Releasing payload."

Moore flipped the switch to disengage the shuttle's load latches.

"Latch release confirmed," MacKay said.

"Rotating engines."

Moore rotated the engine nacelles so they were pointed 'down' from the shuttle cabin point of view.

"Engine rotation confirmed," MacKay said.

"Bring up engines to five percent."

MacKay started a greatly reduced oxygen and fuel flow back into the still-rotating engines. A small amount of gravity returned to the cabin as the shuttle separated vertically off the probe.

"Separation confirmed," MacKay said.

Moore rotated the rear engine nacelles until they were pointed almost straight up, and the shuttle flipped over. As it came back around to be pointing back to Arcadia, he rotated both engines to point straight back, away from Arcadia.

"Bring engines up to full thrust," Moore said.

MacKay increased the oxygen and fuel flow until the engines were at full thrust. The cabin gravity went to several gees of push back into the seats as the shuttle, now released of the heavy probe, accelerated much more rapidly than it had accelerated when loaded.

"Time to head for home," MacKay said.

"Telemetry indicates the shuttle has released the probe. The pilots report successful release. They're on the way back. We have ninety seconds remaining on the five-minute safety margin before the probe's engines start."

Over thirty thousand miles away, the computer's timer ran out, and it began the rocket ignition process by starting the fuel and oxygen pumps. As before, it leaked primer fuel and oxygen out the engine nozzles, then ignited them. The rockets lit, and the computer increased fuel and oxygen flow. With that established, the computer focused the nozzles and went to maximum thrust.

"Sir, probe reports it is now at maximum thrust. All engines nominal."

Seventy-five minutes later, with the fuel and oxygen reserves at sixty percent, the computer shut down the rocket engines. The probe continued to separate from Arcadia at its new velocity. It would take four days to coast to the test location.

"The probe reports shutdown of the engines, sir. The probe is at target velocity."

"All right, then," Borovsky said. "I guess that's it for today. Standby crew is on-shift. We'll see everybody else on Friday."

Friday came, bright and sunny, but there were no operations

out of the Arcadia City Shuttleport related to the project today. All of the action would be a million miles away.

Nevertheless, the command crew all showed up at the control center attached to the warehouse on the shuttleport grounds. Mikhail Borovsky, Karl Huenemann, Chen ChaoLi, and Chen JieMin were there as spectators.

The hyperspace probe's flight over the last four days had coasted along at its terminal velocity. It had not hit any debris and all its systems were operating within nominal parameters.

The probe's computer verified its distance from Arcadia by sending a message to the flight control computer in the control center. It timed the delay until acknowledgement to make sure it was as far away as specified. Then the probe's computer ran up the power levels on the probe's power supply.

"Probe power supply coming up to necessary power levels," the technician in the control center reported.

The probe's computer verified operation of the power supply within nominal parameters, then began the hyperspace transition sequence.

"Hyperspace transition sequence initiating."

A distortion began forming around the hyperspace probe, as if the probe were in an ovoid of glass.

"Hyperspace bubble forming."

The probe's computer sent the signal to the hyperspace field generator, and power consumption spiked. There was a flash, and the probe was gone.

"We lost telemetry on the mark. The probe's transitioned."

As before, the probe was programmed to spend five minutes in hyperspace and transition back. They still didn't know if hyperspace ran on the same clock or not. Was it delayed? Running at some factor from space-time normal? Relativity time-dilation implied it could be.

Five minutes later, the technician reported.

"Telemetry has resumed. The probe has successfully transitioned back."

There were cheers, even tears, in the control room.

ChaoLi stood up and shook the hands of Borovsky, Huenemann, and JieMin.

"Congratulations, gentlemen. You have just changed human history."

The beach was crowded on the Founding Day holiday, but they went anyway. The buses to the beach ran non-stop. ChaoLi and JieMin just sat on the beach and watched JieJun play in the sand and let the older kids run off to the water.

"That was pretty remarkable yesterday," ChaoLi said. "You were right all along."

"Within broad parameters, perhaps. But we also got a lot of new data."

"Like what?"

"Like the timebase of hyperspace and space-time are the same," JieMin said. "At least for condensed matter in the hyperspace field."

"What are the implications of that?"

"It will tighten up some parts of the theory. Where the existing theory allowed that timebase to be different, we now know it isn't, so that will change some things. Make the theory more accurate."

"Anything else?" ChaoLi asked.

"We need to look at all the data in the telemetry, of course. Inspection and testing of the device when we get it back will be important, too."

"They flipped it over and fired the engines to an intercept course for where Arcadia will be by the time it can get here.

Should be a couple weeks, even playing with orbital speeds and such. We need it in the right velocity range or the shuttle won't be able to pick it up."

JieMin nodded.

"You know, we both just broke the rule about talking shop on weekends."

"We'll have to spank each other later," ChaoLi said.

"Deal."

Chen Zufu and Chen Zumu were sitting in his tearoom before having dinner and going up to watch the fireworks later.

"They actually did it," Chen Zufu said.

"Yes. It's marvelous."

"Now what happens?"

"Years of engineering," Chen Zumu said. "Running probes in and back. Trying to accelerate in hyperspace and learning how to do that. Figuring out how close to the planet the transitions can be. Working out how big the components really need to be. Scaling the whole thing up to the size of a ship that can be used for passengers and freight. Lots of work."

"Can we afford it? Or should the government do it?"

"We can afford doing it as a private enterprise. The expenditure will also be spread out over years. What's funny is that the government is so inefficient, they probably can't afford to do it. There just isn't enough money in government coffers to carry that kind of waste burden on a project this big."

"Will we live to see it?" Chen Zufu asked. "Interstellar travel and shipping?"

Chen Zumu considered.

"I don't think so," she said.

She watched a bee, laboring endlessly in the garden.

"Perhaps."

# Epilogue

They had rented the big banquet room at the family restaurant in the Uptown Market. It was something of a double celebration. JieMin and ChaoLi were celebrating their twentieth wedding anniversary.

But the big event was the wedding of ChaoPing and JuMing.

ChaoPing had been promoted two years ago from tea girl in Chen Zumu's entourage to the reception desk, where JuMing already worked. They had gotten along well together, and enjoyed each other's company. When JuMing received his next promotion – up to two years of full-time study to finish his education – the two had decided to marry rather than be separated.

At seventeen and eighteen years old, ChaoPing and JuMing were in the most common age range for marriage on Arcadia. For all that, the divorce rate on Arcadia was low. Children grew up fast on the colony, with most beginning some kind of employment by age fourteen.

Self-paced study via the heads-up displays on the communicators had a lot to do with that. ChaoPing and JuMing were already deeply into their college work. In two years of study, JuMing would likely receive his masters degree in engineering. ChaoPing wasn't far behind, majoring in business, like her mother.

All of the families' friends and close relatives were there, numbering over three hundred people. JieMin's parents, his siblings, and their spouses had come in on a special chartered bus from Chagu. Project people were there, too, including Karl Huenemann and Mikhail Borovsky.

Even Chen MinChao and Jessica Chen-Jasic attended, in a place of honor at the main table. A bigger surprise to many people was the attendance of the prime minister, Rob Milbank, and his wife, Julia Whitcomb.

The hyperspace project was going well. The government had stepped in to assist with the financing in a sweetheart deal cooked up by Milbank and Jessica.

The government would make interest-free advance payments against future deliveries of the first hyperspace-capable spaceships. The Chen family though, under business manager ChaoLi, would continue to independently manage and carry out the effort under the technical leadership of JieMin, with Karl Huenemann as the engineering manager.

As steward of the government funds being invested, the prime minister stopped by monthly for an update on the project from ChaoLi and her technical leads.

Their individual assignments suited each of them and their talents, and they had all grown close.

The public was also excited about the hyperspace project. Not they, perhaps, but their children or grandchildren would gain the stars.

The prospect made Prime Minister Milbank very popular. His party had made major gains in the last elections, and, with a bigger majority, he was able to clean out or knock into line some of the more fractious elements of his party.

Gerard Laporte, in particular, had stepped down from

leadership and begun to tow Milbank's line.

Wedding ceremonies on Arcadia were an amalgamation of cultural practices from Earth. In the Chen-Jasic family, those were primarily Chinese and American.

After ChaoPing and JuMing served tea to each other's parents at the main table, they both consented to the marriage. The 'I do' of an American wedding had not been lost.

MinChao then declared the couple married in the eyes of the family.

And the party was on.

At one point, Jessica beckoned ChaoPing to her. ChaoPing took her husband's hand and they approached their clan leaders and employers.

"Yes, Chen Zumu."

"I have considered the matter carefully, and I think it is best that you also pursue your education full time, ChaoPing. You have shared with me your plans to delay children until you have completed your education, and this way I need not artificially delay ChaoLi's and JieMin's grandchildren."

Jessica said it with a twinkle in her eye, and ChaoPing laughed.

"Thank you, Chen Zumu."

"I have also assigned you a larger apartment together. It is not a family apartment – not yet – but it is bigger than the studio apartment JuMing has now."

"Thank you, Chen Zumu."

Jessica nodded.

"Chen Zufu and I are very happy for you both. Consider it a wedding present from us."

"Thank you, Chen Zumu. Thank you, Chen Zufu."

MinChao nodded.

"May you bear many healthy children," he said.

The festivities were typical for a Chen-Jasic wedding. First dinner – primarily Chinese dishes – then the American tradition of a wedding cake. There was dancing after, beginning with the dance of father with daughter, and the cutting-in of the groom.

Sitting at the main table, JieMin and ChaoLi watched their friends and family celebrate with contentment.

"All is as it should be," ChaoLi said.

JieMin nodded.

"Such a long way we have come," he said.

"And a long way yet to go," ChaoLi said.

She paused before continuing.

"But their children will have the stars."

# Quant #4

RICHARD F. WEYAND

# Geodesic

Janice Quant had been following the hyperspace project on Arcadia with interest. She knew Chen JieMin's mathematics were right, as she had trod the same path more than a century ago. She certainly hadn't expected someone on a colony planet to reproduce that work. He was an amazing talent, the sort the human race produced on occasion, seemingly at random.

Quant then watched with amazement as a political battle developed around a standoff on what was after all an engineering issue. Humans! She could clearly see several possible solutions, but she would not interfere.

Quant had to chuckle at Prime Minister Milbank's solution to the political problem – cancel the project. That had certainly shaken things up. The completion of the project in private hands had been inevitable once it had become, once again, an engineering problem and not a political one.

The Chen family were involved, of course. There was something about that combination of people – the Chen-Jasic group of colonists – that had worked out really well in the colony environment. Some combination of tradition and ingenuity, hard work and thrift. And Matthew Jasic had been a big part of how well Arcadia had turned out.

All of Quant's children – the colonies – were doing pretty well, if none quite so well as Arcadia. That would change, though, if Arcadia developed the hyperspace drive. Trade and travel would help bring up the other colonies, even as Arcadia prospered.

What the advent of the hyperspace drive meant, though, was that Quant had to complete the geodesic transporter. She would not be outrun by events.

The big sticking point had been how to join the five-hundred-mile-long carbon-filament tubes at the vertices. Six such tubes came together at most vertices of the geodesic sphere. The tubes had to be joined at precise angles, and the vertices had to be rigid and not susceptible to fatigue failure.

The solution was to spin carbon-fiber filaments between and among the tubes at the vertices. She had perfected that technology, and built a couple dozen vertex machines to do it. They labored now building the huge sphere.

Tugs pushed the carbon-fiber tubes into place. They were temporarily fastened and the angles meticulously measured and adjusted. Then one of the carbon-filament vertex machines moved into place and worked at bonding the new tube to the existing structure.

Quant watched the early stages carefully, looking for any error, any oversight, in her planning. But things were moving along now. It would still take twenty years to complete, but the process was moving smoothly along.

At the beginning of its construction, the structure looked almost flat. Only as it proceeded did its gentle curvature become apparent. The final structure would be twelve thousand miles in diameter.

The geodesic transporter could transport an entire planet.

Please review this book on Amazon.

ARCADIA

# Author's Afterword

I faced a problem writing Arcadia. There was of necessity a long passage of time between the landing of the colony and the development of the hyperspace drive. While I could have written a separate book about each of the four major events depicted here, it would have been hard to do so and keep up the pace of action and density of ideas I like to write.

There was also what Janice Quant was up to, which would be occurring in parallel with the events on Arcadia.

I had no shortage of interesting characters from the first book, Quant. I had set up the secondary characters of Quant to provide an interesting pool of people on Arcadia, so there was no problem there.

Ultimately I decided to write the eighty-thousand-word Arcadia as four twenty-thousand-word novellas, following the same family through the four major events in separate story arcs. I would follow Quant's activities in short interludes between them.

Of course, those story arcs weren't fleshed out at all. I started writing not knowing what was going to happen or how, just that I was covering the development of the Arcadia colony. I also thought the hyperspace drive would be invented on Earth at the beginning of the next book, given Earth's deeper technology base and long-established centers of learning.

That's not what history teaches, however. The airplane, the telephone, and the transistor were all developed in the United States, not in Europe.

So as I started the third novella of Arcadia, I changed my

thinking and began the build-up to the hyperspace drive being developed on Arcadia.

The third book of the series – Galactic Survey – was the seminal idea out of which this series grew. The idea of lost colonies being searched for by an organization set up to do just that. Something like Star Trek, but not knowing where the other humans were.

Now, though, that search would be conducted not by Earth, but by Arcadia, as the center of dynamism and progress in the human race moves to the colonies. Egypt had once been the center of civilization and technical progress, then Babylon, Rome, Constantinople, London, and the United States.

So, too, with the colonies. Arcadia would be the dynamic center of the human race moving forward, as progress on Earth lagged.

What happens next in the series? Galactic Survey. What happens after that? What do they find? What are the other colonies like? Will Janice Quant have to use her geodesic transporter to break up a war? What else might she do with it?

I don't know. I never do. We'll just have to see where the story goes as it reveals itself to me. Should be fun.

Speaking of fun, I hope you liked reading Arcadia as much as I did writing it.

Richard F. Weyand
Bloomington, IN
May 8, 2021

Made in the USA
Middletown, DE
01 August 2021

45199304R00190